CHEAT CODES

DAWSON FAMILY SERIES BOOK ONE

EMILY GOODWIN

Belinda—
Enjoy Quinn +
Archer's story ☺

Emily xoxo
Goodwin

To my girls. I love you.

"The future belongs to those who believe in the beauty of their dreams." -Eleanor Roosevelt

COPYRIGHT

Cheat Codes
A Dawson Family Novel
BOOK ONE

Copyright 2018
Emily Goodwin
Editing by Ellie, Love N Books
Editing by Lindsay, Contagious Edits
Cover Photography by By Braayden Photography
Models: Jade and Jordan Fisher

―――――――

This is a work of fiction. Names, characters, businesses,

1

QUINN

I am a glutton for punishment. Ever since the tender age of fourteen, I knew there was something wrong with me. Because of all the boys in all the world I could go and have a crush on, I fall for *him.*

My older brother's college roommate. The mysterious boy with the troubled past who could have any girl he wants. The cute boy with the dark hair and deep brown eyes who's as smart as he is cocky, who somehow managed to both get into med school and win over a lifetime friendship from sports-loving Dean, who only attended the same college because of a basketball scholarship.

And those girls? I was never one of them. Not then, and I won't be again now.

I don't expect to see him here tonight, but if he shows up, I won't be surprised. Everyone is back in town for Dean's engagement party, and it's inevitable we all end up at Getaway, the bar owned by my twin brothers. My heel catches on the toe of my other shoe, tripping me and making me slosh my very full Dirty Shirley down the front of my dress.

"Shit," I mutter and sip my drink as I turn around to grab a napkin.

"Smooth, sis." Logan holds out a rag.

"It was that obvious, huh?" I set my glass on the wooden bar top and take the rag.

"In your defense, I did fill your glass to the top. I thought I was doing you a favor, but now I know otherwise."

I roll my eyes at my brother and blot at the stains on my dress. Of course I'm wearing white. Never fails, does it? I slide onto a barstool and wipe the sides of my glass, taking a big drink before returning the rag to my brother. He takes it and tosses it at Owen's face, making him lean away from the girls he's been flirting with all night.

"What the hell?" Owen snaps, throwing the rag in a bin behind the counter. "I had a good thing going."

"You're going to pay for those drinks you gave away, right?" Logan shifts his eyes from me to his twin. They're identical, thick as thieves, but radically different in many aspects, which works out in both their favors. They balance each other out—most of the time.

"Take it from my pay." Owen grabs a bottle from the top shelf, arms himself with a cocky smile, and goes to the end of the bar to refill empty shot glasses. I pull my phone from my purse and see I missed a text from Jamie. She got held up at work and is rushing to get changed. She says she'll be here in fifteen minutes, which could mean up to an hour in Jamie-time. I relax in my seat and sip my drink as I mindlessly surf the internet.

"You're working, aren't you?" Logan rests his elbows on the bar and leans in, peering at my phone.

"Not this time. I'm trying really hard not to even check my email. I'm looking at a castle for sale in Scotland."

Not missing a beat or even questioning me, my brother

just shakes his head. "Mom can hardly handle you being less than two hours away in Chicago. She'd lose her shit if you moved to Europe."

"But look, it has a bookshelf that opens to a secret staircase."

"That is pretty badass." A moment passes as I continue to look through the images of the castle. Logan sets a glass down on the bar next to me and grabs a bottle of whiskey. "So you're just going to sit here, drinking by yourself while you look at castles you're not really going to buy?"

"You say that like it's a bad thing."

Logan just chuckles and goes to take drink orders from new customers. I slowly sip at my drink, mildly entertained by what's on the glowing screen in front of me. A large group comes in, filling the bar with bodies and noise.

Newly expanded, Getaway is a large bar, and it needs every single square foot it can get. I'm proud of my brothers for turning this place around from the hole-in-the-wall bar it was when they first bought it into something people flock to.

The woman next to me gets up and a man immediately slides onto the stool. His cologne is overwhelming, making me gag.

"I couldn't help but notice" —he starts, leaning in— "that you were here alone."

Blinking, I look up from my phone at the man next to me. He's wearing a dark suit with the jacket unbuttoned and is flashing me a bright-white smile.

"I'm Cam, by the way." He extends his hand, showing off his large-faced watch in the process. He's overdressed for the bar which caters to the blue-collar people of Eastwood, Indiana.

"Quinn," I say, finding it hard to be anything but polite.

It's in my nature to assume people aren't assholes. His attention is unwanted, but not rude. Not yet at least. He grips my hand tight, pressing his finger over the pulse-point on my wrist like he's trying out some lame move he read about in a dating-blog article.

"You're not from around here, are you?"

"No." It feels like a lie. I *am* from around here. I just don't live here currently. I always assumed I'd end up back here someday.

"Didn't think so. I've been doing business in Newport the last few months and have stopped in here every now and then. If you'd been in here before, I'd remember it."

I force a smile and shift my eyes to the bar. All I need to do is look at one of my brothers for them to come running, shove a fist in this guy's face and kick him out for life. Three of the four are here tonight, and they all take their roles as big brother seriously. Instead, I grab my drink and fiddle with the straw, wishing I had the power to speed up time and make Jamie walk through the door.

"So, you're here alone," he says more than asks. Of course I'm alone, and it's obvious.

"For now. I'm waiting for a friend."

"Yeah." He gives me a wink. "Me too." He inches closer. "We can wait together. Want a refill?"

"No thanks. My friend is a boy. Well, no, more like a man. Not more like. He is. He's my man-friend." The words keep coming out of my mouth even though I want them to stop. "I'm waiting for my man-friend."

"Right. Man-friend." Cam's eyebrows arch in amusement. "In case he doesn't show, you know where to find me."

"Yeah," I mumble, flashing a polite smile before getting

up and going behind the bar. I fill a glass with a small amount of vodka and then fill it with cherries.

"What are you doing back here?" Owen breezes past me to get a bottle of tequila. I pull a cherry from its stem and pop it in my mouth.

"Making myself a drink."

"That's just cherries and vodka."

"Exactly. I'll give the cherries a few minutes to marinate in the booze then I'll eat them."

Owen responds with a head shake and points to something next to me. "Hand me that glass?"

"Sure," I say and hand it to him. "It's getting busy in here. Where's Heather?"

"Waiting on her sitter to show up. She'll be here...eventually."

"I can help in the meantime."

Owen considers it as he pours a drink, hurrying back across the bar before coming back. "Can you make an Old Fashioned for the guy in the white shirt?"

"A what?"

"Old Fashioned."

I blink and reach into my purse again for my phone. Holding up my finger to tell Owen to wait, I do a quick Google search. "Got it. Well, maybe. What does it mean to 'muddle' a drink?"

"I'll make it. Here." He hands me a bottle of whiskey. "Pour ten shots and take them to Dean's table, along with this margarita for Kara."

"Easy enough." I move my glass of cherries to a safe spot, grab a tray, shot glasses, and carefully pour. I worked at a bar in college and lasted three nights before getting fired for not being able to keep up. I like fast-paced jobs. Hell, I'd go so far as to say I enjoy being in a field I can describe as demanding. But there was something so overwhelming about being surrounded by drunk people all shouting and yelling for their drinks.

Centering the margarita and arranging the shots around it, I lift the tray. A few shot glasses wobble, and the amber-colored liquid sloshes around. I take a step—nothing spills. Holding the tray as level as I can, I slowly make my way through the bar and feel a new appreciation for Heather, who can sprint through here, in heels no less, and deliver drinks without so much as losing a drop of booze on her way to the table.

I spy Dean and my soon-to-be sister-in-law, Kara, at a crowded table at the back. I sidestep to avoid a group of drunk women all wearing matching pink shirts that say "Marie's Last Fling Before the Ring" and grit my teeth as I watch the smallest bit of whiskey roll down the sides of the glasses. Maybe I shouldn't have filled them so high.

Stopping in front of Dean's table, I make my move to set the tray of shots down. Right as I'm lowering it, a drunk guy stumbles and bumps right into me...and the tray full of alcohol.

Boobs.

All I see are boobs. Large. Perky. Round. They're in my face and I'm having a hard time straightening up to look at the waitress's eyes. Alcohol drips off her perfect tits, rolling down onto the table and splashing into my lap.

"Sorry," the drunk asshole who bumped into her slurs, stumbling away. Dean, who's on his way to being just as toasted as that guy, jumps up and takes the waitress by the arm and helps her straighten up. The guy had shoved her forward and she hit the table. In a desperate attempt to save the tray full of shots she brought it closer to her body which resulted in all ten shot glasses and one strawberry margarita sliding down the tray and crashing against her ample chest.

I've never been jealous of an inanimate object before today. She's leaning over, alcohol streaming down the tray. A shot glass hits the table and rolls, landing on my lap.

"You all right?" Dean asks, brow furrowing. He looks through the crowd for the drunk guy who bumped into the waitress. She takes a step back, looking at the alcohol running down the front of her white dress. I raise my gaze from her breasts to her face, and my heart stops in my chest.

It's Quinn, and I haven't laid eyes on her in years. Her green eyes widen in shock, full lips parting ever so slightly. And then red rushes to her cheeks, embarrassed not by dropping the tray, but by having everyone look at her.

It may have been years since I've seen her, but I remember her well. Even though I shouldn't. Even though it's wrong.

"Logan's going to kill you," Dean says with a grin.

She shakes her head. "I do his taxes. He won't kill me." With a sigh, she shifts her gaze, looking at me for the first time. "I am so—" The words die in her throat the second we make eye contact. Everything about her is sheer perfection —even with the booze covering her dress. Her brunette hair falls down her back in waves, and I can see a hint of her freckles dotting her cheeks. She blinks rapidly, long lashes coming together. Then she turns her head down again, wiping away a bead of alcohol rolling down her neck. I can't help but look too, eyes going right to her tits, which are currently covered in whiskey. My cock jumps at the thought of licking it off her.

"Sorry. I'm so sorry," she finally finishes.

"It's okay. It wasn't your fault." I exhale and reach across the table for a napkin. It's damp from the drink that was resting on it, but it's better than nothing.

"Thanks." Her fingers brush mine as she takes the napkin, swiping it over her collarbone. "It's going to be hard to explain this if I get pulled over on the way home." Her hand plunges between her breasts, wiping up as much of the whiskey off her sun-kissed skin as she can.

"You too, Archer." Kara points to the shot glass that's resting on my legs. "You both smell like alcoholics."

Her comment, as innocent as it is, makes me cringe. I *do* know what an alcoholic smells like. And it's often much worse than smelling like straight whiskey and a strawberry margarita.

"Whatever," Quinn says, shaking her head. "It is what it is, right? Could be worse. Want me to get you refills?"

"Refills implies we got the first fill," Dean teases, picking up empty shot glasses from the table. I lean over and grab three from the floor. Quinn does the same, but her back is to me. My mouth goes dry as I watch her bend over, oblivious to how dangerously close her ass is to being exposed in that short dress.

It's just a sundress, white with little pale-yellow birds patterned along the hem. On anyone else, I wouldn't bat an eye. But on Quinn, a potato sack would look erotic.

She's tall and lean, getting most of her height from her long legs. I've wanted to bury my face between her large breasts since the moment I saw her, and those tits are what threw me on day one, thinking she was much older than she really was.

Even when I found out our age difference, I still wanted her. Her brother was my roommate freshman year of college, but it didn't matter.

Until it did.

Dean became more like a brother than my best friend, and I didn't realize how much I needed his family until they took me in. The whole Dawson crew—all seven of them— are good people.

The kind of good that's hard to find.

The kind of good that values family. That means it when they say they'll be there for you. The kind that makes you feel welcome and safe, who invites the guy who's been living with their son for a few months back to the family farm for

Christmas because his own parents had to fly out to Vegas at the last minute to deal with some shit no one should deal with over a holiday.

Then it mattered.

"Thanks," Quinn tells me and puts the final shot glass on the tray.

"Why are you bringing drinks out?" Dean sits back down in the booth and puts an arm around Kara.

"Heather is running late and I tried to be nice."

"That's where you went wrong, sis." Dean picks up his beer only to realize it's empty. "Don't do favors for those dickheads."

"Those dickheads who brought you another beer?" Logan appears behind Quinn, with a towel in one hand and a beer in another. Dean laughs and takes the beer from his younger brother.

"It wasn't my fault," Quinn starts. "Some drunk guy bumped into me. On accident," she adds quickly, knowing her brothers well. All four of them are over-protective, and if it weren't for the fact that I've secretly wanted Quinn for myself for the last several years, I would have felt sorry for her. Dating can't be easy with Owen, Logan, Dean, and Weston always looking over her shoulder.

Logan shrugs it off and mops up some of the booze on the floor with the towel. "There's a reason you're not a bartender anymore."

"Trust me, I know." She picks up the tray. "I'll go get more."

"No!" everyone shouts at the same time. Laughing, Logan takes the tray from her. "I'll get it."

"Thanks," she tells him and pulls her phone from her purse, firing off a text message. "Dammit. Jamie's already on her way. I was hoping she'd bring me more clothes," she mutters to herself. The white fabric of her dress is stained from the margarita, and she has to be soaked down to her bra from the whiskey. Well, if she's wearing a bra. My eyes go back to her chest on their own accord. I don't see straps, and the faint outline of her nipples are visible through the wet fabric.

Dammit. I need to stop.

"I have an extra set of scrubs in my car," I offer before I have a chance to think about what I'm saying. "They're clean."

"I'll take you up on that offer," she says, looking at the stains on her dress again. "The smell alone is going to make me sick."

"Memories?" Dean probes, raising his eyebrows.

"Maybe."

"I didn't know your nerd-friends knew how to have fun."

Not missing a beat, she pops her hip and places a hand on the curve. "Well, between washing our Ferraris and firing our personal assistants, we're known to have fun."

Dean waves his hand in the air. "Yeah, yeah, I get it. Be nice to the nerds because you might end up working for one."

"Exactly. And I don't drive a Ferrari. Or have a personal assistant. And I wouldn't fire one unless they were doing a terrible job." She turns to me, a smile playing on her full lips. "You brought scrubs to a bar?"

"They're in my car. I keep an extra set or two in there. You never know what a day might bring at the hospital."

"Oh, right." The flush is back on her cheeks. "You're a doctor now."

"I am," I reply and get out of the booth. The smell of her floral perfume is masked under the heavy scent of alcohol clinging to her skin. It wafts its way to me, teasing, making me want to lean closer and inhale.

"What do you do?"

"General surgery, for now."

She takes a small step backward, heel sliding on the floor still slick from the spilled drinks. I reach out and catch her, pulling her to my chest to keep her from falling.

"I keep telling you 'thanks' tonight." Her hands slide across my pec as she uprights herself. "And I should probably wipe that up before someone else slips." She moves away, reaching across the table for the stack of napkins Logan left. She wipes up the floor and leads the way out, tossing the napkins in the garbage as she passes it.

We slip out the employee door, stepping onto a gravel path that takes us down to the back lot behind the bar. The heavy door swings back into place, blasting us with cool air-conditioned air once more before shutting out the cacophonous thumping of bass coming from the bar.

The sounds of early summer echo through the night and moonlight shines down on the cornfield behind us.

"What did you mean 'for now?'" Quinn turns to me, slowly walking into the parking lot.

"I finish my residency soon. I've been applying for jobs and I'm not sure what I'll get."

"But it'll be surgery?"

"Yeah, I'm a surgeon."

She smiles and looks up at me. Even in heels, I'm taller than her. "That sounds cool, you know."

"It does," I agree, not at all attempting to hide my smirk. I worked my ass off from day one to get to where I am right now. I motion to my car and pull my keys from my pocket. "What about you? Dean said you invented and sold an app."

"Ah, yeah. I did." She gets a little shy, casting her eyes

back down. Dean also told me how much Apple bought it for, and I'm actually surprised to find out she *doesn't* drive a Ferrari or have a team of personal assistants.

"You were always smart."

"I just like computers and coding and all that stuff Dean says is geeky."

"So what do you do now?"

"I design the structures software systems need to operate. This week, I've been fine-tuning the coding standards for a program with real-time computing for a client that may or may not be the US Government." She gets excited as she talks, face lighting up.

"Coding standards?"

"It's the basic guidelines used when writing out the code to a new program."

Having reached my car, we stop. I turn my head down to meet Quinn's gaze and raise an eyebrow. "I'm not even going to pretend to understand what you do."

She brings her shoulders up and smiles. "That's okay. I don't understand it either." Her smile disappears the moment she realizes what she says, and the flush is back to her cheeks. "Actually I do. Obviously. Since it's my job."

I'd be lying if I said her awkwardness wasn't part of her appeal to me.

I open the back of my Jeep and grab my bag. Being a resident doctor means shit hours, long-ass days, and even longer weeks. Two years into my residency, I got an apartment with my friend Sam, who was working his way to becoming an anesthesiologist. We were farther from the hospital than before but saved a ton on rent. I started keeping necessities in my car on the nights when we were in surgery for hours.

I shake out the blue scrub top and pants. "They're a little wrinkled, but they're clean, I promise."

"As long as there's no blood on them, I'm good." She shakes her head, hair swishing over her bare shoulders. A few strands stick to her collarbone, still damp and sticky from the spilled drinks. If there's ever a lesson in self-control, it's right here and right now.

I swallow hard, talking down my cock.

"Then you're good. They're going to be big on you." I hold up the shirt, using it as an excuse to run my eyes over her body.

"That's okay. It's better than being wet all night. Which I am. I'm soaking wet."

Fuck. It's like she's trying to kill me.

"I mean, look at me." She sticks her finger between her breasts again. "I'm all sticky. I'm pretty sure—" She licks her finger. I readjust my cock in my jeans, trying to stop it at half-mast before it gives me away. "—Yep, that's salt from the margarita. It tastes kinda good, actually. I think I'll go order one after this. Want one? I still feel bad I spilled those drinks on you. But ten shots? Isn't that a little excessive?"

"There were other people at that table, you know."

"Right. I guess I didn't notice them."

Her words make my heart stop, make all the air leave my lungs. I've felt that way for years whenever she's around.

"But I'm sure they noticed me and the spilled drinks."

"They noticed, but probably won't remember."

She smiles again, and we head back to the bar. "This is nice, you know."

"What is?"

"Talking to you." Gravel crunches under her heels. "We've known each other for years but hardly ever talked.

It's like you thought I was just an annoying nerd like Dean did and avoided me."

I did avoid her, but it was the only way I knew how to keep my hands off her. To keep those words in my mouth and my lips away from hers. There were times I was fairly certain she had a crush on me, times she even put herself out there. But I couldn't dare act and risk losing my friendship with Dean.

"It is nice, isn't it?" she asks when I don't respond.

"Yeah."

"Maybe we can do it again sometime."

"Maybe."

But I can't. Not now. Not ever.

There's nothing more I'd rather do than spend more time with Quinn. But if I'm alone with her, I'm going to spill my guts and admit that I've wanted her for years. That I've watched from the sidelines, fighting off jealousy when she'd have a new boyfriend and how I never thought anyone was good enough for her. That she's made me want to be a better person without even trying because being around her showed me what it's like to be a good fucking person.

Or worse, I'll skip all the words that'll get knotted up in my chest and try to kiss her.

Neither of which I can do. I'm in town for my best friend's engagement party, and I'm not going to fuck shit up by making a move on his little sister. She might have liked me years ago, but the time has come and gone.

So I do what I've always done: Swallow everything I feel like a big pill, forcing it dry down my throat and walk away.

3

QUINN

The air leaves my lungs and I'm left standing there, watching Archer walk up ahead of me. What the hell? Did I say something wrong? One minute we were talking, feeling like the old friends we should be, and the next he's acting like he can't get away from me fast enough.

It doesn't matter. More importantly, it shouldn't matter.

He stops at the employee door, needing me to punch in a code to unlock it. I fold the scrubs over my arm, careful not to press them against my wet dress, and take a spot next to him to enter the code. He doesn't look at me, doesn't say a damn thing. The tension rolls off him in waves, and as nice as our chat was a minute ago, I cannot wait to get back into the bar and away from him.

That's how Archer Jones has been since the moment I met him. Closed off. Guarded. Letting the walls inch down just enough for me to get a glimpse of the man inside only to bring them up again.

A little green light flashes after I punch in the four-digit code and Archer opens the door for me. I step in first, shivering almost immediately from the cold air blowing down on us from the vent above.

"Thanks again," I say and turn to him. The door clicks shut and I shuffle forward. "For the scrubs. I'll get them back to you tomorrow. How long are you in town?"

"Until Sunday."

"Me too. I'll, uh, see you again I'm sure."

"I'll be at your parents' house tomorrow for the engagement party."

"Oh, right." I fiddle with a strand of hair, heart beating rapidly in my chest. Archer shifts his weight, lips parting as if he wants to say something. Our eyes meet for a brief moment before he blinks and turns his head, bringing his hand up to his stubble-covered jaw.

"I'm gonna go change now," I blurt, needing to say something. It's getting awkward just standing here.

"Yeah, good idea." He nods and steps forward, following me out of the back hall and going back into the bar. He goes in the opposite direction, back to Dean and company, and I go into the bathroom. I do the best I can to rinse my skin, sticky from the margarita, and change into the scrubs.

Archer was right: they are big. Knowing I look ridiculous in oversized scrubs and heels, I fold my dress and exit the bathroom.

"I don't get it."

I turn, following the male voice I assume is directed to me. It's that guy Cam from the bar, the one in the fancy suit with the expensive watch. He pushes off the wall, drink in his hand, and flashes that same super-bright white smile my way.

"Are you trying to be a sexy nurse? Because if you are, I suggest something with a little less coverage."

I blink. Is that supposed to be a compliment? "I'm not trying to be a sexy nurse."

"Then please explain your ensemble. Because I don't get it."

Is he that drunk or is he for real? "You don't have to *get it*. It's what I'm wearing so..." I bring up my shoulders in a shrug. He continues to stare at me, a smug smile on his lips. I shake my head and turn to walk away. He says something else and I pretend I don't hear it. I go right to the bar again to get a bag for my wet dress and get my glass of vodka-soaked cherries that I stashed in the mini fridge under the counter.

"I heard what happened." Owen looks over his shoulder as he fills a tall glass with beer from the tap. "Way to go, butterfingers."

I make a face. "Someone bumped into me. Hard. It would have happened to you too."

"Doubt it." He makes a face back and gives the beer to a guy at the counter. I pop a cherry in my mouth, shuddering from how strong it tastes. Owen laughs. "Want me to make you a real drink?"

"Please. I'll try an Old Fashioned."

"Give me a minute," he says and hurries off to bring out more drinks and flirt with his female customers again. I move away from the counter so people don't mistake me for a bartender, though right now I look more like an escaped mental patient given what I'm wearing.

A few minutes later, I'm sipping the Old Fashioned and Jamie's walking through the doors. She orders a beer and we snag two seats at the bar.

"Want to go home and change?" she asks.

"Is it that bad?"

"It's not good." She laughs and takes a hair tie off her

wrist. "Stand up...let me fix it the best I can." With a bit of finagling, she pulls the scrub top tighter, securing the band in the back. "At least I can see your figure now. And your tits. Maybe we can get some free drinks."

Since the shirt is big, the V neckline goes down low. "I can already get us free drinks."

"Yeah, but where's the fun in that?"

I laugh and rest an elbow on the counter. Jamie and I have been friends since middle school, and though she still lives here and I'm up north in Chicago, it's always like we just picked up right where we left off whenever we see each other.

We catch up, talking and laughing about any small town drama I missed. About half an hour later, a friend from work comes in, and Jamie's all too excited to see him. She's been crushing on him for a while, and they are seriously cute together.

My gaze darts to the back of the bar, finding Archer still in the booth with Dean and his friends. They have more shots in front of them, and while everyone else seems to be having a good time, something seems off with Archer.

But it's not my problem.

"Want to play pool with us?" Jamie asks, finishing the rest of her beer.

"Yeah, sounds fun. I'll get us drinks and meet you over there." Back behind the bar I go and get Logan to make me three mojitos. I give him my credit card before I leave, opening myself a tab to cover what I spilled as well as what I drank and have him put Dean's party on it as well.

"I have to say," Cam starts, appearing out of nowhere. "The look is starting to work for me."

I've already spilled enough drinks tonight and I'm determined not to shed one drop of the three I'm precariously balancing on a tray this time. Flicking my eyes to him, I keep walking, taking small, level steps.

"This might surprise you, but I didn't get dressed today with the intent of my clothes *working for you*. I wear what I want."

He laughs. "Sure you do. That little dress you had on was just for you, wasn't it, sweetheart?" He winks and then laughs, and I've never been more tempted to throw a drink in someone's face before. Guys like him make me want to throw up. I don't need to be patronized, and I sure as hell don't need him to mansplain how my brain works when I pick out an outfit to wear.

"Yes. It was."

Grimacing, I set my sights on Jamie and her friend Bryan, delivering the drinks with no incident this time. We take turns at the pool table, not playing by the rules but giving us something to do as we drink and talk. Soon, Jamie and Bryan get handsy, and I go a few yards away to throw darts, giving them some privacy. Well, as much as they can get in a crowded bar.

"And then there was one."

Seriously? I close my eyes in a long blink. Doesn't this guy have anything better to do? If he's really stuck in Newport on business, then no, he doesn't. Still...haven't I made it clear I'm not interested?

"Need some company?" Cam asks.

"No thanks, I'm good." I finish the rest of my mojito and set the empty glass on a tall table. I have a feeling this guy's going to give me his company whether I like it or not.

"Are you?"

"Yes. I am." I throw a dart and hit only an inch from the bullseye.

"Nice shot!"

"Thanks," I blurt, my manners coming out automatically.

"How about this: I get one closer and you come have a drink with me."

"Look, you seem like a nice guy, but I'm not interested."

"Come on, sweetheart. What do you have to lose?"

I've dealt with my fair share of pushy guys before, but this guy is relentless. He takes a step toward me and I move back.

"I won't bite." He smiles. "Unless you want me to." He reaches out and tucks my hair behind my ear, then runs his fingers across my shoulder and down my arm. If my drink was in my hand, I'd throw it in his face. Unfortunately, I'm holding a dart, and the last thing Logan and Owen need is a lawsuit over their sister stabbing a drunk guy with grabby hands.

"Hey!" a loud male voice shouts. It's not one of my brothers, and it only takes me a second to place the voice.

Archer.

"She's not interested, man. Back the fuck off." He shifts his gaze to mine. Darkness clouds his chocolate eyes and anger pulls down his handsome face. "Are you all right, Quinn?"

"I am now."

Cam holds up his hands. "Sorry, bro. Didn't mean to trespass on your territory."

Archer gives him a what-the-fuck-is-wrong-with-you look, then before I know what's happening, he coils his fists and goes to hit Cam right in the face. I grab his arm at the last second, the logical part of my mind kicking in. He said he's applying for surgeon jobs. Getting arrested for a bar fight won't look good on a resume.

"He's not worth it," I say softly, and Archer turns, just

inches from me. He unclenches his hands and lowers his arm. I keep my fingers wrapped around his bicep, feeling the heat of his flesh through his t-shirt.

"But you are," he says so softly I'm not sure I heard him correctly.

"What?"

He shakes himself, pulling out of my grasp. "You sure you're all right? You don't need me to punch this cocksucker in the throat?"

It's like one of my brothers coming to my defense, but there's something different with Archer. Maybe I'm the only one who feels it, and there's a good chance I'm only feeling whatever the hell it is because I want to.

And also because I've had a few drinks.

But there's nothing brotherly in the way Archer stands in front of me, eyes narrowed and arms held out slightly to his sides, ready to pummel Cam and defend my honor.

"No, but thanks. Really. You didn't have to do that."

He puts his hand on my shoulder and turns, keeping himself between Cam and me. "That guy's an ass."

"He's been hitting on me all night."

"All night?" Archer tenses again and turns around. Cam is slinking away, but won't get far if Archer decides to go after him.

"Even in the scrubs." I give him a half-smile and sigh. "I'm trying not to go off on a rant right now, but I cannot stand guys like that. There are other reasons for going to a bar, you know. Not everyone wants to hook up with you, Mr. I'm-Doing-Business-in-Newport."

Archer laughs. "That was his line?"

"It was one I remember. It's pretty bad, huh?" I readjust my purse on my shoulder. "I think this is a sign from the universe I'm not meant to be at a bar tonight. I just want to go home."

"Did you drive?"

"No, I came with Kara. So it's going to be a long night."

"I can take you." He doesn't look at me as he offers.

"I don't want to make you leave."

"Honestly," he starts and forces himself to look at me. Our eyes meet for a fleeting second before he brings his hand to the back of his neck. "I'm tired. I came straight from work and I haven't had a day off in over a week."

"That's brutal."

"It is. So let me take you home and use it as an excuse to bail early. I don't think the guys are ready to hear that I'm not the partier I used to be."

"You can use me as your scapegoat." He can use me any other way too. "I'm going to tell Jamie I'm leaving and then we can go."

Ten minutes later, we're walking out into the parking lot.

"Are you staying with your parents?" Archer unlocks his Jeep.

"Yeah, I am." I fold down the top of the to-go bag of burgers and fries I got on the way out, the least I could do for Archer for leaving his friends. Yeah, he said he was tired, but I'm not sure I believe him.

"I haven't been to their house in a long time. Please tell me it's the same." He opens the passenger side door for me and goes around to get in.

"It pretty much is. Plus another dog or two." I click the seatbelt into place, trying to think back to the last time Archer joined us for dinner. Before I went away to college myself, I looked forward to the Sundays where Dean and Archer would make the drive from Purdue University to the house for dinner.

Sunday dinners were a big thing. After church, Mom would spend the day cooking, and even with all four of my brothers plus Archer, there'd be food to spare and she'd send Dean and Archer back to school with enough care packages to last half the week.

Without needing directions from me, Archer drives to my parents' house. We're about twenty minutes away, and suddenly the silence between us is awkward. A mile goes by and I know I need to say something.

Another goes by before I turn and open my mouth.

"So where do you work?" I ask at the same time Archer asks me something.

"You go first," we say in unison.

Laughing, Archer looks away from the road for a second. "Indy. What about you?"

"Chicago."

"I never pegged you to be a big city kind of girl."

"I didn't think I was either, but I love it there. And I love my job, but sometimes I miss this." I wave my hand at the window.

"There's literally nothing there."

"Exactly." I smile. "I miss it. The cornfields, the quiet, the slower pace...I'm not that far away at least."

"Do you come home often?"

"I try to. Mostly to see Jackson, because I miss him too much."

"Jackson?" Archer turns his head, eyes widening and his grip on the wheel tightening. Is he jealous?

"Oh my God, has Dean never mentioned Jackson to you?"

"Why would he...who...I don't think so. Is he your boyfriend?"

My heart speeds up and I lick my lips, eyeing Archer. I

think he is jealous. "No, Jackson is my nephew. Wes's son."

Archer relaxes considerably. "Right. Yeah, he's mentioned him. He always calls him Jax though. Didn't ring a bell right away."

I roll my eyes. "He's watched *Sons of Anarchy* way too many times. Jackson is named after our grandfather, who never went by Jax. Well, never according to my grandma, that is."

Archer smiles. "How old is he now?"

"He just turned three. He's so flipping cute. Hopefully he stays that way and isn't overly influenced by his uncles."

"At least he has a good aunt."

It's my turn to smile. "I try. So...do you like Indy?"

"It's not where I thought I'd end up, but the hospital is great." He gives me a genuine smile, and I ease back in my seat. We talk about work the rest of the way.

Archer puts his Jeep in park outside the garage. He hesitates, and I take it as my cue to leave.

"Thanks again, Archer," I say, and his name feels both good and bad coming from my lips. I extend my arm, giving him the bag of takeout.

"Didn't you get two burgers?"

"Yeah, but you can have them."

He swallows hard, his Adam's apple bobbing. "You should eat. I mean, you've had several drinks, right?"

"Right." My heart speeds up. "Who am I to ignore advice from a doctor?"

He kills the engine and gets out. I unlock the garage door and shimmy past my parents' trucks. My dad's a contractor, and my mom quit her job as a kindergarten teacher years ago to work full-time along with him. It's not unusual for the barn, the garage, and occasionally the house to act as storage from a project they're working on.

"I didn't know your parents were so high-tech," Archer muses when I enter the passcode into a computerized lock.

"They're not. Technology is kind of my thing, though." I open the door and wait for the dogs to come running. Boots, Chrissy, and Carlos are friendly and don't give a care in the world who's walking through the door. All they want is attention. Rufus, on the other hand, is territorial and protective and has gotten worse in his old age.

I slip my fingers under his collar and hold him back before he has a chance to lunge at Archer.

"Hey, buddy," Archer says, holding out his hand. "Remember me?"

All of my parents' dogs are mixed breeds, rescued from the local shelter. Rufus is the oldest of the bunch, and I think my mom had just brought him home the last time I remember Archer coming around.

Rufus growls but sniffs Archer's hand. He considers him for a minute, then wags his tail. He's a German Shepherd and Malamute mix and can be hard to handle when he goes on the defense. I'm glad he's good with Archer, because there's something telling when your dog doesn't like someone they've just met.

"Calm down," I whisper-yell to the others, not wanting to wake my parents. Obviously I'm a competent adult and can come and go as I please, but I'd feel bad waking them, and mostly, I know Archer would leave.

Nothing makes me feel the child I was the first time I laid eyes on Archer than bringing him back to my childhood home and hoping we don't wake up my parents.

"What do you want to drink?" I ask, still greeting the overly-excited dogs. I grab treats from the pantry.

"Whatever you're having," Archer tells me as he drops to his knees to pet Rufus. I stare for a few seconds, hating how freaking adorable he looks with his fingers buried in the old dog's fur.

I pour two glasses of lemonade and put our food on plates, taking it to the large island in the kitchen.

"I never realized how much I missed eating here." Archer looks around the room, flattening his hand on the surface of the cold granite counter.

"You and Dean spent a lot of time in the kitchen."

He half-smiles and takes a bite of his burger, nodding. I grab two fries and dip them in ketchup.

"The food was only part of the reason I liked coming back to the Dawson Homestead."

I raise an eyebrow. "There was more than one reason?"

His eyes meet mine, and something passes between us. My heart is in my throat, beating so fast and so loud there's no way he's not hearing it.

"There was."

I wait a beat, but he doesn't elaborate. "What was it?"

"That's for me to know." He gives me a little grin and goes back to his food. I can only stomach half my burger and a handful of fries before feeling too full. I pick the meat off the bun and divide it up between the dogs, who gobble it up in seconds.

Chrissy goes over to the back door and noses a bell hanging from the knob.

"Is she ringing a bell to go outside?"

"They all do. Well, everyone but Boots. That dog's not the brightest crayon in the box if you know what I mean. And when I let one out, they'll all want out."

Archer finishes his lemonade and stands, taking his plate and mine to the sink. He's right behind me when I unlock the door to let the dogs out, and steps onto the patio with me.

The sounds of the night echo around us and a soft breeze has picked up, moving the sticky humid air. All four dogs take off, running through the grass like idiots. My heart speeds up again when I look back at Archer, and all the things I've wanted to say to him over the years threaten to bubble up and spill out.

He takes a step closer, and the woodsy scent of his cologne wakes up every nerve inside of me, making me curse myself for not staying in touch with this beautiful man.

The breeze picks up again, bringing in a gust that tousles my hair around my face. Archer tucks it back behind my ear and parts his lips. If we were in a romance movie, he'd lean in and kiss me right now. Then he'd tell me how he's always had feelings for me, and even though it's been years, the fluttering in his stomach came back the moment he saw me, just like it did when I saw him.

But this is real life, and real life isn't as carefully crafted and scripted like a movie. Archer has never expressed interest in me, and as far as I know, he thinks of me as a sister. Plus, Dean would throw a fit if I said I've had a crush on his friend, telling me how things will be awkward from there on out.

Sometimes, real life sucks.

Boots barks, and we turn just in time to see Chrissy lower into a crouch at the edge of the pool.

"Chrissy, no!" I shout, but it's too late. The lab mix dives in, happily paddling about. Carlos goes in after her, doing one quick lap before coming out and shaking water all over Rufus, who gives the small mutt the evil eye. Sighing, I shake my head and laugh. "Whatever. You guys can just stay outside until you're dry."

"That dog loves to swim." Archer's lips are pulled into a

smile as he watches Chrissy splash about.

"She loves it, and I forgot. Though I will blame my parents for not shutting the gate around the pool." I grab a squeaky tennis ball from the ground, squeak it a few times and throw it as far as I can into the night.

It doesn't go far.

Still, it's enough to get all four dogs running, and as soon as Chrissy is out of the pool, I shut the gate. Chrissy brings back the ball, and this time Archer grabs it, throwing it much farther than I did.

I sit on the wooden glider my dad made for my mom, figuring I might as well get comfortable. With the breeze and her running around, it won't be long before Chrissy is dry enough to come inside and get toweled off.

"I meant to ask you before," Archer starts, taking the slobbery ball from Chrissy and throwing it again. "How you got into software design for your career."

"I took one of those online quizzes that tell you what you should be when you grow up."

"Really?"

"No," I say with a laugh. Archer takes a step back, closer to me. "I've always been fascinated with technology. When I was a kid, I thought it was crazy people didn't have the technology that we did. Like how the hell did they survive in the olden days?"

Smiling, Archer takes a spot next to me on the glider. He pushes off the ground with his feet, sending us sliding back.

"I guess from there I just got into it even more. I actually started out my freshman year as an engineering major but switched to computer science my second semester. Which is super interesting, I know, but remember that little-known fact about me in case my dad decides to play Cash Table tomorrow."

"Cash Table?"

"His version of *Cash Cab* but he asks random questions when we're all sitting down at the table together. It's like the daddest thing in the world, I know."

Archer laughs. "That sounds like something he'd do."

"So what about you? What made you want to go to med school?"

"I didn't want to face responsibility and chose a profession with an ungodly amount of schooling." He playfully nudges me.

"That was actually my first guess, though you should have wavered more in there and switched your major back and forth at least three times, you rookie."

"Damn it, I should have. But really, I made up my mind to be a doctor when I was a sophomore in high school. I had a sick family member and have always been thankful for what they've been able to do for...for that person."

I bend my knees up, tucking my feet under my legs, and study Archer. He's staring into the dark, eyes narrowed ever so slightly. I don't remember him or Dean ever mentioning a sick family member. My heart aches a little for him, and I hope the illness didn't claim a loved one.

His jaw tenses, and then he leans back, blinking rapidly. "You can't tell anyone about that project you're working on?"

"Nope. Though I'm pretty sure I've convinced Dean we're building a Batmobile."

"Is it sad I'm a little disappointed that it's not?"

I laugh. "Well, I didn't say it's *not* a Batmobile..."

"Don't get my hopes up." He chuckles, and his eyes sparkle in the moonlight. "And if it is, you'll have to pull strings to let me drive it."

"Only if you wear a Batman costume."

"I'd wear a Joker costume if it means I can drive the Batmobile."

I shake my head. "If you're thinking of Heath Ledger's Joker, then his clothes are too cool. You'll have to go with Danny DeVito's Penguin."

Archer makes a face, acting like he's considering it seriously. "Yeah, I'd still do it. For the Batmobile."

"I should probably wait until after you're dressed up to tell you this, but it's *not* a Batmobile."

"I figured such." He yawns, and in just seconds all the humor is gone from his face. Leaning forward, he grabs the ball from Chrissy and tosses it again before standing. "I should go."

"Yeah," I reply, trying not to let him know the abruptness is startling, though it's the second time tonight he's cut me off short right when I was thinking we were getting along just fine. Better than fine, really. "I should, uh, go inside and get some sleep. Tomorrow's going to be a busy day."

Archer's hand lands on the back of his neck, and his brows pinch together. "Right. Tomorrow. Your brother's party."

I pat my leg and make a kissy sound, getting the dogs' attention. Archer stands aside, letting me take the lead back into the house.

"Thanks for dinner. See you tomorrow," he says as he pulls his keys from his pocket. He's gone before I can tell him goodbye.

Perplexed, I stand in the kitchen for a minute before going to lock the back door. Though it's now gone, there's no denying we had a moment. The feelings I thought I could quell for Archer have come back with a vengeance, and my heart demands another moment with him.

But I can't help but feel he doesn't want one with me.

4

QUINN

I pour myself a cup of coffee and sit at the kitchen table, phone in hand. Blinking, still too tired to focus on the bright screen of my phone, my finger hovers over the email icon. I have a handful of new emails, and while I can assume a few are junk, I know the others are from work.

If I open it and see a problem, I won't be able to stop thinking about it. And I already have enough on my mind.

"Want some eggs, dear?" Mom turns, looking at me over her shoulder as she scrambles a skillet full of eggs.

"You know the answer to that, Mom." I open Facebook instead. The emails can wait. If something was terribly wrong, someone would have called me by now.

"What about over easy?" she tries, knowing I detest eggs. "I can make you pancakes instead."

"You don't have to, Mom, but thanks. I'll stick to coffee for now."

"You got in late." She raises her eyebrows and smiles. "Did you have fun at the bar last night?"

"I spilled a tray of drinks on myself, but it was all right. Archer took me home so Dean and Kara could stay out."

"That was nice of him. I'm glad he was able to make it this weekend. Dean said he wasn't sure if he'd be able to get time off from work." Mom turns the burner off and grabs a plate. "I haven't seen that boy in years."

"He's not a boy anymore." The words spill from my lips, and I think of sitting outside on the glider with Archer last night. My pulse increases and heat flows through me. Archer was the subject of my dreams last night, and in my dreams, we did more than just sit and talk.

Mom scoops her eggs onto her plate and eyes me curiously. She's always been eerily—and annoyingly—perceptive.

"Right. He's not." She grabs the salt and pepper and joins me at the table. "You know you all are always just kids in my eyes."

"That's because you're old."

"You say that like you forget you're not getting any younger. Though you are right about Archer. He's a doctor now," she says with a smile. "Which is impressive on its own, but even more so considering all he went through in college."

I almost spit out the sip of coffee I just took. "What did he go through?"

Before Mom has a chance to answer, the back door opens and the dogs go barreling through the kitchen to greet Weston, my oldest brother, and Jackson.

"Grammy!" Jackson squeals and squirms out of Weston's arms. He gets stuck in the middle of the four dogs, who are all wagging their tails with excitement and licking Jackson's face. He's the only person—well, besides Mom—who lets the dogs lick his face. They love him for it.

"Hey, sis." Weston takes off his boots and crosses the

room. I set my coffee down and stand, welcoming him with a hug. "Haven't seen you in a while."

"I know. I've been swamped at work."

"How's the Batmobile coming?" he asks with a smirk. Weston's a cop, and together we keep the Batmobile theory alive in Dean's mind.

"Will you two stop already!" Mom steps over Boots and scoops up Jackson. "Poor Dean actually believes you."

"Mom, not even Jackson believed me when I told him I was building a Batmobile." Shaking my head, I sit back at the table to finish my coffee. Lord knows I need it.

"Right, Grammy. Batman already has the Batmobile."

"My three-year-old son is smarter than our brother," Weston mutters, making me laugh.

"Grammy, I'm hungry." Jackson's eyes are on Mom's scrambled eggs. "Can I have that?"

"Of course, little mister!" Mom puts him down at her spot. "I made those just for you, you know."

Standing to get more coffee, I smile. Mom's been like that my whole life, never stopping to think about herself for even a second when it comes to her family. I chat with Weston for a bit before he leaves to run errands and go home to sleep before working the night shift.

Then Jackson and I go outside to feed the chickens and play with the dogs while Mom rushes around to clean the kitchen. The house is already spotless, but since she's hosting the party this evening, she's in overdrive.

I know something is wrong the moment we step back into the house. Mom's on the phone with one hand pressed to her forehead.

"Don't panic. It's not a disaster. We'll work it out, sweetie. All right, bye now. See you later." Mom hangs up and whirls around. "This is a disaster!"

"What is?"

"The caterer is sick."

I blink and wait for her to elaborate.

"Kara's aunt and cousin started their own catering business a few months ago. She wanted to hire them to be nice." Mom shakes her head and starts madly scrolling through her phone for someone else to call. "Her aunt has been sick with the flu all week and her cousin woke up this morning throwing up. I can't believe she thought it would be okay to make the food up until now! The moment her aunt got sick, she should have canceled, not leaving us high and dry the day of the party."

"It'll be okay, Mom," I reiterate. "I'm sure we can find someone else to cater tonight."

"On such short notice? It'll be a miracle if we do." She trades her phone for her to-do list and takes a deep breath, trying not to panic. Raising four rowdy boys and one wonderful daughter—who might have gone through a super sassy teenager phase—has given Mom an edge on appearing calm when she's internally freaking out. It's something I inherited from her and am thankful for when I get stressed with work.

"Mom, go take a shower. I'll call around. And if I can't get someone, we'll put something together. Dad's still out on a job, right?"

"Yes, he won't be back until the afternoon."

"Perfect. He can pick up whatever we need in that time. And Kara's a pretty good cook, isn't she?"

"She's a wonderful cook. But it's her party and that's the last thing—"

"Mom, it's not the wedding today. If she needs to help make appetizers or whatever, she can."

"Right." Mom comes over and kisses my forehead. "I'm so glad you're home right now, honey."

My phone rings, startling me awake. I rapidly blink, trying to get my eyes to focus. I'm disoriented, and it takes me a few seconds to realize where I am. It's been so long since I've done anything but work, and on my days off I spend most of my time catching up on the sleep I've missed.

I feel around on the nightstand for my phone, and have a minor panic attack when I see my mom's name. Unless it's my birthday, I always do. And even then, my anxiety goes up every time I see her name on the caller ID.

Maybe today is the day the Narcan didn't work.

Maybe today is the day they found him a little too late.

"Hello?" I answer, pushing myself up onto my elbows.

"Hey, Archie." Mom's voice is calm, but that doesn't mean much. "How's my favorite doctor?"

I let out a breath and realize it's going on ten o'clock. She's not waking me up early in the morning with terrible news.

"Tired."

"Hang in there, you're almost done."

"Yeah," I say, though work wasn't the reason I'm tired this morning. I got back to the room late and should have crashed. But I couldn't because I couldn't get my mind to shut off.

Quinn was in my thoughts, in my dreams, pulling on my heart. I almost messed up last night. Almost took things too far.

Twice.

I can't let it happen again.

She's my best friend's little sister, and he's made it abundantly clear the best way to get on his shit list is to make a move on Quinn. No, he's never directly told me to stay away from her, but the unwritten rules of friendship are there. And who's to say Quinn would even go for me?

She's the most interesting person I know, and while being able to introduce myself as a doctor definitely helps me score, the effect is lost on Quinn. She's not impressed by titles or jobs that make lots of money. Though most of the women who fawn over doctors don't realize how little a resident doctor makes.

Quinn is different. She's smart and self-sufficient. She sold a fucking app to Apple before she was twenty-five and works for one of the most up-and-coming software companies in the nation.

"Arch?" Mom repeats my name.

"Sorry, Mom, didn't hear you."

"Are you at work?"

Yawning, I lay back in bed. "No. I was sleeping."

"Oh, I'm sorry. I didn't mean to wake you. Why did you answer?"

I don't say it, but she knows exactly why I answered. I've spent the last fifteen years worried every time my phone rang it was *the call.* "I need to get up anyway. I'm meeting the guys later."

"The guys? Oh, right! You're back in Eastwood with Dean Dawson. Have fun, Archie. You deserve it."

"Yeah. How's...how's everything at home?" It's the most specific I'll get, but Mom can read between the lines.

"Things are looking up. For now. The last few days have been easy. Dad got some time off from work and we've all gone out and did the things we used to, like bowling and dinner."

"That's good to hear."

"We miss you."

"Yeah," I say, knowing not everyone in the "we" even gives a shit. "I'll call and check in next week. Love you."

"Yeah, you too." I hang up, feeling my pulse still race. I waver back and forth between sadness and anger, hating him for doing this to us. Sometimes I think he's a selfish prick. Other times I think he's a victim of his disease.

It's hard not to be mad at him, and even harder not to resent him. I miss him as much as I never want to see him again, and I hate him as much as I love him. Though in the end, he's family. In the end, I just want him to live.

I want him to be my big brother again and not the addict he's become.

"THERE'S BEEN A SLIGHT CHANGE IN PLANS." DEAN SETS HIS phone down and finishes his beer. The plans for today were nothing more than drinking and playing video games. Catching up on the same old shit we used to do in college, besides go out chasing girls.

"Why?" Owen doesn't look away from the TV.

"The caterers got sick and no one else is free."

"How is that our problem?"

Dean gives his younger brother a glare. "There's no one to make the food for the party."

"Again," Owen starts. "How is that our problem?"

"And you wonder why you're still single," Logan mutters.

I laugh, finding the banter between Dean and his brothers to be oddly comforting. "You said plans changed," I say. "What have they changed to?"

"Going to the house to help Kara, my mom, and Quinn cook."

Quinn.

"Sure." I do my best to sound annoyed. Cooking a big, fancy meal on a Saturday afternoon is the last thing I want to do. Hell, cooking a big, fancy meal any day sounds like a terrible time. I don't know how to cook and I hate washing dishes.

But if Quinn's there...

I need to stop. Dean is right there, standing feet from me, and I'm thinking of stripping his sister down and burying my cock between her legs. Fuck. Logan and Owen are right here too.

All three of them would kill me if they knew what I want to do to their precious Quinn. What I've wanted to do...what I've imagined doing over and over again. I've jerked off to the thought of her, fucked her in my dreams more than once.

And it's never enough. Every time leaves me wanting more and I don't know exactly what it is about her that drives me so fucking wild. She's like my kryptonite and the closer I get, the weaker I become. Soon I'll cave and give in... and lose my best friend and his entire family that have become as close to me as my own.

I've never been an impulsive person. Don't get me wrong, I'm far from a saint. But I don't do crazy shit. Yet for some reason, Quinn has gotten under my skin and crazy is all I want to do.

With her.

To her.

The only way to keep that from happening is to shut it down.

———

"You're with me." Quinn slides her bare feet into sandals and grabs her purse. "Ready?"

I blink. Shake myself. Try not to acknowledge how damn sexy she looks in those cut-off shorts and t-shirt. It's loose-fitting, tucked into the front of her shorts. The collar hangs just low enough to be teasing, showing off the top of her perfect cleavage. Her hair is up in a messy bun on the top of her head, and she's not wearing a bit of makeup.

"Yeah. I'm ready."

She unfolds the grocery list her mom wrote out and snaps a picture of it with her phone. "I'll lose the paper," she explains. "And now I'm going to leave the list on the counter and see how long it takes before my mom calls and freaks out." Her smile is fucking adorable.

She walks ahead of me, and I divert my eyes, knowing if I look at her ass I'm done for. We make it three steps before I flick my eyes up. One quick look is all it takes to get my cock's attention. The denim rides up her ass a bit, and I watch her butt cheeks move beneath the material.

Quinn doesn't drive a Ferrari, but she does drive a Porsche. Loud music plays from the speakers as soon as she turns the car on.

"I forgot to turn it down," she says and brings the volume low enough to talk over. "Thanks again for taking me home last night."

"It was on the way."

"Not really, but it wasn't too far out of the way. So, thanks. And it was nice last night talking to you."

"Yeah." I look out the window. I can feel Quinn's eyes on me but don't turn to look at her. I don't want to be a jerk, but I don't know how to act around Quinn.

I've never been so sexually frustrated with anyone in my entire life. I like her. I want her. But I can't have her and being off limits only makes my dick harder. She fiddles with the radio the rest of the way.

"All right," she says when we get to the store. She brings up the picture of the shopping list and grabs a cart. "We should probably start at the bakery and work our way around, getting the cold stuff last."

She's thinking out loud, which is something that usually irritates the piss out of me when people do that. But not Quinn. Every flaw, every little weird thing she does draws me to her even more.

"It makes more sense to split up. You go to the bakery and I'll go to the deli. We can meet in the middle and save time," I say.

"Oh, uh, okay. That's a good idea."

"I know. We can get this over with."

Quinn airdrops me the photo of the list and pushes the cart in the opposite direction. I grab a basket and start walking, not knowing where I'm going, too irritated to stop and figure it out. Quinn has no idea what she's doing to me and is clueless about how hard it is for me to curb what I'm feeling for her. And even if she wasn't Dean's sister, it doesn't make sense to date anyone right now. I have no idea where

I'll end up. I could get a job at a hospital halfway across the country for all I know.

I circle around the store before I find the deli, and get everything from there on the list.

"There you are." Quinn's voice comes from behind me. "I thought maybe you got bored and ran off. I've been waiting for you by the canned goods. They're in the middle, after all, and on the list."

"Right. I don't know where things are here."

"True, and I do. What have you gotten so far?"

I put the basket of groceries in the cart, and she checks things off her list. Cold air seeps from the coolers around us, and Quinn shivers, goosebumps breaking out over her arms. Her nipples are hard, faintly visible through her t-shirt.

Biting the inside of my cheek, I turn away, shifting my cock in my pants to hide the semi I have going on.

"We're almost done." Quinn sticks her phone back in her purse and turns the cart around. "I know where the rest of this stuff is."

She leads the way to the produce, picking out potatoes and carrots. Two carrots are stuck together in a deformity, and the larger one has a growth that looks like a tiny penis. Quinn snickers and puts it in the cart.

"What's so funny?"

"Come on," she says, holding up the carrot.

"What?"

She hikes up an eyebrow. "Do you have to be a serious fuddy-duddy all the time now that you're a doctor?"

"Fuddy-duddy?"

"Yeah, a fuddy-duddy."

"I've never heard an adult say that."

She rolls her eyes. "Well, you are one. You can't say you

didn't think the same thing I did when you saw that deformed carrot."

"It just looks like a deformed carrot to me."

She lets out a small sigh and gets the rest of the produce we need, crossing the last thing off our list. We get in the checkout line behind a young mother, visibly exhausted as she tries to juggle twins who are I'm guessing to be around six months old and a crying two-year-old.

The cashier totals up her order and the mom digs her credit card out of her bag. It's declined. Her cheeks turn bright red and the cashier runs it again. And again. I probably wouldn't have noticed if it wasn't for the way Quinn is staring. She bites her lip and gets her own credit card from her purse.

"I can try entering the numbers manually," the cashier says. The young mom nods, on the verge of tears, and turns to attend to the toddler, who's on the floor crying now. Quinn takes a quick step up and slides her own card through the reader.

The cashier eyes Quinn and she just smiles back at him, then uses her finger to messily sign her name. The mom straightens up right as the receipt starts to print.

Her eyes go from the receipt to Quinn and back again.

"Thank you," she whispers, voice wavering with emotion. "I knew we might not have enough, but they're hungry and..." She stops, looking up to try to keep her tears from coming.

"You're welcome," Quinn says. "You have beautiful children."

The two-year-old stops crying, looking up at Quinn with curiosity. The mom thanks her again and again, wiping away her tears, before she and her children leave. Quinn moves on, acting like what she did was no big deal. She doesn't want recognition from it. Doesn't want anyone to pat her on the back.

That's just Quinn. As kind as she is pretty.

The situation with her just went from bad to worse. Because as I stand here looking at her, it hits me that she's not just someone I want to hook up with. She's someone I could fall in love with.

And I think I already have.

6

I cannot believe I had feelings for that asshole.

A mere few hours ago, at that. Am I stupid for reading too much into last night? We talked. We bonded. We felt like friends, and for once I thought Archer looked at me like I was more than just Dean's little sister, who he puts up with solely out of loyalty to his friend.

"Quinn!" Kara squeals, walking through the foyer with open arms. "Thank you again so much for helping today!"

"Of course," I tell her as she hugs me. "It was fun."

And it was, other than the ride home from the grocery store where Archer did his best to act like I wasn't even there. I don't get it.

And they say women are complicated.

"Everything looks great. The food smells amazing and those drinks are to die for!"

"I had them at a party in Chicago once. They're too complicated for me to make, but that's why we invited Owen and Logan, right?"

Kara laughs. She's had one or two drinks already, I can tell. She was nervous for tonight she admitted while we were cooking, and hates being the center of attention. She actually suggested to Dean they elope just so she can avoid opening presents in front of everyone at her bridal shower.

"And you look amazing," she goes on, looping her arm through mine. We head to the appetizer table. "I'm seriously jealous of your boobs."

I look down at my cleavage and laugh. "I could tell you how annoying big boobs are and how I'd kill to trade with you, but I'd be lying."

"Thanks for the honesty. I've been thinking more and more about getting mine done."

"If you want it, then do it."

"Really?" Kara picks up a plate.

"Sure. It's your body."

"You're the first person to not try and talk me out of it."

"Why would I?" I grab myself a plate as well. "If it's what you want, then go for it. Besides the obvious—going under the knife—I don't see how it's any different than getting up and doing your hair and makeup every day. You're changing your appearance that way as well."

"Right? That's what I told my sister."

I start filling my plate when Dean walks over. Archer is with him, and I don't have to look up to know. The scent of his cologne fills my nose, causing me to tense. Not because it smells bad, but because it reminds me of last night.

"What are you talking about?" Dean wraps his arms around Kara.

"Boobs," Kara responds.

"This is a conversation I can get behind." Dean slides his hands up Kara's waist.

She takes his hands in hers. "I was specifically talking about Quinn's. I'd kill for a set like that. I mean, they're perfect, aren't they?"

Dean's face contorts and he shakes his head. "She's my sister. As far as I'm concerned, she's never had any."

I roll my eyes. "I've had big boobs since I was thirteen. It's the Dawson curse."

"That's not a curse," Kara laughs. "Oh, there's my aunt Jessica. Remember, she's the one who's going to try to get you to campaign with her."

"The conservative one?"

"Yes. And if she asks—and she probably will—we're waiting until marriage."

"For what?" Dean asks, looking at Kara like he's serious.

"You're lucky I love you," Kara mutters before putting on a fake smile. She takes Dean's hand and goes to greet her aunt.

"Want a plate?" I ask Archer, casting my eyes up to him for half a second. His face is set, dark stubble covering his jaw. I might not know Archer Jones at all, but I know for a fact he's not one to turn down food.

"Sure."

I hand him one and move around the table. The tension between us is thick and heavy, and I don't understand why it's there at all. I look at Archer again, wishing I could crack him open and take a look at his internal codes to find out what makes him tick. And to also find out what the hell is wrong with him.

There's a reason I like to work with computers and not people.

I take my plate and turn on my heel, ignoring the sexy, brooding man in front of me, and almost run over my grandma. She's headed in the direction I just came from and wants company. I don't want to step back into the ice storm Archer has raging around him, but it's my nana.

"Hi, Mrs. Dawson," Archer says, offering a polite smile. "It's been a long time. How have you been?"

Nana smiles. "Archer Jones. My, it has been a while! I've been good, busy with my garden and the choir."

"Has Shelly Nicolson stepped aside yet and let you take the lead?"

Nana beams. "You remembered! And yes, she has, but only because she got cancer."

"Oh, I'm so sorry."

Nana leans in. "Between you and me, she deserved it!"

"Nana!" I say, eyes widening.

"The stories I could tell about that woman!" Nana turns to me. "But not here. We'll save those for the bachelorette party." She gets herself a plate. "I hear you're a doctor now, Archer."

"Yes, I am. I finish my residency this year."

"Are you hoping to start your own private practice?"

"No, ma'am. I'm a surgeon, so I'll be staying at a hospital."

"Ohhh," Nana coos. "A surgeon. You must be good with your hands." She winks at Archer. "And I bet you look dashing in that white doctor coat. You know I'm single, don't you?" Nana puts a few appetizers on her plate. "Oh, Barbara, dear!" She waves to one of her friends and takes off.

I push a stuffed mushroom around on my plate. It's too hot to eat but standing here without something in my mouth leaves me at risk of talking. Archer steps closer. Speaking of things to put in my mouth...

"Maybe I'm reading into this too much," Archer starts, looking perturbed. "But was your grandma just hitting on me?"

The effort to control my smile fails me. "She's gotten a little, how should I say it—crude. Her memory is all there and she drives and lives alone, but she kinda says whatever is on her mind now."

Archer laughs. "I'll take it as a compliment then. And you do look nice tonight, Quinn." He swallows hard, looking me over for a brief moment.

"Thanks. And you do too." I look at him and he looks away, and we're left standing there in awkward silence.

"Everything turned out nice."

"Yeah, it did," I agree, internally wincing. I didn't think anything could be worse than not talking but making forced small talk is.

"The stuffed mushrooms are good."

Shoot me now. "It's Nana's recipe."

Archer nods. "Well, I should go find Dean."

"He's right there, still talking to Kara's crazy aunt."

"Oh, right." Archer steps back from the table, letting another partygoer get some food. My mind flashes to my dream about Archer last night, and as annoyed with him as I am, there's no denying how fucking sexy he looks in dress pants and a button-down shirt.

"I should, uh, go check on the chickens," I blurt.

"The ones outside?"

"Yeah." Cursing myself, I go into the kitchen and pour myself a glass of wine. I get a mouthful down when Mom comes in, carrying a stack of dirty plates.

"This is so much fun," she says with a broad smile. "Just think of how much more fun it'll be when it's you getting married. I get to plan the whole thing!"

Kara threw Mom a bone by letting her plan tonight's party since it'll be her family taking care of the bridal shower and then the wedding.

"Someday."

"Oh, it'll happen, sweetheart. You are looking for someone, right?"

"In a sense."

"Whatever happened to that guy two floors down?"

"Our first date didn't go so well."

Mom raises an eyebrow. "Maybe you're being picky."

"He ate nachos with a fork. A fork, Mom. You can't stab a chip with a fork."

"He didn't want to get his hands dirty." She smiles then quickly changes her mind. "What kind of first date did you go on where you were ordering nachos?"

"A Cubs game. He has really good seats too. I might have been able to let the fork thing go, but then he put ketchup on a hot dog."

"Chicago has changed you. What about your new intern?"

"Mom, he's my intern."

She opens the cabinet and takes out her own wine glass. "So he's not good enough for you because he's an intern?"

"He's a lot younger than me because he's my intern."

"A younger man isn't a bad thing, you know. Men typically die first. This could be your insurance you don't end up a widow."

I take another gulp of wine. "You're not much better than Nana," I mutter and set my wine down and wrap my fingers around my wrist. "Do you have any Advil?"

"There's some in the cabinet next to the fridge. Is your wrist hurting again?"

"Yeah, that dull ache is back and it's traveling up my arm when I extend it." I make a face and shake out my hand. "I'm sore from being on my computer for hours every day."

"You should get it checked out. My girlfriend Gloria had something similar, always in pain, then had some sort of surgery done. I can ask her—wait! We have a surgeon here with us! Let me go find Archer."

"Mom, no, he's not here—" And she's out of the kitchen. "To work," I say to myself. I grab the Advil and pop a pill in my mouth, washing it down with wine.

"Are you taking painkillers with alcohol?" Archer gives me a smug smirk.

"Relax, Dr. Fuddy-Duddy. It's just an Advil."

"You still shouldn't do that."

"Noted." I raise my eyebrows.

"Your mom asked me to come in here because you're in pain."

I wave my hand in the air. "I'm fine. It's just random shooting pains in my arm that go up to my shoulder."

"Which arm?"

"I'm not having a heart attack," I sass. "It's my wrist and really, I'm fine."

"I can take a look."

"I guess it won't hurt anything." I set my empty wine glass in the sink and cross the kitchen. My heart starts to speed up and heat rushes through me, settling between my thighs. I stand before Archer Jones, left arm extended, fighting off the insane attraction I'm feeling.

Archer gently takes my wrist in his hands. "It's not swollen. Does it hurt now?"

"It's off and on. Like a dull ache."

"What makes it hurt more?" He turns my arm over and runs his thumb down my forearm. I suppress a shiver, licking my lips as I watch his fingers slide over my flesh. I tear my eyes away from his hand to look up at his face, but that only makes things worse.

His brow is furrowed, and there's genuine concern in his eyes.

"Extending my arm and being on my computer."

"Do your fingers feel tingly?"

"Actually yeah, they have a few times when the pain gets bad."

"You have carpal tunnel syndrome, which is quite common for someone who types or is at a computer all day."

"I figured so." His hand is still around my wrist. "A handful of my co-workers have it. They're a lot older than me, but it is what it is, I guess. So, am I damned to live like this forever, doc?"

"No, there are treatments. Start with ice and Advil for the pain and try a wrist brace."

"I will. Thanks."

Archer steps closer and hasn't let go of my wrist yet. "You said it makes your shoulder hurt?"

"It does, but I think part of that is bad posture. I know I slouch at my desk." I put my free hand over Archer's. "It's not something a massage can't fix, right?"

The floor in the butler's pantry creaks and Archer drops my wrist and steps back. Dean emerges into the kitchen.

"Are you guys hiding too?" he asks.

"Why are you hiding? This is your party. And no," I say. "We're not hiding. Mom's overreacting—surprise, surprise, I know—and made Archer look at my wrist."

"What's wrong with your wrist?"

"Carpal tunnel. It's seriously no big deal. Archer told me what to do and I'll be fine."

Dean gives Archer a nod. "You're a good friend for putting up with our mom."

Archer laughs. "She's not that bad."

"She can be a bit overbearing," Dean grumbles.

"Go back to your party," I tell him. "Before Kara notices you're missing."

"She's the one I had to get away from," Dean admits.

"You're hiding from your fiancée at your own engagement party?" I hike an eyebrow.

"She's still going on about your boobs. And then Mom came over and was talking about her boobs." He shudders. "I had to leave or throw up."

I laugh. "Watch out, Dean, we might start talking about our uteruses next." I give him a sweet smile. "I hope you two only have girls."

"As long as they're not twins. Twins do run in our family."

"It doesn't matter on the guy's side," Archer explains. "It only matters on the girl's side, and identical twins aren't hereditary anyway."

"Really?"

"Really. Identical twins are a random event."

"Well, that's good news," Dean says. "I guess I'll go back out there. Might as well enjoy the party you all threw in my honor, right? You're my best man," he says to Archer. "You gotta come save me. I mean join me. Keep me away from Aunt Mary. She thinks modern medicine is witchcraft so she'll avoid you."

"Best man," I repeat as Dean walks out of the room. I turn my gaze back to Archer. "I wasn't sure how that was going to go. Logan and Owen were taking bets on which one of them Dean would pick. You are Dean's oldest friend. It makes sense."

"Yeah...we have been friends a long time." His brow furrows again, and he flicks his eyes up to me, looking at me almost as if I'm suddenly offensive.

"So...I'll, uh, try to have better posture. Would that help my wrist pain?"

"Maybe. I'm a surgeon. I don't deal with this sort of thing. Make an appointment with your general practitioner." He turns to leave.

"What the hell is wrong with you?" I snap.

"Nothing," he retorts, whirling around. "What the hell is wrong with you?"

"Seriously?" I ask.

"Yeah." He inhales deeply, and I'm not sure if he's going to tell me off or push me up against a wall and kiss me.

"It's like you're a rescue dog and I don't know if you're going to let me pet you or if you're going to bite. At least I can understand the dog's unpredictable behavior, but you...I haven't got a clue with you and you are driving me nuts."

"You want to pet me?"

"Yes. No. Kind of. It's a figure of speech." I throw my hands up. "Whatever, Archer. I don't know what I did to offend you."

He strides forward so quickly I take a step back, pinning myself against the fridge. Archer's hands land on my waist and he moves in, legs spread, so his hips are against mine. I inhale the scent of his woodsy cologne, heart beating so fast I think it might explode. So many times I've imagined his hands on me. For years, I've yearned for his touch. Begged and pleaded with the universe to have him look at me and *not* see me as Dean's little sister.

And right now, he's not. I'm not his friend's sibling to put up with, but he's not looking at me the way I'd hoped. He stares at me with a combination of hatred and lust, more intense than anyone has ever looked at me before. It turns me on and terrifies me.

I'm hot and cold up against him.

I want to push him away and bring him closer.

He leans in, taking one hand off my waist to move my curls over my shoulder. He licks his lips, and the light above us shines off the trail of wetness left from his tongue. The heat between my thighs intensifies, and my pussy begs to be touched. Stroked. Fucked hard.

Just like in my dream.

I swallow my pounding heart and turn my head up to Archer, refusing to let him see how close to coming undone this is making me. He tucks my hair behind my ear and traces the outline of my jaw with his thumb, bringing it up to my mouth. I part my lips, feeling intoxicated by his touch.

"You didn't offend me, Quinn." He spits each word out, eyes narrowing. Then he blinks and his face softens. His hand trails over my collarbone and down my arm until our fingers meet. He intertwines his with mine for a brief moment. "You didn't. But I should go."

He pushes off me and goes back to the party like nothing happened. I lean onto the counter for support, heart racing and nerves tingling. That asshole did it on purpose. He knew he could get that reaction out of me. Knew he could easily unnerve me with a few simple touches.

Fuck him.

If I never see Archer Jones again, it would be too soon.

7

ARCHER

"Well, kids, it looks like you're going to be here for a while." Mr. Dawson hangs up the phone and goes to the window, watching the storm. "A tree fell and knocked out power lines. The road is blocked."

"How bad?" Dean asks.

"Weston said there's been a lot of damage in town they have to get to first. He'll keep us posted. I know Quinn and Archer need to leave soon to make it home in time. Though you shouldn't drive in this rain anyway."

Quinn shifts in her seat, and the collar of her oversized sweatshirt falls down her shoulder. Her hair is in a messy braid, she's not wearing any makeup, and she's refused to look at me all morning. She's done an impressive job of pretending I'm not here, actually. No one else has noticed her go about the kitchen, getting coffee and helping her mom make breakfast and act like it's just her family sitting around the large island counter.

"Should we go into the basement?" Mrs. Dawson asks.

She tightens her grip on Jackson, who doesn't seem bothered by the storm at all.

"Nah," Mr. Dawson says, looking out the window. "This house has survived for over a hundred years. It'll go a hundred more. I'm not worried."

A loud crash of thunder booms overhead, startling the dogs. The lights flicker. Once. Twice. And then the power goes out.

"Quinn, can you call your brothers and make sure they're awake and aware of the storm? Owen can sleep through anything." Mrs. Dawson gets up, keeping Jackson's hand in hers as if she's afraid the small boy will blow away in the storm, and gets battery-powered candles and a flashlight out from under the kitchen sink.

"I've been texting Logan all morning," Quinn responds, not looking up from her phone. "They've been up doing inventory at the bar."

"The bar? Maybe they should come here where it's safer."

"Jackie," Mr. Dawson starts. "It'd be far more dangerous to have them drive. The bar has a basement."

"Grammy will you read to me? I'm tired." Jackson tugs on Mrs. Dawson's hand.

"Of course, baby! Let me get another flashlight and we can go snuggle on the couch."

Kara goes into the living room with them to work on her lesson plans for the week, and Mr. Dawson tells Dean he needs him to sort through a client's file so they can get a head start on a project for tomorrow.

And now just Quinn and I are in the kitchen. I'm pretty sure her coffee mug is empty, but she brings it to her lips and pretends to take a drink, turning away from me to look outside at the storm.

It's just now ten AM, and I'm not at all worried about making it back home in time. But being stuck in this house with Quinn...it's not uncomfortable at all. Especially after last night.

Hah. The tension is so thick it's hard to fucking breathe.

Regretting the second helping of bacon and eggs I got, I push the last bit around on my plate and steal a glance at Quinn. She's holding her coffee cup—which is definitely empty—and frowning as she reads something on her phone.

"Is something wrong?" I ask.

"No." She doesn't look away from her phone, but at least she answered me. She sets her mug down and types up a reply then fires off the email. "I get no service here," she mutters and trades her phone for the coffee mug again. This time, she takes it to the sink.

Those little bitty shorts ride up her tight ass as she walks. I want to put my hands on it. Press my cock up against it as I kiss her neck, gathering her hair into one hand and move it over her shoulder.

I swallow hard. I can't think like that. Not here. Not now.

Not ever.

"Are you done?" Quinn puts one hand on her hip and for a split second, I think she knows what I'm thinking.

"Yeah," I say, picking up my last piece of bacon. I pop it in my mouth and stand, bringing my plate over to the sink. Quinn takes it from me and bends over to let the dogs lick the remnants of eggs. Her ass is in the air right in front of me, and I wonder if she's doing it on purpose to get a rise out of me.

Because she is, and I have to change my stance thanks to my hardening cock.

"Quinn," I start, not sure what to say, but I have to say something. "We should talk."

"About what?" She straightens up and rounds on me, crossing her arms. Her eyes meet mine, drilling in with an intensity I've never seen from her. She has little flecks of blue in her brilliant green irises that I haven't noticed before.

I move closer, stepping over Boots. If I say it now, there will be no more wondering. No more waiting. She'll either take me or leave me, but at least I'll know. I can kiss her now or move on. Somehow, someway.

It's not hard. All I have to do is open my mouth and let the words come out, speaking with unwavering vehemence as I tell her how I feel.

Yet, I can't.

Standing here looking at Quinn, with her messy hair, thick sweater hiding her perfect tits, and dogs circling around her feet in hopes of more food, I feel more nervous that I did the first time I stood in front of a patient on the operating table with a scalpel in my hand.

"Archer?"

"Your wrist. How's your wrist?"

"My wrist?" she questions, nostrils flaring. She lets out a sigh and picks up the plate the dogs licked clean. "Same as yesterday. I ordered a posture brace on Amazon to help with my shoulder pain, not that you care."

I'd offer to massage her shoulders, but the moment my hands land on her back, all bets are off.

Suddenly, Quinn advances. She's inches away, arms crossed tightly over her chest and head tipped up to mine.

"That's not what you wanted to talk about." She pulls her bottom lip between her teeth and cocks her head. "Is it?"

"Quinn."

"Don't *Quinn* me, Archer Jones. You know as well as I do you weren't going to talk to me about my wrist." She lets out a frustrated breath and lets her arms fall to the sides. Her fingers brush against me, and my skin feels electric just from that small touch.

Goddammit.

"But fine. I'll play that game. Here." She holds up her hand. "Examine me, doctor."

Her words are meant to mock, but they do the opposite. I'll examine every inch of her body. Twice. Three times. Just to be certain nothing was missed.

I take her wrist and tug her forward, knocking her off balance so she falls against me, both her hands flat on my chest. I slip my other hand around her waist, stopping at the small of her back. Quinn's lips part and she gasps.

Instead of struggling to get away, she relaxes in my arms, and nothing has ever felt more right.

Even though this is wrong.

Quinn is in my arms, back arched and tits against my chest. My cock is hard, pulsing against the confines of my jeans. Thunder booms above and Quinn shivers.

"Do you still want to talk?" My voice is gruffer than I intend, but the harshness does something for Quinn. She slides her hands up my chest and around my shoulders.

"There are other things I'd rather do," she says, voice breathy. Fuck. She's killing me. She brushes her hips against mine, feeling my erection through my pants. "And I think you would too."

I do. I so fucking do and she knows it.

"Archer," she says softly and hearing her whisper my name is almost enough to make me come right then and there. I slowly bring my face down to hers. I'm going to kiss her. After all this time, it's finally fucking happening.

Then the floor creaks and Dean and Mr. Dawson's voices echo through the house. Dean's been a better brother to me than my real brother. Mr. Dawson stepped in and filled the role of a father when my own was bailing Robert out of jail or going to the hospital to confirm the identity of the unconscious junkie the paramedics brought in.

"Stop," I tell Quinn, ripping my heart out of my chest as I speak. "You're Dean's sister."

"I know who I am, and if that's all you see me as..." She pushes away and walks out of the kitchen without looking back.

"I'm TELLING YOU, YOU GOTTA FUCK HER OUT OF YOUR system."

I carefully make the incision, not taking my eyes off my patient to look at Sam. "And that means?"

"You've been hung up on this piece of ass for years. She's always been your forbidden fruit. And trust me on this: the fruit looks better than it actually tastes. Drive back up to that Podunk town, fuck her hard and dirty, kick her out as soon as you're done, and she'll be history."

"That is terrible advice," Shelly, one of the OR nurses says. "If you like this girl, tell her. Take her out on a date and treat her like an actual human being and not a piece of meat."

"That's not a way to get over her," Sam counters.

I can feel Shelly's eyes on me. "I don't think he wants to get over her."

Shelly's right, but I don't let anyone in the operating room know. I used to agree with Sam, having thought Quinn was someone I sexually desired, but seeing her again over the weekend changed things.

Though really, it's always been the same.

I never let myself think about it. I shut down the thought the moment it came into my mind. Quinn had to be the girl I wanted to fuck, not the girl I wanted to settle down with. Because I couldn't. I still can't.

"She doesn't live in that Podunk town." I exchange tools and go back to the mass we're removing from this guy's abdomen. "She lives in Chicago."

"Then drive your ass up there so you can tap *her* ass."

"You're disgusting," Shelly says.

Sam laughs. "I do what I have to do. And now it's time for Archer to figure this shit out. I mean, look at him. He could be out fucking the world, but he's gotten less ass in the last five years than I did those months I had mono."

Shelly shakes her head. "I'll say it again. Disgusting."

"If you're not willing to fuck her out of your system, then at least fuck someone else. You'll be doing yourself a favor in more ways than one. If you're never going to make your move, then you need to move on."

We finish the surgery, and I think about what Sam said, wondering if there's any validity to it. Not the part about using Quinn like a real-life sex doll, but the part of her losing her appeal if we finally hooked up. I've thought about and pined after this woman for years, unable to get her out of my head.

Maybe that's all I need. One night with Quinn to snap me out of this fucking annoying-as-hell funk so I can get on with my life.

I meet with my patient and his family in the recovery unit and talk about how the procedure went and what he can expect in terms of healing. Stomach grumbling, I head out, telling Sam I'll meet him in the cafeteria. We have about an hour before our next scheduled surgery and I'm fucking starving.

"Archer Jones," a familiar female voice says, coming from behind me. "Just the man I was looking for."

I turn away from the elevator and see Melissa Miller, one of the attending physicians I worked under, making her way over.

"Hello, Dr. Miller." The elevator opens and she motions to step in.

"I was going to tell you I've finished your letter of recommendation, but you might not need it. I have a friend on the surgical team at another hospital, and—I'll cut to the chase. Are you still interested in a trauma fellowship?"

"Yes, I still am."

"Great." She smiles. "I was supposed to go to a conference at the end of the week and can't now due to work obligations. The Board has everything already paid for and set up. One of the speakers is particular, to say the least. Talking to him before applying could be a foot in the door since the fellowship is extremely competitive. You're one of the best resident surgeons I've seen, it never hurts to get a leg up."

"Absolutely."

"What's your schedule like this week?"

I laugh.

"That bad?" She raises her eyebrows. "Let me pull a few strings. I know a good surgeon when I see one."

"Thank you, Dr. Miller. Where is the conference?"

"Chicago."

8

ARCHER

I look out the window, watching the ground come closer and closer. The plane lands smoothly, and I lean back, yawning for the millionth time on this one-hour flight. I left the hospital at two AM, got home, showered, and slept for an hour and a half, before having to get up and get to the airport in time for my flight into Chicago. Even though it's early, I'll still be pushing it to get to the hotel in time to change before going to the conference.

Feeling like I'm walking through a heavy fog, I get a coffee with extra espresso on my way to the baggage claim, and down the whole thing by the time I get my suitcase. There's a car waiting for me, and it takes effort not to fall asleep on the drive over. Traffic is slow, and while I don't want to miss anything, the thought of dozing off while stuck in a jam sounds nice right now.

Quinn works in the city. I don't know where she works, or exactly what she does to even begin to describe it to someone, but she's here. And so are three million other people. I won't run into her. I shouldn't even worry about it.

But I'm not worried.

I'm hopeful.

I close my eyes, remembering the way she felt in my arms. The way she smells. Her smile. Her laugh.

And the way she looked at me. Lust. Want. She was a little bit afraid but determined not to show it. But all that melded into anger, and that final look made my stomach churn. Hurting Quinn is the last thing I want to do.

I need another coffee once I get to the hotel. The room is nice, and the king-sized bed is calling my name. I don't know why I thought working a nineteen-hour shift before coming here was a good idea.

"Jones, you coming?"

"Yeah," I tell Dr. Tyler White. Also a surgeon, he's here for the conference but isn't interested in the same fellowship. It's the afternoon, and we've already sat through several panels. If I don't get up and move around, I'll be asleep in my seat before the next panel starts. Before the convention began this morning, I was able to talk to renowned surgeon, Dr. Crawford, who knew my name from talking with Dr. Miller. It was enough of a small victory to keep me awake and alert through the morning, but now the lack of sleep is hitting me hard.

Tyler and I step out onto the busy sidewalk, both blinking in the bright light. He's from Texas and isn't familiar with the city either. We have a break for lunch, and the next panel is geared for OB/GYNs, which I don't mind missing.

"I'm thinking we should go to one of those pizza places," Tyler starts. "That serves the famous Chicago-style pizza."

"Pizza sounds good right now." Hell, anything sounds good right now. I didn't have time for breakfast and I had another cup of coffee. Yeah, yeah...I know...doctors make the worst patients. My eating habits turn to shit when I'm working nonstop.

We do our best not to look like tourists as we go to Giordano's. It's busy, and we talk about work and the shit hours you pull as a resident. Two women, wearing tight pencil skirts and low-cut blouses, are eyeing us, doing their best to get our attention.

"Are you guys doctors?" one of them asks. She's petite, with bright eyes and sleek black hair.

"We are," Tyler says with a smile.

"That's what we thought," the other says, flipping her blonde hair over her shoulder. "We heard you talking. So you're both surgeons?"

"Yes, ma'am." Tyler shuffles closer through the busy lobby.

"Wow, that's amazing." The blonde flashes another smile. Both women are pretty—very pretty. She's tall and fit and her tits are practically falling out of her shirt. While I can appreciate how good she looks, and have my cock react accordingly, I don't feel drawn to her.

I know why, but I refuse to admit it to myself.

"Do you want to join us?" the woman with the dark hair asks. "Our table should be ready any minute now."

Tyler looks at me, no question in his eyes. These women are flirting, attractive, and will probably be up for something this evening. Sam's words echo through my head. Would hooking up with someone else make me stop wanting Quinn?

A few minutes later, we're all seated together. The women—Rene and Charlene—ask us about being doctors and tell us about the city. They're nice enough, a bit obvious with their attempts at flirting for my liking, but Tyler is eating them up. The blonde, Charlene, has cozied up to him, and they're already talking about meeting up tonight.

"We're done at four-thirty," Tyler tells them.

"Perfect!" Charlene wiggles closer. "We're having this little office party at five and you should totally come crash it with us."

"Your boss won't mind?"

"Nah." Rene waves her hand in the air. "She's cool. Or at least she tries to be," she says with a laugh. "She'll probably be in her office working the whole time and won't even notice. Talk about a bore."

"Yeah," Charlene coos. "You should totally come. It's catered and everything, and it has free drinks."

"You got me there," Tyler laughs. "I suppose we can swing by."

"Great!" Charlene beams and gives him the address, as well as her number. We make small talk as we eat, and Tyler pays the whole bill at the end of our meal. Charlene fawns over him on our way out.

"You know," he tells me as we head back to the convention. "I didn't want to go to this fucking thing. I think after tonight I'll be glad."

"Yeah," I chuckle. "All I was hoping for was a foot in the door for that fellowship."

"You'll be getting more than that."

I go along with it, acting like I'm looking forward to meeting up with the women tonight and the prospect of getting laid. Looking around the busy city, I wonder where Quinn is and what she's doing right now.

We get to the convention with time to spare before the next panel. I go up to my room, setting the timer on my phone for twenty minutes. I stretch out on the bed and close my eyes. Five minutes later, my phone rings. Grumbling, I sit up and see it's Mom.

"Hey, Mom," I answer, heart already in my throat.

"Archer," she says, voice strained, and I know something bad happened. "Is this a bad time?"

"No, Mom, it's never a bad time. What's going on?"

"I found a bottle of pills in Robert's room when I was cleaning."

"What does the bottle say?" I pinch the bridge of my nose.

"Lorazepam."

"That's Ativan. What do the pills look like?"

"Round and orange."

I sigh. "That's not Ativan. Give me the numbers scored in the pill." I've been over this with her before. She can enter this information into a Google search and find the pill. But I know she's anxious and upset. I know how guilty she and dad feel over their oldest son becoming an addict.

They feel like they failed him, like they weren't good enough and didn't give him enough attention. I've tried to tell them that's not the case. They're not bad parents. They gave us everything they could. I turned out okay. Better than okay, according to some.

"It's amphetamine and dextroamphetamine."

"Is that bad?"

"Yes, Mom, it's bad. It's Adderall."

Mom doesn't say anything for a few seconds. "That doesn't mean he's taking it. It was in the back of the closet, along with a pack of cigarettes. And I know he doesn't smoke anymore. I'd smell it on his clothes if he did."

"Yeah, I guess." I lost all faith in my brother recovering after his third failed attempt at rehab.

"Would it show up on a drug test?"

"Depends on what they are looking for. Given his history, I'd assume they'd check for a wide range."

"Good. He passed the test last week."

"Then maybe he isn't taking it."

"I just want my Bobby back," she says softly. "I miss him."

"Me too, Mom. How's Dad? Is he taking his blood pressure medication every day?"

"I make him. And remind him that his doctor son won't hesitate to call and yell." I can hear the smile in Mom's voice. I let out a small breath of relief. "I'll let you go. Thanks, Archie."

"Anytime, Mom."

I lay back down and close my eyes but am not able to fall back asleep. It's been a long time since I spoke with my brother. We're not on the best terms, with me struggling not to blame him for everything and him being jealous I actually did something with my life. When my alarm goes off, I'm glad to get up and get Bobby out of my head. He's pretty much out of my life.

The final panels are interesting, and once they're over, Tyler and I get a cab into the city. Charlene texts and says she'll meet us in the lobby, and once we get there, it's apparent why. They work in a high-rise, and security clearance is needed to go up into their office.

The place is open and modern and Rene sits behind the front desk. She bats her eyes and smiles when she sees me. Then the phone rings, and she answers it, holding up her finger, signaling me to hold on a minute.

"There's an open bar," Charlene tells us. "And after this, a bunch of us are going out for more drinks."

"Sounds fun," Tyler says. Rene transfers the call and comes out from behind the desk. "What do you guys do?"

"Well, we answer the phones," Rene tells him and leads the way into the office. Music comes from the back, and people are gathered around a makeshift bar. "So nothing too exciting. Not like surgery, I bet!" She giggles. "But this place is a software company."

"Software?" I ask. There's no way. There are tons of software companies in the city.

"Yeah. Don't ask me to explain it because I can't. The nerds design programs or whatever." She slows a bit, looking down the hall into an office with a large, glass door. "Speaking of nerds, my boss is still working, so let's get this party started early!"

I can't remember the name of the company Quinn works for, and before I can ask, the name on the large glass door comes into view.

Quinn Dawson.

I do a double take and catch a glimpse of her brunette ponytail. Taking a step back, I see her sitting behind her desk with a smile on her face. She leans back in her chair, laughing.

And then he moves in, sitting on the edge of her desk. She points to something on the computer screen in front of her, and he leans closer before turning to face her. The smile broadens on her face and she blushes.

I have no idea what's actually going on. All I know is it's making me want to Hulk out and flip tables. Quinn isn't mine. She has no idea how much I want her, or how long I've wanted her at that.

And yet I'm instantly jealous to see her with another man.

Goddammit. She's so much more than a piece of ass to

me and it's about damn time I admit it to myself: I'm in love with her.

And now I'm standing in her office, walking next to her bitchy secretary who's insulted her more than once in the little amount of time I've spent with her. I need to get out, or at the very least, away from Rene.

I don't want to mess this up any more than I already have.

But it's too late because Quinn looks up and stares right at me.

"**Y**ou have got to be kidding me." I blink. Once. Twice.

Archer Jones is still there. He's staring back at me, and good Lord, that man looks fine as hell in that navy blue suit. His dark hair is a little messy, and the scruff on his face enhances the strong, masculine features.

I'm instantly turned on. And equally annoyed. What the hell is he doing here?

"Quinn? Is everything all right?" Jacob follows my line of sight out the glass door. "What's wrong?"

"Nothing, nothing's wrong." I force a smile and look back up. Jacob McMillan works at our sister company and is partnering with me on this new big project. We dated for a while a year ago, and are better friends than lovers. He's a nice guy, too nice really, and working with my ex isn't as awkward as I thought it would be.

Don't get me wrong, it *is* awkward to work with an ex when he's still in love with you. But it's manageable.

"I'll be right back," I say and stand, moving quickly out

of my office. Archer steps in my direction. "What are you doing here?"

"Hi, Quinn, nice to see you too." He gives me his trademark smile, and if I wasn't still pissed at him for whatever the hell he was trying to do before, I might have gotten weak in the knees.

"Are you stalking me?"

"I'm not doing a very good job at it, am I?" He laughs and lets his eyes wander over me. "I like professional-Quinn. You look very...proper."

I cross my arms. "Seriously, what are you doing here? Do I need to call security?"

Jacob comes up behind me. "Is he bothering you, Quinn?"

Archer pushes his shoulders back and stares down at Jacob.

"No," I say. "This is my brother's friend, Archer. I didn't expect to see him, that's all."

"Oh." Jacob holds out his hand. "Nice to meet you. I'm Jacob. Which brother's friend? She's got a lot," he says with a chuckle.

"Dean's," Archer says and shakes Jacob's hand. Something changes in his demeanor, and it's then I notice how tired and worn Archer looks. "I'm attending a physician's conference in the city."

"But that still doesn't explain why you're *here*," I press.

"I'll let you guys catch up," Jacob says, reaching out to take my hand. He gives it a squeeze. "Call me if you need anything. See you later." He turns to Archer. "Nice to meet you." He walks past us, going to the party to celebrate the successful launch of our new program. The shock starts to wear off and my heart speeds up. Archer is here. In my office. The last time I saw him, he grabbed me and almost kissed me.

And I wanted him to.

I still can't think of that incident without growing wet. I've dreamed of it over and over, and in my dreams, he finishes what he started. I want to tear off his suit jacket and untuck his shirt, slowly undoing every button before peeling it off his muscular body.

Archer closes the distance between us. He smells even better than I remember, and the scent of his cologne triggers something animalistic inside of me, making me think there's a good chance I might actually rip his clothes off.

"Sorry to startle you," he says. "I really had no idea you worked here."

At a loss for words, I just nod.

"I was going to text you and tell you I was here, but I wasn't sure if you wanted to see me after..." He trails off and looks away.

After he made it clear getting close to me bothered him. I think. Maybe? I can't get a read on him.

"Well, welcome to Chicago. You've never been here before, have you?"

"No. It's nice."

"You sound surprised." I inhale and try to get my heart rate to go back to normal. Usually, I complain that it's too cold in this office, but right now I'm sweating. And it has nothing to do with Archer. Nope. No way.

"I didn't know what to expect, really." He casts his eyes in the direction of the party. "And it was a last-minute thing. One of the surgeons I worked under when I first started my residency got me into the convention."

"That was nice. Right? Or are conventions awful? I kinda hate going to them. I have to talk to too many people and I don't like most people." Shit. I probably shouldn't have said that.

Archer laughs, eyes brightening. "Honestly, it's nice to sit down for hours at a time. I haven't done that much lately. And I'm hoping talking to one of the surgeons speaking will get me a foot in the door for a fellowship I want."

"A fellowship? I'm guessing it doesn't have anything to do with taking a magical ring to Mordor."

"Unfortunately, no. But if it was, I'd just ride the giant eagles, right?"

I hike an eyebrow. "You do know that wouldn't have— you like *Lord of the Rings*?"

"Now you sound surprised."

"You and Dean always seemed so alike, so yeah, I guess I am." I bite my lip, wrestling my libido down. "What are you doing here though? Like in my office here?"

"Oh, I, uh," he starts, diverting his eyes to the ground for a second. "Another doctor and I went out to lunch together and ran into your secretaries. They invited us back for some sort of work party." He's trying not to cringe as he talks, and it's both adorable and repulsive.

"You were hoping for a booty call."

"It's not technically a booty call if I'm not the one calling."

I put a hand on my hip. "You're not helping your case, Jones."

"Fine. Yes. But not me. Just Tyler."

"I thought all doctors referred to each other as 'Doctor Whatever' and not your first names."

"It depends on where we are. In the hospital setting, we do. Mostly. Hey," he says and playfully nudges me. "We spent over a decade in school. We've earned being called 'doctor' all the time." He smiles again and dammit, I'm going to have to change my underwear. "I didn't know you were so high up in the company."

"Unlike you doctors, I don't need to go around bragging."

Archer chuckles and I suddenly realize there are other people in the office, including Rene, who keeps looking over her shoulder at us.

"Do you want to go find your date?"

"No," he answers quickly. "I didn't want to come, but I'm glad I did."

"Yeah." I find myself smiling. "Me too." Our eyes meet, and I want to ask him to walk back with me, introduce him to my co-workers, and get a drink or two at the bar.

Then I remember I'm mad at him.

He's an asshole, getting me all hot and bothered just to turn around and walk away like it was nothing at all.

"I have to go back to work."

"Isn't your day over at five?" he asks, looking at the clock on the wall behind me.

"Who told you that?"

"Your secretary."

"Her day is, but I stay late sometimes."

"Even on a Friday?"

"Especially on a Friday," I retort, then realize it wasn't the best comeback. Wit has never been my strong suit.

He gives me his best cocky smile. "And you said I was a fuddy-duddy."

"So now you're not too cool to use that word?"

"Oh, I am way too cool. I'm cool and a doctor, remember?"

I can't help but laugh. What's the harm in getting one drink and one piece of cake? Maybe he's not an asshole.

Or maybe I'm really naive.

There's only one way to find out.

"Are you hungry?" I ask.

"My answer to that will always be yes."

I motion to the back of the building. "We have food. And drinks. And it sounds like Dillan has fired up the karaoke machine."

We fall in step together, going through the rows of empty desks. "Is this a regular occurrence?"

"Parties? Kind of. We always celebrate a successful launch, and doing stuff like this keeps up morale in the workplace."

"All I want is an eight-hour shift."

"How long do you work? I know residents have crappy hours."

"Usually around eighty hours a week."

I give him a horrified look. "How is that legal? You're all doctors, so you know how bad it is to not get enough sleep."

"Yeah, I'm shortening my life so I can extend it for others." He's joking...kind of. "I worked nineteen hours before getting on a plane to come here."

"Ouch." No wonder he looks so tired. "And you landed this morning?"

"Yeah. I landed at O'Hare around six this morning."

"Ohhh, that's a rookie mistake. Fly out of Midway next time. O'Hare is crazy busy. Or just drive. It's like four hours from here to Indy. Traffic permitting, at least."

"Noted. I did consider driving, but wasn't sure if I could stay awake."

"That's sad."

He shrugs. "It's been my life for the last several years. I'm used to it. Though my ideal vacation would be any quiet hotel room with a comfortable bed."

"That's mine too, though I'd prefer that room to be in a Disney hotel."

"I've never been."

"What?" I give him my best I-can't-fucking-believe-it look. "We've been a few times, and the last trip, all my stupid brothers thought they were too old and too cool to go to Disney. They missed out."

"I remember that. You went our junior year over spring break and Dean had a party at your house."

"No way."

"Yeah. It got out of control and Weston had to come shut it down. He was just a rookie cop then."

"Oh my God. And no one ever found out. I can't believe Wes didn't tell me!"

"I probably wasn't supposed to tell you. It seems like it was so long ago."

"Were Logan and Owen there?"

Archer raises an eyebrow. "Why do you think it got out of control?"

"I wish I could give them hell for this!"

"There might be pictures. I know some were taken."

Archer tells me about the crazy things that went down that night as we go back to get cake and drinks. We take it into the hall, away from the noise. And right now, I'm forgetting to be mad at Archer.

"There you are," the man Archer came in with says. He looks from Archer to me, curious but not questioning anything.

"Quinn," Archer starts. "This is Dr. White. And this is Quinn."

"Nice to meet you," I tell Dr. White.

Holding a beer in one hand, he tries to put this all together. "You're in charge here?"

"More or less."

"And you two know each other?"

"Yeah," Archer answers. "I've known Quinn since my freshman year of college, but I didn't know she worked here."

He didn't introduce me as his buddy's sister. I grit my teeth and force another smile. I need to stop.

"I'll see you tomorrow," Archer tells Dr. White. "Have fun."

Dr. White smirks. "Oh, I will. And you too. It was nice meeting you, Quinn."

I turn to Archer as soon as we're alone again. "You said 'doctor' instead of his first name."

"I know. Fine. We do like saying it. Sometimes I'll purposely 'forget' to take my lab coat off when I run errands after work so people know I'm a surgeon. I'm not proud to admit that, but it's true. Happy now?"

Giggling, I bring my drink to my lips and take a sip. "I like this side of you, Archer."

"What side?"

"The honest one."

He moves so his leg touches mine. "I am honest."

"Really?" I don't mean to sound as bitchy as I do. Maybe I'm still a little mad at him after all.

"Yes," he breathes, eyes trying to convey what he won't say.

I don't budge. An apology goes a long way, buddy. Looking away, I stick my fork into my cake, carefully slicing off a flower made of frosting, and put it in my mouth. A few seconds tick by and neither of us speak.

And a few seconds turns into a minute. And another, until my cake is gone and I have nothing to occupy myself with. I turn to Archer, telling him—for real this time—that I need to get back to my office.

"Can I take you out to dinner?" he asks before I have a chance to get a word out.

"Like a date?" I blurt. Shit. I wish I had more cake to stuff in my mouth to keep me from talking. Though his answer could change everything.

"Do you want it to be a date?"

Damn you, Archer. Every time I think the ball is in his court, he throws it back at me.

"Depends on where you take me."

He grins, and I hate that I want to impress him. "Considering I've never been here, you might not want me to be the one picking where we go. Unless you like pizza, because the one restaurant I've been to so far was good enough to go back to."

"I do like pizza."

"Well, then." He stands and offers his hand. "Shall we? Or do you have to stay?"

"I should probably walk through and pretend to be social." I finish my water and take his hand.

"You never answered me," he says, his deep voice rattling everything inside me.

"About what?"

"Do you want it to be a date?"

I swallow hard, throat suddenly thick. This is the type of pressure I crack under, and it's always because I put said pressure on myself. I get ahead of my own thoughts and end up saying something I regret. "What do you want?"

"You're Dean's kid sis. He'd give me shit if he found out I was in Chicago and didn't check up on you."

Archer is right. Dean would be pissed. Logan and Owen too. Even Weston...and my parents. Archer is basically part of the family, and it's not like he's being rude. So why is my blood starting to boil?

I look at him out of the corner of my eye, frustration building. God, I hate that I want him. I hate that I want him to see me as more than his friend's little sister.

I just wish I could hate him.

"Yeah, he'd be pissed for sure." I toss my empty plate in the trash and my cup and fork into the recycling and wait for Archer to do the same. Not saying a word, we walk to the party. With each beat that passes, I'm tempted to break my own rule of not drinking at work.

We're pretty casual around here. Some may even accuse us of being too hipster or crunchy for a company that develops software. We have drinks and massages at the office, and anyone without children are welcome to bring their pets on 'bring your child to work day.' As long as work gets done, anything goes.

But since I got promoted, I've tried to uphold a certain standard and make sure I stay professional at work. I'm far from uptight and have often been caught dancing to the Disney Descendants soundtrack in my office. Yet I don't like to drink at work because I'm the type of person who says she'll have one shot of whiskey and then keep drinking until I've had five.

"Quinn!" Marissa, a co-worker and my best friend in Chicago, sets down her empty cup and opens her arms. "Yes! I was hoping you'd stop working and—who is this?"

"This is Archer. My brother's friend," I introduce. "Archer, this is Marissa. She works with me." I shake my head. "Obviously. We're at work."

Archer smiles, eyes lingering on me a moment longer than I'd expect from someone who's only here out of loyalty to their best friend.

"*The* Archer?" Marissa whisper-talks.

I flash her a you're-talking-way-too-loud glare and give her the tiniest nod. She hooks her arm through mine.

"Do you have a drink? No, we need to fix that. I'll bring her back in just a second," she says to Archer and spins me around. "What the hell is he doing here?"

"I don't know. Wait, actually I do. He's in town for some doctor convention. Medical doctors, not Doctor Who doctors."

We stop at the bar and Marissa gapes at me for a moment. "So what are you going to do about it?"

"About what?"

"Oh, come on, Quinn. You've had a giant crush on this guy for years, even if you're not willing to admit it to yourself. I've known you since you started here, and every time you mention the name Archer Jones, you get all googly-eyed."

"I do not."

"Seriously?"

"Yes, seriously. I don't get googly-eyed when I talk about him. And for the record, I never talk about him."

"Then how do I know about him?"

The bartender comes over and against my better judgment, I order a cranberry and vodka.

"He's Dean's best friend. I know I've talked about my brothers before."

"You have, and I don't know Logan's best friend."

"It's Owen," I counter. "Who I've talked about."

Marissa responds with pursed lips. "Owen is your brother too. Weston—I don't even know his wife's name."

"I wish I could forget it too," I grumble, intense anger surging through me at the mere mention of my sister-in-law. No one has seen her in years, but the anger is still strong.

"That's not the point here. The point is, you have the hots for this guy. And now he's here."

"He's attractive," I tell her. "Obviously."

"Fuck yes. If you're not interested, I'll climb all over that. Do I have your blessing to strip him down and put my lips around his cock?"

My left eye twitches.

"See!" Marissa points a manicured nail at my face. "You want him!"

"Keep it down," I say through gritted teeth, fighting the blood rushing to my cheeks. "I'm attracted to him. I always have been. I'd love to spend the night in his bed, but I'm pretty sure he only sees me as his friend's sister. I'm probably like a sister to him too."

"You need to show him you're not. Go home, get changed into something that shows off your boobs, and make him realize you're a sexy, successful, totally awesome *single* lady."

"You make it sound so easy."

"It is easy!" She grabs both our drinks and hands me mine. "Just be you, Quinn Dawson, boss lady extraordinaire. If he doesn't like you, it's his loss."

"I love you, you know that, right?" I bring my straw to my lips and suck down a mouthful of watered-down cranberry juice and way too much vodka.

"You can prove it by taking that hunk of a surgeon back to your place tonight."

"I'm not making any promises, but he did say he wanted to take me to dinner."

"Give him a good dessert." She wiggles her eyebrows and leads me away from the bar.

I suck down another mouthful of my gross drink before

tossing it and find Archer standing near a window looking out at the city below.

My heart stops in my chest for a brief moment when I look him over.

"Ready to get out of here?" I ask, not recognizing the woman talking. I don't say things like this. I don't go to dinner with a guy I'm wildly attracted to hoping for a one-night stand.

I'm a romantic.

I like tender moments.

Feeling what can only be described as magic.

"Yeah." Archer's smile melts my panties right off. "Where do you want to go?"

"Home first," I say, then panic he thinks I'm insinuating something I'm not. "I'd like to change, and I need to feed my cat."

Feed my cat? This isn't the way to show him I'm a sexy, single lady.

"You have a cat?"

"Not just one. Three and a half."

We start to walk away from the party. "How do you have half a cat?"

"He's not really mine. I have three cats and am fostering another and I said I wasn't going to keep him, but I think I might."

"Oh, that's nice of you. I miss having pets."

"I grew up with them. You know that."

"Yeah," he says. "I remember. Though I'm a little surprised you went with cats instead of dogs."

I laugh. "I do love dogs. I'm not home enough to have one. And my mom has enough to give me a dog-fix when I need it. And if you promise not to tell her, I'll let you in on a little secret."

"You can trust me. I already know about the Batmobile, after all."

Smiling, I lean in. "I'm more of a cat person than a dog person."

"You're risking getting disowned."

I make a face. "What can I say? I live on the edge." I make a detour into my office to grab my purse and computer. Archer offers to carry the laptop for me, and I let him take it, even though it's not heavy at all. The gesture is nice, and not something I see too often anymore.

"Do you drive from your house to work? Or is it as big of a pain to drive around Chicago as they make it seem in the movies?" he asks when we get in the elevators to leave.

"It can be a pain. And I do sometimes. I have a spot in a garage nearby, and a spot at my loft so at least I'm not looking for a place to park. But it can be a headache, so unless it's really cold, I usually walk. I'm not that far and consider it my work out for the day."

"Good point. The winters here are brutal, aren't they?"

"They're awful and make me question my sanity. It's not that much worse than at home, though, but being closer to the lake does amplify things."

We make it a block in silence, but this time the noise of the city is loud enough to drown out the awkwardness. And then we stop at a crosswalk.

"I don't know if I should say this or not," Archer starts.

I hike my designer purse up on my shoulder, heart lurching. "Say what?"

"Your secretaries are bitches."

"Oh, well, I know."

"You do?" He's taken aback.

"Yeah. But why do you think so?"

"They casually insulted their boss. I didn't know it was you or I would have said something."

I shrug. "Thanks, but no need. They do that from time to time."

"You're okay with them talking about you like that?"

"I wouldn't say I'm *okay* with it, more so I just don't care. Rene is vapid and shallow. Charlene is a gold-digger. I knew that when I hired them. But I needed someone to answer the phones and greet people when they walk in, not a humanitarian. And you know what they're good at? Answering the phones and greeting people when they walk in. It might not be what you want to hear, but I've been dealing with girls like that my whole life, and compared to some of them, Rene is harmless."

"I had no idea. I'm...I'm sorry, Quinn."

"It's water under the bridge now. I learned to embrace being the computer nerd years ago. Yeah, girls like Rene threw their fair amount of stones. But you know what I did with those stones? I used them to build a foundation, and not to sound cliché, but look at me now."

The light changes and I step forward to move with the crowd. Archer stays rooted to the spot, looking at me like he's seeing me for the first time.

"Archer?" I say softly as I turn around, and he snaps back, shaking himself. He takes my arm, pulling me into him at the last second to avoid being hit by someone on a bike. I stumble just like I did the last time he pulled me close, with my hands landing on his chest and my eyes going right to his.

This time, there's no denying the spark that passes between us.

10

QUINN

"So, this is my home," I say, stepping into the loft. I pull my purse off my shoulder and take my laptop from Archer, setting them on the bench next to my door. I traded my heels for comfortable walking shoes before leaving the office, and kick those off, using my foot to push them under the bench.

Archer takes his shoes off as well and moves close behind me, looking around. A fat orange cat trots over, meowing when he sees us.

"This is Neville." I pick him up and he instantly starts purring. "The half-cat."

Smiling, Archer holds out his hand for Neville to sniff. Deciding Archer isn't a threat, Neville rubs his face on Archer's fingers. "I can see why you don't want to give him up."

"He's a lover. I wasn't sure how the other cats would react to him, but they get along fine. The other three are all females and boss this fat guy around." I walk inside, letting Neville jump out of my arms. "They're all from the same litter. Someone a few floors down found them in the alley and as soon as I saw them, I couldn't resist."

A little voice in my head is yelling at me to stop talking about cats.

"They're easy to take care of and keep me company."

Why can't I stop talking?

"And I don't have to worry about them throughout the day."

Neville runs into the kitchen and starts meowing, signaling the others to come join him.

"I always feed them when I get home."

A dark gray and black tabby winds around my ankles, almost tripping me.

"Bellatrix," I say, bending over to pick her up. She darts forward, jumping onto the large island counter. The living space in the loft is open, with the living room, kitchen, and dining area all melding together. The entire building was renovated not all that long ago, given a crisp, modern appearance that's a little bit too contemporary for my liking. My decor is mostly bohemian, and the clash of styles works in a weird way.

It's home, and I love it.

All too aware of Archer's eyes on me, I get a can of cat food from the pantry and dish it up, feeling very much like a crazy cat lady as I carry the bowls from the counter to the floor, trying not to trip over the four loudly meowing cats snaking around my feet.

When I turn back around, Archer is standing next to the floor-to-ceiling window in the living room, looking out at the city below. He took off his suit jacket and button-up shirt, leaving just his undershirt on. I run my eyes over him, taking in every inch of his tall body. The white fabric of his undershirt is stretched tight over his muscular arms. It's untucked, hanging unevenly over his belt. I can't help but notice the nice curve of his ass and the bulge from his cock behind his dress pants.

My lips part and I remember how it felt, just for that short moment, pressed against me as we stood in the kitchen as the storm raged around us. Through his pants, I could tell his cock was big.

His touch was deliberate, meant to get under my skin, but he knew what he was doing. My nerves tingle as I think about it and some of that annoyance comes back. Good. I need to hold onto it, or my resolve will crumble.

Archer runs a hand through his hair, messing it up, and angles his body toward mine. I shift my gaze from his crotch to his face at the last second, but it might have been too late.

"I'm going to get changed. You can watch TV or whatever." I whirl around and take off so fast I walk right into the counter. Trying to internalize my pain, I press my hand over my hip where it hit the corner and hurry into my room.

I shut my door and lean against it, hand flying to my chest like that will slow my pounding heart. *Get it together.* Pushing off the door, I pull the hair tie from my ponytail and go into the bathroom, giving myself a hard look-over.

I wear makeup to work most days, nothing crazy, just a little bit of foundation and mascara to make me look put together. I grab my makeup bag and hesitate, not wanting to look like I tried too hard.

This isn't a date.

Deciding to do my makeup after I agonize about it some more, I plug in my curling iron and quickly run my brush through my hair. While it heats up, I strip out of my clothes and trade my comfy t-shirt bra for an uncomfortable pushup, topping it with a low-cut shirt and tight black pants.

I curl my hair in record time and go with light eyeliner and red lipstick. Just enough to make it look like I tried, but not that I'm trying too hard.

I think?

Maybe?

I roll my eyes at myself and unplug the curling iron. Grabbing a pair of heels, I go back into the living room and find Archer lying on the couch. Neville is curled up on his chest, and Archer's eyes are shut.

"Archer?" I say quietly. His breathing is slow and rhythmic. He did say he was running on hardly any sleep. Frodo's voice gets my attention; Archer had turned on *Lord of the Rings*. Smiling, I pull the blanket off the back of the couch and spread it over Archer.

"MORNING, SUNSHINE."

Archer sits up, blinking. "Shit. I fell asleep." He stretches his arms up over his head, and the hem of his shirt goes up an inch or so, showing off his fit abdomen. My eyes go right to the little trail of hair leading to his big cock. "How long was I out?"

"The movie isn't over yet, so not that long."

"You should have woken me up."

"Nah." I wave my hand in the air. "It was much more fun to draw all over your face in Sharpie while you were sleeping."

His eyes narrow ever so slightly. "You wouldn't."

I lean in. "Oh, I would. But I didn't. Not this time. You looked a little too helpless. I knew you were tired."

"I'd say I'm surprised I fell asleep, but I'm not."

"That's why I didn't want to wake you up. I haven't worked a hundred-hour week at the office, but I've pulled some long nights and know how awful it is when you're running on no sleep."

"I'm used to it."

"That doesn't mean it's good for you. We can order takeout and you can go back to sleep if you want."

"And stay the night here?"

"Don't get any ideas, Dr. Jones. Your ass will be sleeping on the couch again."

"The couch? This place is too big to only have one bedroom."

"True, but that doesn't mean you can sleep in it."

He rolls his neck. "You'd really make me sleep on the couch over a comfortable bed?"

"No, I wouldn't. But I don't have another comfy bed. The second bedroom is set up—"

"For the cats?" His perfect lips curve into a smartass smirk.

"As a home office." I cross my arms, wondering if I'd be able to slip the cat-tree into the closet before he walks past. I twirl a curl around my finger. "Want me to order Chinese?"

"No, I said I wanted to take you out."

"So you do want this to be a date."

"Would it be a bad thing if it was?"

My body is saying no, it wouldn't be bad. It's begging and pleading for me to go, reminding me just how long it's been since I felt the touch of a man. But my heart...it's screaming even louder, telling me yes, it would be a very bad thing.

"I don't know."

Archer stands, and his cock is right at my eye level. I turn my head up, meeting his eyes.

"What do you have to lose?" he asks.

Everything.

"Fine. Let's go on a date."

"Don't tell Dean."

I roll my eyes and let out a sharp breath. Of course he has to bring up my brother. "I send selfies from all my dates to my brothers."

"Really?"

"Yes, for their approval," I say seriously before shaking my head. "You know what's kind of crazy?"

"What?"

"I'm my own person and I'm able to function without telling my brothers everything." I put my hands on the arms of the lounge chair and stand up. "I'm going to get changed."

"Again?"

"I'm wearing my pajamas. I changed after you passed out on the couch."

"Oh." He looks me over. "You look good. I didn't even notice."

I will not blush. I will not blush. I will not—dammit. "Well, I think everyone else will notice my pants have little dancing elephants on them. And I'm not wearing a bra."

"I did notice that."

"Pig." I cross my arms over my chest.

"That's making it worse, Quinn."

A quick look down tells me crossing my arms just pushed my tits together so they're almost spilling out of my tank top.

"I'll be right back." I clamp my hands over my breasts to cover my nipples and do my best not to run away. Deciding not to go with the sexy outfit I'd previously picked out, I pull a blue dress over my head. I discovered a while ago a cute yet comfy dress can make it look like you put more effort into your outfit than you actually did. Dresses seem to have that effect, fancying-up your appearance simply by not being pants.

"I still think you looked good in the pajamas," Archer says when I emerge from the bedroom. "But I do like this too."

"Thanks." He put his button-up back on and has the sleeves rolled up. I don't know why that look is so damn sexy, but it is. "The professional look works for you."

"I prefer my scrubs with a stethoscope hanging around my neck so everyone knows I'm a doctor. But, unfortunately, I didn't bring them."

"You're going to have to pretend to be a lowly peasant like the rest of us."

"If that's what it takes to get you to go on a date with me, I'm willing to take one for the team." He moves to the door and puts on his shoes. "Shall we?"

"Hang on, I need to get my selfie to send to Dean." I put my arm around him, doing the cheesiest pose I can think of, and snap a picture. "And now to caption it..." I pretend like I'm writing a text message. "Archer is taking me on a hot date tonight. Don't worry, we'll use protection." I flick my eyes to him, smiling. "Sent."

"Hilarious, Quinn. We both know Dean would try to kill me if he thought I was hooking up with you."

"He would kill you."

"He'd try." Archer hands me my purse. "I could take him."

The image of Archer's bulging biceps is seared into my memory. "Yeah, probably." I punch in the code on my alarm and open the door. "I guess we better not tell him then."

"Now this one is serious," I say, tipping my head up to look at Archer. We're slowly making our way along the Riverwalk after getting dinner and drinks. I might be a little buzzed. Whether it's from the alcohol or the electricity humming between Archer and I, there's no way to tell.

"I'm ready." Archer takes my hand, lacing his fingers through mine.

"You're alone in the car and 'Living on a Prayer' comes on. What do you do?"

"I turn that shit up and belt it out. Which I'd do even if I wasn't alone, just to warn you." He pulls my hand back, bringing me to him. The wind picks up, and I shiver. Archer lets go of my hand to wrap his arms around me. The feeling he gives me can only be described as butterflies, and I haven't experienced anything like this in years.

"Did I pass the test?"

"Yes," I tell him. "But things are about to get more intense. "What if 'Shake it Off' comes on next?"

"I'm alone?"

"Totally alone. On a country road."

"Hmmm." His hands slide up and down my back. I shiver again, but not from the cold. "That song is catchy. I'll be singing and dancing."

I laugh, throwing my head back so the wind doesn't blow my hair into his face. "Do you even know the words?"

"No. I know what song you're talking about. I think. Maybe? I don't want to fail your test."

Hooking my arms around his shoulders, I shuffle closer until my hips brush his. "There was no test. Mostly because I wasn't keeping score."

"You put me through all that for nothing?"

"Guilty. What are you going to do about it?"

In a sudden and swift movement, he scoops me up and turns to the river.

"Archer," I squeal, clinging to him tighter. "Don't you dare!" We both laugh and his hands linger over my body as he sets me back down. We stand there, close together, both of our hearts pounding. The wind blows my hair again and Archer gathers it in one hand, moving it to the side of my neck.

"Have you decided yet?" His deep voice cuts through the night. He looks into my eyes when he talks and the confidence is sexy on him. It's not over the top. It's not hyped up to over-compensate for something. It's completely genuine and is doing bad things to me right now.

Bad things that would feel so good.

"On what?"

"On whether you want this to be a date or not."

I bite my lip. "You have to answer one more question first."

"If your question is if I put out on the first date, I have been known to."

Laughing, I bring my hands down from his shoulders, splaying my fingers on his chest. An attractive man who can make me laugh...I need to run far, far away. Because as much as I want this to continue, I know it won't.

It can't.

"That's kind of along the lines of my question."

He wiggles his eyebrows. "I like where this is going. What's your question?"

"If this *is* our first date, will you take me out on a second?"

11

"Yes." The word leaves my mouth before I have a chance to think about it. Quinn doesn't say anything, doesn't react. Her lashes come together in a blink, and she looks at me, almost as if she's waiting for me to tell her I'm joking.

Then she smiles.

It's the most beautiful thing in the world. And right now, with her hands on my chest and my arms locked around her waist, I want to kiss her hard and tell her I'd take her on a thousand dates and it wouldn't be enough.

The moment is over as fast as it started, and I'm sure she's thinking the same thing I am. She lives in Chicago. I live in Indy. We're not worlds away, but a four-hour drive makes starting a relationship hard.

I don't know the next time I'll be able to get away from work long enough to come see her. It could be weeks before I'm able to drive back up north and take her on a second date.

My heart starts to ache, even though everything I want is right in front of me for the taking. Quinn slides her hands down my torso and around my back. She rests her head on my chest and admires the skyline above us.

This is exactly what I've wanted, what I've wished for. And now that I had a taste, now that I know how fucking good it feels to finally let my feelings surface, it's going to hurt. I need to disengage.

"It's getting late."

"Yeah," Quinn agrees, pulling away. Instantly, I miss her touch and the warmth of her skin. "We should head back. If you want to crash on the couch, you can. Do you have to be back at the convention thingy tomorrow?"

"There are a few more panels to sit in on, but I don't have to be there until nine. It's the last day and they'll be done around two."

"That was a short convention."

"It started earlier in the week, but I couldn't get off work."

She clasps her hands on her elbows, holding her arms in tightly against her body to stay warm. Not pulling her close goes against every fiber of my being, like I'm wired to do everything and anything to make her comfortable.

"Do you like being a surgeon?"

"I do. I better, right? I've put enough into it."

"Yeah. You'd have wasted a lot of time if not."

We go a few paces without talking, and I hate how much the dynamic changed between us. It's because of me, and Quinn has to fucking know it. A gust of wind blows in off the lakefront. It's cold, chilling me and I'm in long sleeves and pants.

I can't help it. My arm wraps around Quinn and the moment we connect, I relax.

"Do you want my shirt?"

"Then you'll be half-naked."

"I have an undershirt," I remind her. "I should have worn the suit jacket just so I could give it to you."

She tries not to smile. "That would have been very gentlemanly. Though you'd think I'd learn to dress for the weather. I have lived here for quite some time. When the wind blows over the lake, it's always cold."

Not wanting to make her walk in the cold, I hail a cab. There's not much traffic this time of night, and we get back to the loft quickly.

"You really can stay," she says again, taking off her shoes. I don't move out of the entryway. I shouldn't stay though I want to. "Or you can call an Uber to take you back to your hotel."

I pull my phone from my pocket and see that it's dead. Quinn says she has an extra charger and that I shouldn't leave until my phone has some battery life in case I need to make an emergency call. She reminds me of her mother there, and it's more endearing than I thought it'd be. She goes into her room to get the charger. I step out of my shoes and sit in the living room, looking around at the decor. The stark modernity of the space isn't something I'd guess Quinn would have gone for, but the view is amazing and she's close to her office. She's done a good job making this large, white space look homey and feel cozy.

Everything is so *Quinn*, tasteful yet a little quirky.

"Here ya go." She comes back into the living room, holding a phone cord, and crouches down next to the couch to plug it into the wall. Then she takes my phone from me and hooks it up.

She takes a step back and crosses her arms over her body again. I hate that she feels like she has to physically guard herself from me. Hurting her is the last thing I want to do, which is exactly why we need to stop this before it starts. "I'm going to get some water. Do you want some?"

"Yeah, thanks."

I watch her go into the kitchen, cats following her in hopes of more food. Her dress hugs her curves in all the right places. It's loose around her legs, hiding her tight ass until she moves and the outline can be seen through the thin fabric. The neckline of her dress goes to a deep-V, tight against her tits.

She moves her hair over her shoulder and picks up the cats' water bowl, rinsing it out and filling it up before she grabs two water bottles from the fridge and comes back to the couch. Taking a long drink, she recaps her water and sits back with a sigh.

I thought she was a little drunk before. Nothing like pulling a Dr. Jekyll and Mr. Hyde to make a girl sober up.

My phone buzzes back to life, beeping from a missed text. I glance over, curious to see who it's from but not really interested in opening it. Then I see it's from my mom. There's only one reason she'd text me this late. I put the water bottle on the coffee table and turn away from Quinn to unlock my phone.

My heart speeds up and I try to prepare myself for the worst. I always do. Because someday, the worst *will* happen.

Mom: Bobby passed out. We just got to the hospital. I tried calling you, but it went straight to voicemail. I hate leaving you messages like this, but I wanted to tell you in case...you know. I'll update you when I can.

The next text was sent sometime later.

Mom: It's his kidneys again, and they're putting him on some new medication. We'll be home in the morning. Don't worry about calling tonight. We're all exhausted

and I know how hard you've been working. We're proud of you, Archie. Love you.

"Archer?" Quinn's voice is as soft as her touch. Her hand lands on my arm. "Is everything okay?"

I read the text again. One of these times, medical intervention isn't going to be enough. One of these times, my brother is going to take it so far there's no coming back. Years of drug use have already taken their toll on his body, and he's only a year and a half older than me.

"Is everything okay?" she asks again.

I put my phone down, shifting my gaze from the bright screen to Quinn's beautiful face.

"It will be."

She pushes her hair back and nods. "Are you tired?" she asks carefully, and I read between the lines. She's wondering if I'm going to stay or go, though I can't tell what she's hoping for.

"Not really."

"Oh, uh, okay."

Silence falls between us, and over the noise of the city below, I can hear my own heart pounding away in my chest. Quinn tucks her legs up under herself and leans forward to pet Neville, who jumped up next to me, purring. Quinn's dress gaps and her tits almost spill out. The will of the gods couldn't keep me from stealing a glance. The faint outline of her nipple is visible through the thin material of a light purple bra. There's no padding. No pushup. I want to bury my face between her breasts and kiss my way down to her sweet cunt.

My cock jumps as an intense wave of desire crashes over me. I don't know how much longer I can resist her. It was one thing when I wasn't sure if she wanted me too, but after tonight I know she does.

I want her so fucking bad. But I shouldn't.

"Well, I had a nice time," Quinn starts, not looking away from the cat. "Even if you didn't, I did. So, uh, thanks for taking me out on our non-date."

"What makes you think I didn't have a nice time too?"

She brings her arms back in and shrugs, shyly flicking her gaze to mine. "I don't know."

"I did, Quinn. I had a nice time, too."

She brings her head up, this time staring at me dubiously. "You seemed to like it until the end. Again. And I just—" She cuts off, letting out an exasperated sigh. "You know what, it's fine. Never mind. It's like you're playing a game whenever we're together, giving me just enough of yourself to make me want more. You open up only to shut me out, and even if I had all the cheat codes to force a win, this isn't a game I want to play." She closes her eyes, jaw tense, and stands. "I'll call you an Uber. It's late and I'm sure you're tired."

"Quinn, don't."

"Why? One minute I think you like me and the next you can't get away from me fast enough. I can't figure you out, Archer, and it's making me feel really fucking stupid."

I get to my feet and grab her wrist, gently pulling her hand toward me. I take her phone and toss it on the couch.

And then I kiss her.

M y heart pounds with indignation as anger surges through me. I don't know who I'm more mad at: myself or Archer. Though right now, with his lips pressed to mine, it's hard to be anything other than stunned.

He moves in, hands landing on my waist. Pushing his tongue into my mouth, he brings me in tight against him. My breasts crush against his chest and heat floods my veins.

I'm not stunned anymore.

And I'm not pissed.

Archer's lips are soft and full. His kisses are hard and desperate. Together, it's a recipe for disaster. My resolve is crumbling. I should stop him now before there's nothing left.

But I don't want to stop him, not when it feels so good.

"Quinn," he pants, pressing his forehead against mine. I bring my arms up around his neck and shuffle closer, parting my legs and pushing my hips into his. Archer has never held me like this before. We've never been so close. And he's certainly never kissed me. Being in his arms is the most familiar new feeling in the world. It doesn't make sense. All I know is I never want this to stop.

"If you don't want—"

"Shut up," I say and bring one hand down to his chest. I twist the material of his shirt in my fist and put my lips to his. Heat rushes over me, and feeling the same fervor, Archer cups my face in his hand and kisses me. His tongue slips past my lips, and he tips my chin up, the gesture more intimate than anything.

I melt against him, hand falling from his chest to his waist, and my fingers curl around his belt. I fumble with the buckle and Archer breaks the kiss, stepping back only so I can undo it. I pull the leather from the buckle, heart hammering as I flick my eyes down, watching the belt fall free from the loops on his pants. I drop the belt onto the floor and grab the hem of his shirt, untucking it.

It's like Archer can't wait any longer, and he advances, kissing me in a fury and sliding his hands down my body. He squeezes my ass and pulls me to him. His hard cock presses against me, and I arch my back to press my pelvis into him.

Enveloping me in his arms, he gathers the material of my dress in his hand, bringing it up over my ass. He moves his lips from mine to my neck, and I run my hand over his muscular chest, trailing my fingers along the buttons on his shirt, along the waistband of his pants, and over his cock.

He moans at my touch, kissing a trail from my neck along my collarbone. I put both hands on either side of his head, curling my fingers in his hair, and urge his mouth to my breasts.

"You are so fucking hot," he breathes, letting go of me for a brief second to widen his stance. With deft fingers, he unzips my dress with one hand and cups my face with the other. His eyes are closed, and his heart is racing.

I pop the button on his pants, and his zipper goes down from the force of his big, hard cock protesting against the tightness of his pants. He lets out a moan when it's freed, and the top sticks out over the band of his boxers.

A bead of precum dots the tip, and I wrap my fingers around his thick shaft, using my thumb to spread his wetness down. My dress, now unzipped, hangs loosely from my shoulders. I pump my hand up and down Archer's cock as he bends his head down, running his tongue over my earlobe. I shiver, though I'm far from cold.

He pushes one of my sleeves off my shoulder, moving his lips to my neck again. He finds a sweet spot, one that sends tingles through my body, making my pussy pulse with anticipation for his cock.

Archer Jones is going to fuck me.

Suddenly, I feel nervous. Too inexperienced. I'm not sure I can handle this huge cock that's in my hand. I'm no virgin, but I've never been with someone like Archer. I want this to be good for him too.

In one swift movement, Archer pulls my dress down, and it melts into a fabric puddle around my feet. I'm standing before him in only my bra and panties. He pulls his mouth off me, brows pushed together, and stares at me.

"Is something wrong?" I ask timidly.

"Fuck no," he growls. "You're even more beautiful than I imagined."

My heart leaps and somewhere in the back of my mind, it registers that Archer just admitted he's imagined me naked, but that takes a backseat to my libido. And right now, Archer needs to get inside of me.

I push his pants down, but they don't fall smoothly like

my dress. Using his foot to bring then down one leg at a time, he kicks them off and pounces on me again, hands wrapping around my waist. He picks me up, and my breasts are in his face.

Wrapping my legs around him, I bend my arms and rake my fingers through his hair. Archer walks forward and presses me up against the wall. We're right next to the window, and the lights are on. Anyone from a neighboring building can look out and see us, but right now I don't care.

If we stop, I might implode.

We kiss again before Archer sets me down. He drops to his knees, urging my legs apart. Starting at my knee, he kisses his way up my thighs, his touch getting rougher the closer he gets to my core. I'm breathing fast, heart close to beating out of my chest. His lips settle on my lower abdomen, right above the elastic in my black panties.

He flicks his eyes to me, a devilish look in his eye, and brings his mouth over me, warm breath a tease through the fabric of my underwear. Closing my eyes, I bring my head back and hit the wall a little too hard. Archer hooks his fingers around either side of my panties and slowly starts to bring them down.

Oh. My. God. My knees are already weak. I don't know if I can physically stand it. My panties hit the floor and he gently lifts up one of my legs, letting my underwear slip free one foot at a time. He licks his lips and puts his mouth over my clit. I inhale sharply, eyes fluttering shut.

But then he brings his face up, kissing his way up my stomach. He gets back on his feet and slips one hand around me to unhook my bra. I'm completely naked in front of him, so overcome by desire now I forget to feel shy.

Archer looks at me like I'm the only woman in the world. Seeing the lust in his eyes, knowing what the sight of my naked body is doing to him, gives me power. I lick my lips and bring my hand down, plunging it inside of his boxers.

He lets out a groan, standing there enjoying me jerk him off, and then grabs my wrist, pulling it away from his cock. He grits his teeth, bracing himself for the sudden stop of being pleasured, and brings my hand up over my head, and does the same with the other, holding them both with one hand, leaving his other free to continue touching me. Keeping both of my wrists locked in his grasp, he kisses me again and drops one hand down to my thighs.

He urges my legs open, running his fingertips over the tender flesh inside my thigh. With slow, deliberate movements, he brings them up closer and closer. Inch by fucking inch. My pussy is screaming. Begging. Dying to be touched. He finds my clit and sweeps his fingers over it so lightly it's the biggest tease, almost as if this is a game to him and he's seeing how long I can hold out before I shove his boxers down, take hold of his cock, and push him inside me.

If it is a game, I'm not going to win, because I can't last much longer. And if it means that monster cock thrusts inside me, I'm okay with being the loser.

"I want you," I whisper, and those three words are all it takes for Archer to become the one unable to hold out. He brings his hand up, rubbing my clit. I press my back hard against the wall, needing the support.

Fuck, he's good with his hands. He slides a finger inside me, pressing against my G-spot and then going back to my clit. The back and forth winds me up, and it doesn't take long before I'm riding on the edge of an orgasm.

And he knows it. He fucking knows it and slows down, lightening his touch until I move my hips down, pressing myself against him. I'm right there, so close to coming. I need to come.

"Are you getting greedy, Quinn?" he groans, voice deep and throaty in my ear.

"Mhhh," I moan, tipping my head up to his. Fighting against his grip, I try to free my arms. Archer's fingers tighten around my wrist, pressing them harder into the wall. His lips meet mine again, but this time his kiss is slow and tender. He releases my wrists and brings his hand down to my shoulder, gently squeezing as he slides it to the back of my neck.

Though I'm still desperate for him to throw me down and fuck me hard, I can't ignore the tenderness in his touch. The way his kisses feel as natural as breathing. How well we meld together like we were made for this.

"What do you want, Quinn?" he asks gruffly, sweeping his fingers over my most sensitive parts.

"You."

"I know that." He slowly slides a finger between my folds, spreading my wetness. "What do you want me to do to you?"

"I want you to fuck me," I pant, hands settling on his arms. It would be easy to feel shy and vulnerable right now, standing here completely naked while Archer still has most of his clothes on. I'm pinned between his body and the wall, dripping wet with his hand between my legs.

But I don't.

I bite my lip, taking in a shaky breath, and slide one hand down his chest. My fingers dance over his cock, and I watch his eyes flutter as I circle the gleaming tip for a moment. Then I grab his wrist and push his hand away.

"And if you won't, I'll have to finish myself."

Archer's eyes widen and he looks down, lips parting as he watches me touch myself.

"You got me so hot, Archer," I moan. "I need to come."

"Holy shit, Quinn," he breathes.

"What?" I ask innocently. "Jealous?"

"That is not what I am right now."

"Archer," I start, rubbing my fingers over my clit. I let out a moan. "Take your shirt off."

Not taking his eyes off me, he starts to unbutton his shirt, giving up halfway through and rips it off. He pulls his white undershirt over his head, then dives forward, moving my arms so he can pick me up. I fasten my legs around him, holding onto his neck as he carries me into my bedroom.

It's dark in here, but enough light spills in from the living room to illuminate his handsome face. He lays me down, moving overtop. I bend my legs up, feeling his hardness press into me, and tug at the elastic in his boxers. Ignoring my attempts to strip him bare, Archer moves down and parts my legs.

I gasp when his tongue lashes out against me. There's no hesitation. No teasing with a light touch. Not this time.

Archer slides his hands under my ass and lifts me up just a bit, bringing my pussy to his mouth. He's not only good with his hands, but his tongue is magic as well. And right now, it's flicking my clit with fury. I flatten my hands on the bed, only to grab the comforter and twist it in my grip.

Setting me back down on the bed, Archer throws my legs over his shoulders. I cross my ankles and steal a look down, watching him eat me out. He flicks his eyes up at the same time, and being caught watching turns me on even more.

He kisses and sucks between licking, and I'm right back to where I was not long ago. My muscles tighten and I twist the blankets tighter in my hand. Archer slides one finger into my pussy, going right for my G-spot again. He lightly presses against it, and that's all it takes for me to come.

The orgasm hits me hard, rolling through me and making every nerve in my body come alive. I cry out, moaning loudly. Archer doesn't let up, doesn't stop. He keeps his mouth on me, feeling my pussy spasm around his finger. It's almost too much and I squirm against him, pushing him away.

Ignoring me, Archer keeps finger fucking me as he works his tongue, and another orgasm hits me as soon as the other ends. They blend together, and my ears ring and my heart beats so fast I think it might explode. No one has ever made me come like this. Hell, no one has even come close. The things Archer's doing to me...the way he knows exactly where to touch me to bring me the most pleasure possible...it's like he has an advanced degree in my body, knowing me better than I know myself.

I'm writhing with an overload of pleasure, heart racing and chest rapidly rising and falling as I try to catch my breath. Archer gently pulls away, wipes his mouth with the back of his hand.

"Breathe, Quinn," he whispers and lies next to me, wrapping his arms around my body. Unable to speak, I just nod and wait for the feeling to come back to my fingers before rolling over and cupping his face.

"Okay," I pant. "You can leave now."

"Funny."

"I'm serious. You have to get up early."

His hand lands on my stomach, fingers inching down to my core. "Are you sure you want me to leave?"

"Fuck no." I grab his arms and tug him onto me, spreading my legs. Still breathing hard, I push his boxers down and wrap my hand around his large cock. Archer sits up a bit, removing his boxers, and I push myself up on my elbows, wanting to take a look at the dick that's about to destroy me.

"Good Lord," I whisper, not meaning to say it out loud. I'm not one to describe a penis as beautiful, but that thing is pretty. Pretty, and big. I bring my hand up to my chest and lick my lips. Archer smirks and moves back on me, falling between my legs. The tip of his cock rubs against me, and I shudder in pleasure.

"Fuck, you're so wet," he groans, rubbing his cock against me again.

"I'm wet because you made me." I buck my hips and Archer lets out a breath.

"I don't think I can hold out much longer," he admits, burying his face in my neck. "I'm going to fuck you now, Quinn," he tells me, but it's more like a warning for what's to come.

I bend my legs up and widen my thighs. Archer reaches down, taking hold of his massive cock, lining it up with my core. He brings his head down, lips pressing against mine, and slowly enters me.

I'm not sure all of him will fit inside me. I've never been with a man this large, and never one this skilled. Dragging my nails down his back, I grab his ass. He lowers himself onto his elbows, squishing my breasts against his chest. He thrusts in and out, cock rubbing against my inner walls. His pace is slow, and I think it's for his benefit as much as mine.

He doesn't want to come yet.

I'm still reeling from the double orgasm he gave me.

We both want this to last. I bring one hand to his face, tipping it toward me so I can kiss him. He fucks me slow as we make-out until my breathing quickens, and I turn my head to the side, mouth falling open as another climax starts to slowly build.

Archer drops his head down, groaning. He's close to coming too. I angle my hips up, and the tip of his cock hits my G-spot again. And again. I slide my hands over his back, skin hot and sweaty, and bring one leg up, hooking it around him.

Suddenly, Archer sits up, moving to his knees. He grabs my leg and holds it up in the air, pounding his cock into me. He rubs my clit with his other hand. His eyes fall shut and he slows down, and I know he's doing everything he can to keep from coming until I do again.

Reaching down, I put my hand over his, feeling him touch me. My pussy contracts and a moan escapes my lips. No sooner, Archer pitches forward, cock pulsing as he comes. He lets go of my leg and moves back on top of me, cock still buried deep inside. My inner walls spasm around him, and I bring my arms up, hands landing on either side of his face.

We're both panting. Both unable to move or form a coherent sentence. He rests his forehead against mine, and we stay like that for a while. Then he slowly pulls out and lies by my side, snaking his arm around my waist and curling his body around mine. I roll toward him, not caring about the mess left on the bed, and snuggle in closer.

Archer presses his lips to my forehead, and reaches down, grabbing the pink fuzzy blanket I have folded at the foot of my bed. He covers us up, wraps his arms tightly around me, and I feel like I'm exactly where I'm supposed to be.

13

ARCHER

I pull Quinn closer, pressing my lips against the side of her neck. I'm half asleep and fighting it. As much as I need sleep, I want to soak up every minute of this as I can. Who knows what the morning will bring. Or even the moment we get out of bed.

I kissed Quinn.

Felt Quinn.

Touched every inch of her. Fucked her. Finally. After years of wanting and waiting for the time to come, it did. I think back to Sam and what he said about idealizing sleeping with Quinn. How there's no way the real thing could be as good as what I've imagined in my mind.

He had a good point. Often, when you want something so bad and it's so out of reach, you romanticize it, make it seem better than it ever can be. I thought that was the case with Quinn.

But it couldn't be further from the truth.

There's no fucking her out of my system. There's no spending one night with her and being able to move on with my life. In fact, it's only making me want her more, because everything was better than I could have imagined. Physically, I've never had more satisfying sex in my life. I've never come so hard, never felt an orgasm so deep through every part of me.

I used to think it was lame when I'd hear someone say there's a difference between fucking and making love. It's all the same in a sense, right? I would have sworn that to be true until a few minutes ago.

I fucked Quinn good. She'll feel it in the morning. Thinking about my cock in her tight, wet pussy arouses me. We definitely *fucked* hard.

But there was something more to it. I can't quite place it, yet at the same time, I'm terrified it'll slip away. We connected on a different level, and that's how I know there's a transcendental difference between the two.

Quinn rolls over, sliding her hand across my chest. She wiggles closer and rests her head on my shoulder. I brush her hair out of her face and pull the blanket up, keeping us covered.

Running my hand up and down her arm, I suddenly feel anxious. I haven't been in a relationship in a while, though ever since I met Quinn all those years ago, I've had a hard time committing to anyone.

It wasn't her, and I was painfully aware of it every single day.

I've had my share of casual sex, and while leaving after has been awkward a time or two, it's never been like this. There's more on the line than being embarrassed or doing the walk of shame.

I finally hooked up with Quinn, and I don't want our first time to be our only time. Quinn runs her nails up and down my side, further relaxing me. My eyes fall shut and my head turns to the side, face buried in Quinn's hair. Everything about her is intoxicating, from the smell of her shampoo to the way her body feels, naked and pressed up against mine.

"Archer?" she whispers, not lifting her head off my shoulder. "Are you asleep?"

For a brief moment, I panic, which isn't like me at all. I'm a surgeon, for fuck's sake. I don't panic. Don't freak out. I can maintain a level head and think clearly in stressful situations. But Quinn...she's doing something to me, and suddenly I'm worried she's going to tell me this was a mistake and I should leave.

"Kind of," I mumble.

"I wasn't sure." She slowly starts to pull out of my arms. Shit. I brace myself. This is it. The moment she tells me Dean will have my head and we need to pretend this never happened. The moment I go back to wanting her so bad it hurts, but only worse now because I know how good she feels.

"I have to pee."

"Oh." I move my arms. "Okay." I sit up, kissing her on the lips before she gets out of bed and goes into the bathroom. A few minutes later, she comes out, wearing a short satin bathrobe with no panties underneath.

"Do you want anything to eat?" She climbs back into bed, going right back to my arms. I grab her around the waist and pull her on top of me. Her legs go around mine, and dammit, I'm getting hard.

"Again?" she asks, raising her eyebrows. She kisses my neck and wiggles her hips.

And now my semi is a boner. "You're so fucking hot, Quinn. And—" I stop, not sure how to even word it. Instead, I kiss her, soft and tender. She lets out a quiet moan and presses her core against me.

"And now I want to again."

She doesn't need to say anymore. I flip her over and move on top. The tip of my cock rubs against her, and she bucks her hips, repeating the motion. I reach down, taking hold of my cock in my hand, and rub it over her clit. Her mouth opens and she keeps one hand on my shoulder, bending her fingers and digging her nails into my skin. She's still hot and sensitive from before. It doesn't take long before she comes, and as soon as she does, I move my cock down, guiding it into her entrance.

I push in balls deep. She's so tight around me and it feels so fucking good. I thrust in and out a few times before Quinn plants her hands on my chest and shoves me away. I pull out, eyes wide and dick aching to be back inside of her. She sits up, breasts rising and falling from breathing hard, and pushes me down onto the mattress.

Then she climbs on top. She wraps her slender fingers around my cock, and the sight alone is enough to make me want to nut right there. Looking down at my cock in her hand, Quinn's lips part and she flicks her eyes to mine before guiding me inside of her.

She leans forward as she moves, hair falling into my face. I hold onto her, watching her breasts bounce, relishing in how fucking good this feels. She slows down, then starts circling her hips at the same time.

I didn't think I'd be able to come so fast after just having sex, but it's different this time. Quinn feels fucking amazing around me, and being with her—finally being with her— feels so damn right.

Quinn sits up, and the new angle pushes me over the edge. She's getting close to coming again as well, but there's no way I can stop myself. Not when it feels so good. Her mouth opens and she lets out a moan and dammit, she's right there. I grit my teeth and lift my hips, doing everything I can to hold back until she finishes.

"I'm so close," she pants as if she can read my mind. Then she falls forward, tits in my face, and I can't help it. I bury my cock inside her, coming hard for the second time tonight. Quinn presses down, widening her legs even more, and my pulsing cock hits her in the right spot. Her pussy tightens around me—and fuck—the end of the orgasm feels as good at the start.

"Wow," Quinn pants, rolling off me. We both lay there, breathing hard. Her hand is on the bed next to mine, and I twist my wrist and interlace our fingers. We stay like that for a few minutes, until Quinn turns her head.

"Are you hungry?"

"A little," I tell her. "You?"

"Yeah. What do you want to eat?"

"Anything, really. What do you have?"

"I don't know." She lets out a breath, turning in to face me. "I can't really think straight right now."

"Yeah, I know I'm good," I say with a teasing smile. Quinn laughs and rolls over, hooking her leg over mine. I clasp my hand on the back of her thigh. There's no way I'm letting this be our last time.

No. Fucking. Way.

I'll fight for her. Do whatever it takes.

Because I'm in love with this woman.

"Stay here," I tell her. "I'm not the best cook, but I'll make you something."

"You don't have to, Arch."

I kiss her. "I know."

Getting out of bed, I grab my boxers from the floor, missing Quinn's body against mine already. I resituate the blanket around her, kiss her once more, and go into the kitchen. It feels slightly invasive to look through her drawers and cabinets. Everything is more or less well organized, and it doesn't take long until I find a pan and ingredients to make grilled cheese.

It's not fancy by any means, but I already knew there was no hope of impressing Quinn with my cooking skills. The cats watch me cook, and I give them each a little piece of cheese, which was like opening Pandora's box. They won't leave me alone now.

I turn off the burner and put the second sandwich on a plate when Quinn comes out of the bedroom. She's still wearing the bathrobe, but this time she has on shorts and a tank top, made out of the same satin material. Her hair is a mess and her cheeks are still flushed.

Seeing her like that is a huge turn on, and it does more than make me want to strip her and fuck her all over again. It makes me want to have this every night. Fucking Quinn into oblivion. Bringing her something to eat.

Being together.

"I love grilled cheese," she says with a smile.

"I remember." I slide the plates to the opposite side of the island counter where we can sit on the high-backed bar stools. "Cheese and Chinese food are your favorite. Not necessarily together, though now I'm wondering what fried rice would taste like topped with cheese."

"I've never tried it." She gets the water bottles from the living room, coming back and sitting next to me at the counter. "But now I want to."

"Maybe for breakfast," I joke and Quinn laughs.

"Thanks for making me a sandwich."

"You're welcome, though it was easy."

She takes a few bites, looking from her food to me every

few seconds. "So...it's late," she says after she's eaten half her sandwich.

"It is."

"And you have to be up early."

"I do." I swallow the food in my mouth and grab my water, slowly twisting the cap off, and try not to think ahead. I fail. I think and plan ahead by nature. I risk a quick glance at Quinn. She's looking at me at the same time, and we both look away.

How can she be shy around me after two rounds of mind-blowing sex?

"Are you going to stay?" she finally asks.

"Do you want me to stay?" Answering her questions with a question irritates her, I can tell.

Her eyes narrow ever so slightly in a two-can-play-this-game sort of way. "Do *you* want to stay?"

"Depends on if you want me to."

She purses her lips and leans back with a sigh. I close my eyes in a long blink and look away, hating the tension that's creeping back up on us. I like her. I've liked her for years. *Years.* So why the fuck is it so hard to tell her that?

She picks the crust off her grilled cheese, neither of us talking. A sleek white cat jumps up on the counter, trying to steal food from Quinn's plate. She picks the cat up and puts her down, only to have the cat do the same thing again. And again.

"Luna," Quinn says sternly. "Stay down."

"Luna, Bellatrix, and Neville...are your cats named after Harry Potter characters?"

"Yeah. The fourth cat is Lily." Quinn gives up and goes to the pantry to give the persistent cat a treat. "You like Harry Potter?"

"I do. I've seen the movies and read the books, because I know you're going to ask."

The smile comes back to her face, but it's not the same one as before. I'm back to feeling like a jerk and am getting afraid it might be too late. We just had sex—twice—and I'm acting like none of it mattered. If only she knew how much it did. How much it always has. "They're modern classics."

"Yeah, they are. Obviously, I'm a fan."

"I got sorted into Ravenclaw. I did the quiz online."

"I got Gryffindor."

"It suits you." I finish the rest of my sandwich. "Quinn," I start and turn around. She's back at the counter, picking at her food, but hasn't sat back down yet. She's uncomfortable, thinking I'm looking at this as a one-night stand and is trying hard not to let it show.

"I do want to stay. With you."

"You don't have to if you don't want to."

I internally wince. "If I didn't want to, I wouldn't. Just like I wouldn't have asked you out to dinner if I didn't want to spend time with you." I wipe my hands on a napkin and pick up my plate, taking it to the sink before Luna comes back. My heart thumps inside my chest and I'm cursing myself for putting this distance between us after we'd come so close. I need to fix it.

"You're not going to make me sleep on the couch again, are you?" The second the words come out of my mouth, I wish I could take them back. My failed attempt at a joke makes Quinn's face go slack.

"I, uh, I wasn't going to but, uh..."

"I'm joking," I say and go to her, pulling her into my arms. Her body is stiff against mine, worlds different than how we were not long ago. I'm smart. I got into Duke

University School of Medicine for fuck's sake. How is it possible I'm such a complete idiot at the same time?

It's Quinn, and I'm not blaming her for turning me into a bumbling fool whenever I'm around. It's either this or shut her back out.

Fuck.

There was a reason I hated my psych rotation. I'm not good with feelings in general. I'm even worse when it comes to my own.

"I would very much like to sleep in your bed next to you," I tell her, gathering her hair to the side of her neck. With each passing second she doesn't relax, I feel like I'm losing her. "I want to wake up next to you," I say softly, letting the honesty she likes so much come out. "And I'd like to take you out to breakfast. And then dinner again after the conference is over."

"I do like eating."

"Yeah? Me too."

"So much I do it every day. Sometimes multiple times a day." She clasps her hands around my shoulders. "Out of context that could sound a bit dirty."

I kiss her neck, remembering how incredible she looked with her hand between her legs touching herself. "I like thinking about it the dirty way."

EARLY MORNING LIGHT SHINES THROUGH THE LARGE WINDOWS in Quinn's bedroom. My alarm sounds and I scramble to turn it off, not wanting to wake up Quinn. She looks fucking adorable in her sleep, buried under her thick blankets. I was hot five minutes after snuggling up with her, but wouldn't change a thing.

Quinn stirs but doesn't open her eyes. She rolls onto her back, hand going up on her pillow above her head. It physically hurts to keep my eyes open, but I want to remember this moment the best I can.

Losing the battle against sleep, I fall back and doze off. What feels like seconds later, the snooze alarm sounds. Blindly, I reach out on the nightstand for it.

"Archer?" Quinn says quietly, voice thick with sleep. Her eyes flutter open and she smiles when she sees me. "Do you have to get up?"

I slide my arms underneath her and pull her close. Her head rests on my shoulder and she hooks a leg over me.

"I don't *have* to."

"You can't skip your...your...whatever that thing is."

"I only came here to talk to Dr. Crawford about the fellowship, which I did. He's not there today anyway. I'd rather stay here and give you a thorough medical exam. Hone my skills that way."

"Well, that does sound educational and I'm very willing to help you expand your areas of expertise." She pulls the blankets around her shoulders. "Or go back to sleep. You can do a sleep study on me."

"I like the way that sounds." I let my eyes fall shut, head dropping to the side to rest against Quinn's. All the awkward tension melted away the moment we got into bed together last night. We didn't have sex again, but the moment we laid down together, things felt back to how they should be.

The world feels right when Quinn is in my arms. Her fingertips dance up and down my arm, lulling me back to sleep. And then my snooze alarm goes off again. Dammit. It's a habit to just hit it again instead of turning it off. I didn't actually intend on not showing up to the panels I signed up to attend, but if I 'accidentally' forgot to turn on an alarm, no one could blame me.

Quinn sits up, brushing her hair out of her eyes. "I can make you breakfast." She runs her hand down my chest, fingers brushing over the tip of my cock, teasing me on purpose. "Go back to sleep. You didn't get much last night and I kind of feel responsible."

"You didn't get much either."

"Yeah, but I can take a nap after you leave. I'm assuming I'll need my strength for later, right?" She bites her lip, looking so damn sexy.

"Fuck yes." I wrap my arms around her and bring her to me, giving her a quick kiss before she gets out of bed.

"Turn your alarm off. I won't let you oversleep."

I watch Quinn leave, admiring her ass in her short sleeper shorts. With her on my mind, I lay down, falling back asleep in minutes.

"Archer?"

The mattress sinks down next to me and the sweet smell of maple syrup fills my nose.

"Archer," Quinn repeats softly.

I open my eyes, and her face is the first thing I see. Yawning, I push myself up. "Breakfast in bed? You know I'm never leaving now, right?"

"That was ultimately my plan. Lure you in with food and sex then hold you hostage and kill you."

I take the tray from Quinn, stomach growling at the sight of the pancakes, bacon, and eggs. "As long as I get to eat all this and fuck you one more time, I'll die a happy man."

Quinn smiles, brushing her hair back. "You said it's over at two?"

"Yeah. Will that work with your kidnapping plan?"

"I was hoping to have you tied up and bleeding by one,

but I can delay things a bit. It'll give me more time to get the kill room ready."

"Kill room? You are serious."

"I'm a serious person, Archer. Which you'll find out later."

I cut into my pancake. "When you kill me?"

"You'll be begging for death by the time I'm done with you."

I laugh and put the piece of pancake in my mouth. They're good. Light and buttery and the exact same recipe Mrs. Dawson uses. I used to think it was weird how everything she made was from scratch because what's the point of all that pre-made stuff you can conveniently just add water to if you're not going to use it?

"Want any?" I ask her, seeing as she's not eating.

"No thanks. I don't like eggs, and I already ate a ton of bacon while waiting for the pancakes to finish."

Nodding, I pick up a piece of bacon and pop it into my mouth. Quinn stretches her arms out in front of her and lies back against the pillows.

"When do you go home?"

"Tonight," I say, and the word is like a punch to the gut. "My flight is at five-thirty."

"Oh." Quinn looks down, and we're both thinking the same thing. Our desire for each other smoldered over the years, sparking here and there but never getting hot enough to ignite.

And then it exploded into a wildfire.

The thing about wildfires is they burn bright and they burn hot, but eventually, they die out.

14

I've shaved every piece of unwanted hair off my body. I've plucked and tweezed, applied makeup only to take it off and do it again, and re-curled my hair three times.

But I'm not trying to look good for Archer Jones.

He saw me in my natural element yesterday at work wearing office attire and my hair in a ponytail. And then he saw me in all sorts of ways last night, and it's not like I woke up looking like an Instagram model or something.

I take my sunglasses off my head, and my hair gets stuck. Yanking it free, I put them on and pay my fare as I get out of the cab. It's nice out today, a little breezier than yesterday, but the air is humid and the wind is welcome.

Archer texted me not long ago and said the convention was over, but the medical director from a big hospital invited him out for a drink at the hotel bar. He didn't think it would take long and was too good of an opportunity to pass up. I encouraged him to go, because that hospital happens to be in Chicago and, for selfish reasons, I'd love Archer to get a job in the city.

I look through the crowd of people and somehow see him right away. He looks up at the same time and smiles as soon as our eyes meet.

"Hey," I say when we meet. He stops just inches from me and takes me in his arms, dipping me back a bit for a kiss.

"Hey to you too." He runs his hands over my arms. "What's this?"

"Oh, I got you something."

"You did?"

"I got it on a whim. I saw it at a market I walked through and thought—well, just look at it and you'll know."

He takes the shopping bag from me and opens it up, pulling out a wool fedora. Looking it over, I worry he won't get it.

"Is this an Indiana Jones hat?" he asks.

"Yes!"

"I like it." He smiles and puts it on, and even Harrison Ford would be jealous. "But, uh, why?"

I lean back, staring at Archer like he just asked what color the sky is. "You're Dr. Jones. Please do not tell me no one has ever said 'okey-dokey Dr. Jones' to you."

"It's surprising now that you've pointed it out, but no, they haven't." He pulls me in and kisses me again. "Wait, there's an Indiana Jones market going on?"

"No, just some weird guy at a pop-up selling hats. He told me I had nice feet."

Archer chuckles. "I guess you do, though, in that dress, it's hard to look past your tits."

I shimmy and wiggle my eyebrows. "That's the point of a pushup bra." We break apart and Archer takes my hand, moving down the sidewalk. "Are you hungry?"

"Starving."

"I assumed so. We can get the famous Chicago pizza you

like. Oh! Or try fried rice with cheese. What are you in the mood for?"

"Other than you? Pizza."

"I knew it. And good, because I made us a reservation."

I GRAB MY LEMONADE, SLIDING IT IN FRONT OF ME, AND TAKE A drink. Even with the wind, the walk from the hotel to the restaurant was a warm one. I'm sitting across from Archer, and we're waiting on our pizza to come. Neither of us has said much, and the conversation ceased halfway here.

I don't get it.

We were so great before. Even better after. And now...it's weird again, like neither of us knows what to say. Probably because we don't, and trying to talk about it is going to be really freaking awkward. He lives in Indy. I live here. Eastwood is in the middle, and while I have a good reason for making the trip as often as I'd like, he doesn't.

He and Dean keep in touch, but they don't hang out like they used to. And Archer works so much.

"Have you and Dean started planning the bachelor party yet?" I ask, needing to say something before things go from bad to worse.

"We've thrown some ideas around. Vegas was one of them."

"That sounds fun."

"What about the bachelorette party?"

"I'm not sure I'm invited. I like Kara, and I think it's mutual. What's not to like, right?" I joke and Archer laughs. "But she's down there and I'm up here. Plus I don't know her friends."

"I thought people in small towns knew everyone."

"Oh, I know who they are. They're older than me so we never talked in high school or anything. And then I left and never went back."

"You said you like it here, didn't you?"

I nod. "I do. Despite the high crime rate, it's progressive and fun and I've made some really good friends here."

"That's good."

I sip my lemonade again, wondering how long it's been since we ordered that pizza. Archer leans back in the booth, looking out the window.

"If you make the drive to Eastwood, you'll have to, uh, let me know."

"Yeah. I will." He puts one hand on the table, drumming his fingers. He wants to say something but is nervous. It's kinda cute. "I'm not sure when it'll be though."

"I figured as much. I know you're super busy with work and you haven't come up in, what, years?"

"It's been a while."

"It's nice you guys are still friends. Not a lot of people stay friends that long."

Archer's brow furrows. "Yeah. He's been a good friend." He looks at me, inhales, and opens his mouth to speak. I know the words about to come out will hurt. I brace myself, expecting him to remind me how I'm Dean's little sister and how he regrets everything that happened last night and how we can never speak of this again.

That sleeping with me was a mistake.

"Quinn!" a familiar voice calls before Archer can get a word out. I turn toward the source and have never been so grateful to see an ex-boyfriend before in my life.

"Jacob, hi," I say as he starts to make his way over. Okay, maybe I'm not so grateful to see him. The server at the table next to us moves, and Archer comes into Jacob's line of sight. He almost comes to a halt when he sees him.

Geez. It's been over a year since we broke up. Poor guy needs to move on already. It's not like we had a great relationship anyway. It wasn't bad, not at all. He treated me well and was respectful, but there was no passion. No fire. No drive.

We got along. Have similar interests. The sex was okay. I only faked it a few times.

But it was nothing like last night. Jacob doesn't get under my skin and annoy me so much I want to slap him across the face one minute, and the next have me cooking him breakfast so he can get a few extra minutes of sleep.

"Quinn." He settles his gaze on me for a few seconds too long before turning to Archer. "Dean's friend, Archer, right?" He holds out his hand for a handshake.

"Right."

"I have to ask" —Jacob starts— "is that an Indiana Jones replica hat?"

Archer gives me a half smile. "I think it's supposed to be. Quinn got it for me."

"His last name is Jones," I explain. "And he's a doctor. Get it?"

Jacob let out a forced chuckle. "I do. Dr. Indiana Jones. You were always clever, Quinn. It's one of the many things I like about you."

And now things just got awkward again.

"I'll let you two enjoy your meal. See you Monday morning, Quinn." He goes back to his table.

"Did you date him?" Archer asks.

"Yeah, for a few months."

"And he works with you?"

I shake my head. "Not at the same company. I design

software and he builds robotics. Our companies work together a lot, which is how we met and why we're doing a project together now. So fun to work with an ex."

"He's still hung up on you."

"I know. I feel bad."

Archer looks puzzled. "Why do you feel bad about that?"

"I don't really know…I feel bad he's not happy, I guess?"

"You're a good person, Quinn," he says softly, and then leans forward. "Software and robotics. You really are building some sort of badass car for a vigilante, aren't you?"

"If I tell you, I'll have to kill you."

"You already established you were. So you might as well tell me."

I laugh and take another drink of lemonade. "All I can say is if robots really do take over the world, at least I'll know the code to shut them down."

I REACH OVER THE BED, FISHING MY UNDERWEAR OUT OF THE little space between the nightstand and the bed frame. After lunch, we had some time to kill before Archer needed to get to the airport to fly back to Indy.

Hand in hand, we walked the few blocks from the pizza place to his hotel, going up to his room for the sole purpose of having sex. In any other situation, this would have been weird. Tense. Embarrassing maybe.

But not with Archer. Things change the moment we take our clothes off, and there's no awkwardness. No hesitation or waiting to see if Archer is going to tell me what's on his mind. He's very open and even more personal. We're amazing together, making me feel bad for doubting the validity in the sex scenes I've read about in romance novels.

It is possible to have multiple orgasms, and I think Archer was going for a record this time.

Lifting my ass off the mattress, I slip on my undies and lay back, heart still racing. Archer hasn't put his clothes back on yet, which is fine by me, and is lying next to me, chest glistening with sweat.

He rolls to his side, slips his arms around my middle, and pulls me to him.

"I don't want to go," he whispers.

"I don't want you to either." I rake my fingers through his dark hair and move as close as I can, needing to feel every inch of him against me. I close my eyes, trying to commit this feeling to memory. I have no idea when I'll see Archer Jones again.

He lets out a breath and brushes my hair out of my face.

"I'm glad I ran into you, Quinn," he says. "The last twenty-four hours have been incredible."

"Yeah, they have. I wish we could do it again."

"Me too." His lips meet mine. "Me too."

We stay tangled together until the last possible minute and then scramble to get dressed. Archer's already packed and ready to go, all he has to do is leave. Finally, and now at risk of missing his flight, we get in the elevator to go downstairs.

The tension starts to come back, and I'm not sure quite what to do. Say goodbye? See you later? I knew getting into a long-term, committed relationship wasn't on the horizon. Yeah, I really like Archer, but we live very separate lives. But I have to say something, right?

I don't know what to expect, or if he even wants to hear from me after this. Do we need to talk about this? Archer's been a part of our family for a decade. If we don't talk and then see each other at the rehearsal dinner...I internally shudder. And I thought riding down to the lobby was an awkward moment.

I hang back while Archer checks out, and we walk together in silence out of the hotel.

"Well," I start, turning to face Archer.

"I'll call you," he says, and his deep brown eyes catch mine, and my heart aches already. There is no one else for me but him. He gets me. Goes along with my weird sense of humor. Makes me feel in-fucking-credible in the bedroom.

He's so close yet so far away, and that little voice of hope that lives deep inside my heart screams at me to tell him how I feel. My brain overrides this time, going into self-preservation mode. It already hurts enough leaving after the amazing weekend we had together. Telling him that I think we should see each other again—soon—will only make it worse.

The timing is all wrong.

Archer is finishing his residency, who knows where he'll end up.

Not to mention how much of a fit Dean would throw if he found out Archer and I hooked up. Though really...I don't see what the big deal is. Everyone likes Archer.

Archer's eyes sear into mine, and I wish so badly for super powers right now. I'd will him to say exactly what's on his mind, because even if it's not what I want to hear, at least I'd know what the hell is going on inside his brain.

Not going with words, Archer takes me by the waist, pulls me close, and kisses me hard. Tingles run all the way through me, and someone catcalls as they walk past us. He doesn't need words to say what his kiss is telling me.

He's saying goodbye.

Once the kiss ends, he rests his forehead against mine,

eyes falling shut. His arms wrap around me, and he gives me a tight hug. I never want it to end.

"I'll see you," he says, breaking away. And then he gets into a cab.

I know I will see him again. But the question is, how will he feel when I do?

15

QUINN

Two weeks later...

I stretch my arms out in front of me, slowly rolling my wrist. It's aching today, and I forgot my wrist brace at home. I remembered my posture brace, at least, and stand for the first time in hours to get it from my bag.

My office is warm today from having multiple computers running and my door closed. I found a snag in the software design and have been pulling my hair out all day trying to fix it. I think I'm the only one left in the office. Opening my office door, I twist my hair into a bun and use a pen to secure it on the top of my head. Grabbing the posture brace, I unbutton my blouse and take it off, tossing it in my oversized purse. I'm wearing a sheer white cami underneath, so it's not like I'm just sitting in here in just a bra. I slip the brace on and sit back at my computer, feeling a bit better to have my shoulders held back into place.

As soon as I sit down, the nausea I've felt all day hits me hard. I get up to get some water, and as soon as I set foot out of the office, I run into Jacob.

"What are you still doing here?" he asks with a smile. And then his eyes drop to my chest. The brace smooshes my breasts together and up, working better than a pushup bra. If only I could hide it under clothes...

"Working. But what are you doing here?"

"Same thing. Well, kind of. I had to pick up files to sign off on."

I casually pull up the collar of my cami, trying to cover my breasts as much as possible. "You should have asked me. I could have dropped them off to you. I go by your office on my way home."

"Yeah, I thought about it, but wasn't sure if your boyfriend would be mad."

I let out a snort. "Archer isn't my boyfriend." Anger surges through me, but I should be proud. It's the first time in two weeks I've said his name without sneering. Though, I really shouldn't be mad, right?

There was no promise of commitment. My feelings for him stemmed from a teenage crush and it was my own naivety to think sleeping together would make him suddenly love me.

"Oh, you two looked, uh, close?"

I wave my hand in the air. "I've known Archer for years." A twist of nausea hits me, and I put my hand over my stomach, grimacing.

"Are you all right?"

"Yeah, I think all the coffee I've been chugging is finally catching up with me."

He laughs. "I've been there. So, since you're not dating the doctor..."

Shit. Shit. Shit. *Please don't ask me out.*

Jacob shuffles closer. "I know it's only Monday and things come up, but do you want to grab dinner Friday?"

"Oh," I start, and watch the hope rise in his eyes. Dammit. "I'm going to my parents' this weekend. I haven't seen my nephew in a while."

"Right. I forgot about that. It's nice you do that. Is Daisy still out of the picture?"

"Thankfully, which might sound awful to say."

Jacob's face softens. I'm not interested in dating him anymore, but it's nice to have someone who knows my family history to talk to.

"I don't think it's awful. She's the awful one. I mean, who can just walk away from their family like that?"

"She's got major issues. The only reason I hope she shows her sorry ass is so she can get served with divorce papers." I shake my head, feeling sorry for Wes. "Anyway, I guess I'll see you Wednesday for that meeting."

"Yeah," he says. "Maybe we can grab lunch."

"I think we can do that." I smile, already knowing Marissa will tag along and keep it from feeling anything like a date.

I FALL INTO BED AS SOON AS I WALK THROUGH THE DOOR OF MY room. "I'm literally dying," I grumble to the cats, who followed me in wondering why the hell I went in here and not the kitchen. "Feed yourselves."

It's Friday and I just got in from the office. I have a laundry list of stuff to do before driving down to Eastwood, but this week has killed me. I pulled a late night at the office Monday and was so tired by Tuesday it physically hurt to keep my eyes open. I crashed on the couch when I came home and was in bed by eight-thirty. Wednesday wasn't much better, and I was cramping so bad from my impending period I didn't have much of an appetite. I think the lack of food furthered my exhaustion and coupled with the stress of this project that I *finally* figured out today, I'm just done.

I lazily strip out of my office attire and snuggle into bed. Not meaning to fall asleep, I feel a bit of panic when I wake up about an hour later. Shit. I sit up too fast and get hit with dizziness. Rubbing my eyes, I force myself up, chug some water to try and feel better, and get a move on.

"Sorry, guys," I say to the cats. Going as fast as I can, I feed them, set cans out on the counter to make it easier for Marie, my neighbor who comes and feeds them when I'm out of town. I quickly pack a bag, make my bed, and try to muster up the energy to vacuum. I'm not a neat freak or anything, but I like things to be tidy when I come home after a weekend away.

There are dishes in the sink, but I don't want to load them in the dishwasher and leave it running after I leave just in case it leaks or something weird. I pull on my pink rubber gloves and turn on the water to hand wash what's in there.

The smell of my yogurt bowl from this morning makes me gag. It hasn't spoiled or anything, yet that fruity scent is sickening. I turn my head and inhale, trying not to breathe as I scrub out the bowl. I'm feeling so sick by the time I finish the dishes, I'm worried I came down with the flu. I crawl to the couch and curl up, closing my eyes for just a minute.

Half an hour later, my phone rings. I sit up, blinking, realizing I fell asleep again. I don't feel nauseous anymore at least. I grab my phone and answer.

"Hello?"

"Hey, honey," Mom says. "Are you still coming? I haven't

heard from you and you're usually getting here around now. I saved a plate of dinner for you."

"Yeah." I sit up, blinking rapidly to try to force my eyes to focus. "I'm leaving here in a minute. I fell asleep on the couch. It's been a long week."

"You're not too tired to drive, are you? Should you stay home and come in the morning?"

"I'm okay. I'll regret it in the morning and wish I'd left tonight. I'll swing by Starbucks on the way. I'll grab my stuff, say bye to the cats, and be out of here in ten minutes."

"Be safe, honey. Love you."

"Love you, too, Mom."

I hang up, grab everything I need and haul it to the door and say goodbye to the cats, who are more interested in the handful of treats I scattered on the kitchen floor before making my exit.

I wait until I'm out of the city to get coffee and sing along to the radio to help keep myself awake. As much as I love my loft, there's something so comforting about my childhood bedroom. We moved into the old house when I was twelve, and back then it was in really rough shape. It scared me at first, and Logan and Owen had fun telling me how haunted the place was. Obviously, it doesn't scare me anymore, but I still think it's haunted. The ghost is friendly at least and I'm pretty sure her name is Anna Beth. Or at least that's what the spirit board told me one night when I was sixteen.

By the time I pull into my parents' driveway, I have to pee so bad it's not funny. I'm already strategizing where to park, how I'll only grab my purse, and then run straight to the bathroom. There's another car in my spot, one I don't recognize right away. Then I get closer, and I know exactly who that Jeep belongs to.

Archer Jones.

"**D**o you boys want a second helping?"

"Yes, please," I tell Mrs. Dawson, even though I'm already full from the first plate of chicken potpie I had. But it's homemade and delicious.

"Your interview was pushed to tomorrow?" she asks as she puts another helping on my plate and moves on to give Dean another scoop.

"Yeah. The chief surgeon wanted to talk to me as well but couldn't. There was a nasty car accident and he's been in surgery all day."

Mrs. Dawson grimaces. "I don't know how you do it. I'm so thankful you can, of course. We need more good doctors like you in this county." She gives me a warm smile. "You're staying here tonight, don't even try to tell me otherwise." Mrs. Dawson smiles. "I love to have both my boys back! It'll be just like college. Except you're both much more mature," she adds with a wink. "What about dessert?"

"Kara was right," Dean says and puts a hand on his stomach. "You are trying to fatten me up."

"Oh hush." Mrs. Dawson opens the fridge and pulls out

a carton of eggs. She's from the southern part of the state, and has that southern hospitality thing down pat, showing her love through feeding us constantly. I don't mind one bit.

"Mom, I know you mean well, but I don't think either of us want eggs."

"They're for Rufus," she tells Dean. "Poor old guy hasn't been feeling well. I think his new medicine for arthritis upsets his stomach. I stopped giving it to him, but he's being finicky with his food."

Part of the reason I don't have any pets is because I can't stand to see them get old. They don't live long enough. Plus, I'm probably emotionally traumatized from finding our Doberman seizing on the kitchen floor after he got into pills Bobby left laying out.

The dog had to be put down the next day. The drugs destroyed his stomach.

I haven't thought about Max in a while. It makes the resentment toward my brother bubble back up. I take a deep breath and push all thoughts of him out of my mind. Dean and I talk about a new video game while Mrs. Dawson makes scrambled eggs. She was right: it does feel like college.

All four dogs get up and run to the back door a moment before it opens. I turn, seeing who's coming in at this hour, and my heart falls out of my chest when my eyes lock with Quinn's.

"Finally!" Mrs. Dawson steps away from the stove to peer down the hall. "I was getting worried."

Like a deer in headlights, Quinn stares at me, unaware of the dogs jumping up around her. Then she blinks, shakes her head, and takes off her shoes.

"What is he doing here?" she blurts, and her words are

like a knife to the heart. She didn't expect to see me, and more importantly, she doesn't *want* to see me.

"Hey, sis," Dean says, looking a little perplexed at Quinn's disdain over seeing me. "How are you?"

"Good," she says shortly. Setting her purse on the floor, she eyes me one more time before stepping down the hall to the bathroom. I turn back to my food, and the implications of what I did hit me in the face like a sucker punch. Which is something I'll probably get from Dean—and rightly deserved—before the night is through.

I slept with Quinn. Three times. And it's not that I regret it, because I don't. Not at all. I've spent the last three weeks missing her more than ever, wishing I could be next to her again so bad it hurt. But I can't.

We can't be.

Not only would Dean hate me for it, but it would create a huge rift between him and Quinn, and they've always been close. The whole Dawson family is tight-knit, and something causing strain between them is like upsetting the balance of the fucking universe.

If this family has issues, then there's no hope for the rest of us.

Pushing my food around on my plate, I wait for the inevitable. The dogs scramble around Quinn once she comes out of the bathroom, all pushing to get her attention. She pets Rufus first, then takes turns greeting the other dogs.

Mrs. Dawson steps away from the stove to give Quinn a hug. I can smell Quinn's sweet perfume, and my heart lurches. She crosses her arms, not sure how to proceed. I don't either. I've seen her naked, kissed and touched every inch of her. Fucked her hard until we soaked the sheets. And we haven't spoken since.

I went through a maelstrom of emotions after that, from hating myself, to regret, to an intense sadness I haven't been able to shake. I miss Quinn, and no amount of distracting myself or trying to tell myself otherwise is going to change that.

I'm in love with her.

Sleeping with her furthered that truth in my mind.

She's the only one I want.

"How was the drive in?" Mrs. Dawson asks, going back to the stove.

"Fine. Leaving a bit later than normal helped avoid traffic, I think."

"That's good. Are you hungry, honey?"

"I am. Whatever you're cooking smells good."

Mrs. Dawson turns to Quinn, raising one eyebrow. "You're joking, right? I'm making scrambled eggs."

"Oh," Quinn says, just as surprised. "Well, I still think it smells good."

"I'll gladly make more." Mrs. Dawson turns down the burner. "I've been trying to get you to eat eggs for years. Take a seat. These are almost ready."

Quinn looks at the island counter. It's long, custom made so all the Dawsons could sit together, and the place we always eat unless it's a formal dinner. Our eyes meet, and the way she looks at me pushes the knife deeper into my heart.

"Hey, Dean," she says, taking a spot next to him. "And Archer."

"Hi," I say back, glad she's not doing her routine of pretending I'm not here today. It would be too obvious, and Quinn is above that.

"Where's Kara?" she asks Dean.

"Home, doing homework. I think she's regretting going for her master's degree now."

"That doesn't sound fun." Quinn wrinkles her nose and dammit, she looks so adorable. "I'm so glad I'm done with school."

"Me too." Dean gives me a look. "How long have you been in school now?"

"I've lost count," I say back with a smile.

Quinn shifts her gaze to me, and our eyes meet for half a second. "What are you doing here?"

"I have an interview at the county hospital."

"The county hospital?" she repeats in disbelief. "I thought you—never mind." She forces a smile. "Good luck. I'm sure you'll do great."

Ouch. The indifference hurts. I'd rather her be mad at me.

"I'm sure he will." Mrs. Dawson brings Quinn a plate of eggs. She eats every last bite.

"Where's Dad?" she asks.

"At a house trying to finish some last minute things for the inspection tomorrow," Dean answers.

"Why aren't you there?" Quinn asks pointedly. "You do still want to take over the family business, right?"

Dean motions to me. "Archer's in town. I rarely get to see this guy." He puts his hands on the counter, pushing his stool back. "But I should get going and go to bed. The inspector is coming early tomorrow, I want to get there before he does, which means getting up at the asscrack of dawn."

"It's weird seeing you act all responsible," Quinn jokes.

"Hey," Dean starts. "You and Wes aren't the only ones who can have adult jobs."

"Right. But we are the only ones who know the details on the Batmobile. I wish I could show you the new developments." Quinn bites her lip like she's thinking. "Well, maybe I can. I have a few seconds of footage I recorded on my phone. We have cell-scramblers all over the place, but I know the codes to get around it. Still, the footage is a little fuzzy."

Quinn gets her phone from her purse. "I don't know...I really shouldn't."

"Quinn," Mrs. Dawson says sternly.

"I can show you too, Mom."

"Better not risk getting in trouble with work," Mrs. Dawson counters, but Dean's already leaning in, eyes wide.

"Right." Quinn puts her phone on the counter. "The cell-scramblers can encrypt footage taken and might be alerted when I press play anyway."

She's making it all up but sells it convincingly. I try not to laugh at Dean's interest. Putting her fork on her plate, Quinn stands, only to grab onto the counter to steady herself.

"Are you all right, hun?" Mrs. Dawson asks.

"Yeah," Quinn says, blinking rapidly. "Just got dizzy. It's been happening lately from stress." She shrugs. "It's normal."

"It's actually not," I counter. "You could be slightly dehydrated."

Looking right past me, she nods. "I'll drink some water." She puts her plate in the dishwasher. Without a word to me, she goes into the living room with her mother to talk.

Before we slept together, I wouldn't have thought anything of it. But now everything is painfully obvious. I can only hope it's obvious to only us.

I wake up around two o'clock. After tossing and turning for a bit, I give up and get out of bed. I'm in a guest room upstairs, the one right next to Quinn's room. Knowing she's in bed alone just yards from me is part of the problem.

She's so close yet so far and I can't go to sleep knowing she's *right there*. There's so much I want to say—hell, so much I need to say—but don't know how to start. My bare feet hit the cool hardwood floor, which creaks slightly under my weight. The entire house has been restored top to bottom, but holds onto its century-old charm, including the original creaky floors.

Opening the bedroom door, I pause before going down the hall. Quinn's door is cracked open to allow the dogs to come in and out. Moonlight streams through her open window, and I can see her dark silhouette lying in the bed. She rolls over, and my heart skips a beat.

Fuck, I miss her.

Rufus, who's sleeping on the foot of her bed, looks up at me, lazily seeing who's walking about before going back to sleep. I go downstairs to the kitchen, where I get myself a glass of milk and a few of the cookies Mrs. Dawson made earlier.

Looking out the windows at the dark yard, I eat and try not to think. Even on nights when I'm exhausted from being on my feet for hours on end, this happens. Random thoughts go through my mind, keeping me from sleep. Coming to the Dawson's farm used to be my reprieve when I was in college, but now, I'm uneasy.

And it's all my fault.

I'm finishing my last cookie when the stairs creak. At first, I think it's one of the dogs, but the lack of jingling dog tags lets me know it's a human.

"Oh," Quinn's voice comes from behind me. I turn,

taking in the sight of her in her pajama shorts and tight tank top. She's obviously not wearing a bra, and her long, lean legs are hardly covered by the shorts.

If she turns around and I see her sweet, supple ass, I'm screwed.

"I didn't know you were down here," she murmurs.

"I couldn't sleep," I say, brushing the crumbs from my hands. I'm only in my boxers, not expecting anyone to join me. Quinn lets her eyes linger on my body for a moment before looking away. She smooths out her shirt, pulling the collar up, trying to cover herself, and looks so uncomfortable.

"Neither could I," she admits and opens the fridge, rooting around until she finds a can of ginger ale.

"Not feeling well?"

She pops the top and shrugs. "I've had an upset stomach off and on all week."

"As well as feeling dizzy?"

"Don't try to diagnose me, Archer," she snaps and takes a sip. "I'm tired and stressed from a current work situation, that's all."

"I can relate to that. I'm glad you're here then. You can rest and relax."

"Really, Archer? You're *glad I'm here*? Could have fooled me." She starts to leave.

"Quinn, wait."

"What do you want?" she snaps. Her hand flies to the space between her eyes, rubbing her forehead as if she has a headache. "Sorry. Wait, no. I'm not sorry."

"Fair enough. I think we should talk."

"Listen, Archer," she says and takes another sip of ginger ale, looking a little green. Letting out a sigh, she pushes her hair over her shoulder. I swallow hard, wanting more than anything to trail my fingertips over her collarbone again. To taste her lips on mine, to feel her under me. "It's okay. You don't have to."

One of the dogs comes down the stairs and goes right to the back door, ringing the bell.

"Really?" Quinn sighs, setting down her drink. "You don't have to go out, Boots."

The little dog hits the bell again.

"Fine." She disarms the alarm system before opening the back door. "Oh, shit."

She disappears onto the deck. I stand and go out after her, shutting the door behind me.

"Quinn?" I call into the dark, catching a glimpse of her long hair in the wind as she runs toward the gate at the back of the fenced-in yard. The open gate.

Oh shit is right.

"Boots!" she calls. "Get back here!" She stops at the edge of the yard, hand over her mouth.

"Did you see where he went?"

"No," she says, close to tears. "I didn't know the gate was open. It's dark and it's late and there are coyotes out here."

"Stay here and keep calling him. I'll go get your shoes and a flashlight."

I hurry back into the house, shove my bare feet into my running shoes, and grab Quinn's sandals. Remembering the flashlights and candles Mrs. Dawson got out from under the sink during the storm, I open the cabinet and find two.

The Dawsons own the farmland surrounding their house but lease it out to farmers. About half an acre of grass is fenced in, and that's divided with another fence, keeping the pool locked up safely from the animals or any children.

"Here," I say, giving Quinn her shoes and a flashlight. The night air is chilly, and she's covered in goosebumps. Her pert nipples are obvious through her thin tank top, but now's not the time to lust over how incredibly sexy Quinn is.

"Boots!" Quinn calls once her shoes are on. She steps onto the dirt perimeter of the cornfield. The corn is tall, but not so much we can't see over it. Still, I'm not above admitting it's a little creepy out here at night. "My mom is going to kill me."

"She won't kill you."

Quinn flashes me a look. "Have you met my mother? You know how she is with her dogs."

"She is quite devoted."

"I don't get why the gate was open. It's never open." We walk a few more yards and stop. Quinn calls for Boots again and waits.

I look out at the corn, wondering if Boots is big enough to make the corn rustle like it does in movies when something is lurking. I look at Quinn and am taken aback by her beauty. Inside and out, this woman is gorgeous. And now that I know we're phenomenal in bed together, it makes everything more complicated.

Because that's exactly what it is.

We pick our way down the space between the fence and the corn, swatting away bugs and breaking spiderwebs. We're out here alone, with no one to overhear us or get in the way. I need to open my mouth and say everything I want to say, because every second that passes without saying it makes things worse.

Quinn already thinks I saw her as a one-night stand.

"Quinn, I—"

"Shhh," she cuts me off. "Do you hear that?"

I tip my head, listening to the night. And then I do hear it: the jingling of dog tags followed by panting. A few seconds later, Boots leaps from the cornfield, excitedly greeting Quinn. She scoops him up, scolding him and then kissing him.

"It is way past your bedtime, mister," she says, hurrying back into the house. I shut the gate once we're in the yard, and double check to make sure it's latched. Quinn doesn't put Boots down until we're inside, and as soon as she does, she sits heavily on a kitchen chair, eyes closed and hand pressed over her mouth.

"You don't look so good," I say gently. "Are you feeling okay?"

"Can you get my drink?" she asks, voice tight. I grab the ginger ale and hand it to her. She sips it slowly, then leans back. "Thanks. For this and for helping me look for Boots."

"Of course. Are you sure you're all right? You look a little pale."

She shrugs. "I think the adrenaline of Boots running away is wearing off too fast. I feel a little shaky."

I grab a cookie off the counter and give it to her. "Here. You could have low blood sugar. Nausea, dizziness, and feeling shaky are all signs."

"I eat way too much sugar, but I won't turn down a cookie." She takes a bite and makes a face that lets me know it doesn't agree with her. She forces herself to finish her bite, then drinks more ginger ale. Maybe she has a bug. I hate that I can't comfort her.

"Well," she starts, putting the cookie on a napkin on the counter. "I'm going back to bed. I, uh, hope you can fall asleep okay."

The air between us is thick with tension. She bites her lip, eyes running over my body. They linger on my crotch, and I wonder if she's thinking about us making love. I know I am.

She grabs a ceramic coffee mug with a to-go lid from the

cabinet and pours the ginger ale inside. "I have this weird thing with bugs," she casually explains. "I can't have a drink on my nightstand at night without a lid. What if a spider falls inside and I'm too tired to notice and accidentally drink it?"

I chuckle. "If you drink it down you probably won't notice. But I suppose it could bite your lip or your tongue. And now I think I have a weird thing about open beverages at night. Thanks."

"Hey, you really should thank me. No one wants to drink a spider."

"No, I can't say anyone would." I step closer.

Quinn pulls on her hair with her free hand, twirling it around her finger. She lets it go and her hand falls onto her chest, sliding over her breasts. I don't know if she's aware of what she's doing or not, but damn, she's so fucking hot. She turns her head to the side, and I see a mosquito on her neck.

I stride forward and gently slap my fingers on her neck, trapping it before it can escape.

"Mosquito," I quickly explain, pulling my hand back to show her.

"Oh, uh, thanks."

We're standing close, and I can feel the heat radiating off Quinn and can smell the fabric softener she uses on her pajamas. My heart is beating so fast I'm sure she can hear it, and I want nothing more right now than to kiss her.

And that's exactly what I'm going to do.

y stomach gurgles and my throat feels thick. A telltale sign I'm going to throw up. I pride myself on saying I have an iron stomach and often bring up how I survived the Dawson Family Picnic disaster, over seven years ago, with just a twist of nausea when everyone else was riddled with food poisoning.

But right now, there's no stopping what's coming up.

And also right now, Archer's hand lands on my cheek, gently cupping my face and turning my chin up to his. He leans in and I know he's going to kiss me. I want nothing more than to kiss him back, but I can't.

Not right now.

I push his hand away and turn, barely making it to the sink before I throw up.

"Fuck, Quinn," Archer says and moves in, grabbing my hair and holding it back. My stomach heaves again, and I shudder. Throwing up is awful. Just fucking awful.

I turn on the faucet and rinse my mouth, washing away any vomit that might be on my face. Archer's hand lands on my back, gently rubbing it, and he's still holding my hair. I'm suddenly hit with emotion, and tears spring to my eyes. I splash cold water on my face. I don't feel sick anymore at least.

"Let me walk you to your room," he offers. "Do you want anything? More ginger ale or ice chips or anything?"

"No, but thanks."

Archer hands me a towel for my face, and I rinse out the sink, thankful for the garbage disposal.

"You're sick," Archer says.

"Really? What gave that away, doctor?" I don't mean to snap—again—but I do. Archer's back to irritating me, especially with him looking all hot and bothered, sitting there in his boxers as he tries not to look at me. Add in him rushing to help me find Boots and then springing in to hold my hair back and I'm close to having feelings for him again.

Close.

But I'm not stupid. I went to MIT, for fuck's sake. I'm an overall rational person who likes science and technology. I do believe in ghosts and like to think that maybe unicorns and dragons used to actually exist, but that's as far as my belief in fantasy goes.

And believing I could be more than a hookup to Archer Jones is definitely fantasy.

"It did take me over eight years of college plus several years as a resident to figure out that vomiting is not a normal reaction of the body when someone tries to kiss you."

"It wasn't because of—" I stop, realizing he's razzing me. I'm not in the mood. I just almost lost one of my mom's dogs and then threw up in the kitchen sink like a drunk college student sneaking in after a night of partying. "Thank you, Archer. Really. You didn't have to help me, and you did, so thank you, for what you did."

God, I need to learn how to stop talking. I don't know why I ramble and repeat myself so much.

Archer's lips press into a thin line, and he nods, grabbing my coffee mug from the counter.

"You should get some sleep."

His hand settles on the small of my back again, and I love and hate the way his touch makes me feel. I've missed his touch badly, but my sex drive has gone into *over*drive in the last few days, and my dreams have all involved him naked and with me, who is also naked.

In itself, it's nothing new. Archer has been the subject of my sex dreams for many years, though knowing what he's really like in bed makes me want him even more.

But I shouldn't. He's not good for me and what happened was a one-time deal.

We go upstairs, and I'm feeling more and more exhausted with each step. Something in the back of my mind nags at me, saying everything I've been feeling isn't normal. I don't see how I could have a bug lying in wait for a week, making me feel nauseous for days before it hit me hard enough to cause further damage.

But what else could it be?

I make a mental note to go to bed earlier this coming week and to lay off the coffee. Usually, I do pretty well with healthy eating, and when I veer off the healthy path, my insides take a beating. Maybe that's it. I have been eating more junk than usual this week.

Stopping at the threshold of my bedroom door, I turn around to look at Archer. Out of all the rooms in this big house, he's in the one next to mine. It wouldn't be hard to sneak into his room in the middle of the night or invite him into mine. Hooking up again would be easy. Heat spreads between my legs thinking of it, and I'm aching to have his big cock inside me again.

Blushing, I flick my eyes to his crotch, feeling weird that I know what's behind his boxers. It's like a hidden secret, and knowing Archer not only has a monster cock but knows how to use it well makes me feel a little dirty.

And dammit, I like it.

Archer is looking at me as if he's remembering what I look like naked as well, and when our eyes meet, it's not awkward. He mirrors back the lust I'm feeling, and if I hadn't just barfed, I'd be tempted to grab him and kiss him, dragging him back into my room with me for the night.

I've never been thankful for throwing up before. Getting back into bed with Archer is like a death sentence. I can only withstand so much before I crumble and fall, and trying to convince myself that I'm not upset, that it's okay, that I didn't have expectations for things to continue has taken its toll on me.

Because I am upset.

I do have feelings for him.

And I thought maybe, just maybe, he'd call me and tell me he missed me. That he'd try to come up and see me on his weekend off, or he'd invite me down for a mid-week booty call.

I'm a hopeless—and hopeful—romantic at heart and I can't help it.

"Well," I say, pushing my shoulders back, trying to regain as much composure as I can for someone who just threw up in the kitchen sink. "Thank you again, Archer. Goodnight, and good luck on your interview tomorrow."

Instead of giving me his cocky smile, his brow furrows and he looks, dare I say, *sad*. His hand lands on the back of his neck, a subconscious gesture I'm starting to realize he does when he's uncomfortable.

"Of course, Quinn," he says my name softly, and it rolls off his tongue like velvet. "If you get sick again, you can come get me. I am a doctor after all."

"Right. I'm glad you reminded me because I almost forgot."

His frown starts to turn. "We can't have that now, can we?"

"You probably should start wearing your white doctor coat around the house. And have one of those gold-plated stethoscopes around your neck like the TV doctors do."

"Mine's platinum."

I laugh. "Even better. Goodnight, Dr. Jones."

"How do you do this every day?" I fall into a lounge chair, over exaggerating my exhaustion. Though I am dragging, even with sleeping in past ten this morning.

Wes shrugs, a slight smile on his face as he watches his son run around the yard with the dogs. "You just do."

"You're like a superhero. Literally. Saving lives as a cop and rocking the whole single-parent thing."

He bypasses the compliment. "Keep your shoes on, buddy!" he shouts to Jackson. "He's going through a barefoot phase right now."

"Better than his bare-butt phase when he wouldn't wear pants."

Wes laughs, adjusting his gun on his belt before sitting on a chair next to me. He's on his lunch break, and came by for a homemade meal and to see Jackson.

"You do know the crime is really low here, don't you? Or

have you been away so long you forgot? I'm not saving lives in Eastwood."

I shoot him a look, trying desperately hard to ignore the sick feeling in my stomach. "Fine, you're no Avenger, but you keep this town safe. We'd have higher crime if we didn't have good police on our force." Wes rolls his eyes. "Can't you just accept a compliment?"

I flatten my hand over my stomach, swallowing down the lump rising in my throat. "He starts preschool this fall, right?" I grab the can of ginger ale I brought out and pop the top. This is my third one today and the only thing so far that helps. I've made a point to avoid junk food, even though the cookies that made me sick last night look oh so appealing today.

"Yeah, he'll go two days a week."

"Are you sad about it?"

"Not right now," Wes says. "On the first day, I think it'll hit me. Though it'll be good to have him in school for a few hours those days. Mom loves watching him while I work, but Dad's been getting busier and busier. Mom will never admit she's crunched for time, but I'm sure she is."

"Have you thought about hiring a nanny?"

"I shouldn't have to hire a nanny," he grumbles, looking away. I know where his thoughts have gone, and I feel bad for directing them that way. Wes's wife left when Jackson was only a few months old, leaving a note saying she cracked under pressure. She showed up on his first birthday, played the role of perfect housewife for a while and then left again.

Jackson doesn't remember her, but he still asks if his mommy will come home. I hate her and I never want to see her again. Well, only so Wes can divorce her once and for all.

"So," I start, changing the subject. "I made a fake video of the Batmobile for Dean. Want to see it?"

Wes chuckles, blue eyes sparkling. All my brothers have blue eyes like our parents. I'm the odd one out with green eyes.

"Of course."

I show him the video, and we both laugh. Then Mom calls us all in for lunch. She made homemade mac and cheese, along with a cucumber and avocado salad that I usually devour. But right now, a small bowl of mac and cheese is all I can handle.

After Wes leaves, Jackson and I go into the living room to watch a movie and hopefully get the crazy kid to nap. I end up falling asleep before him.

I wake up to the sound of Jackson playing with *PAW Patrol* on in the background. Archer is sitting on the ground with Jackson, pushing toy cars around on the ground. He's still wearing the suit he wore to his interview. His tie is loosened around his neck, and the top few buttons are undone.

Good Lord. It should be against the law for a man to look that good.

Don't even remind me of the fact he's sitting on the ground talking in funny voices to a three-year-old who I just happen to love more than life itself. Feeling hot and bothered, I sit up and push my hair out of my face.

"Aunt Winnie!" Jackson exclaims. Quinn was too hard for him to say, and 'Winnie' just stuck. "Come play with me!"

Archer turns, eyes meeting mine. He looks happy and relaxed sitting there playing, and it's doing bad things to me. Fuck, I want him so bad.

"How was the interview?" I ask, deciding it's best to just

stick to polite conversation. He did hold my hair back as I threw up last night. And as much as I want to hate him, I can't.

"I think it went pretty well," he says, eyes meeting mine. "How are you feeling?"

"Better."

His eyes go to the ginger ale on the coffee table in front of me. "Really?"

"I haven't thrown up again, so that's a plus, right?"

"Right."

I get up and move to the floor, tucking my hair behind my ear. Jackson can be a little bossy when he plays and tells us all what to make his toys say. It's nice sitting here with Archer, and with Jackson here as well, there's no risk for drama.

Not yet. Not until Archer and I are alone together. Which is something I'm going to make sure doesn't happen.

About fifteen minutes later, Jackson's finally tired. Mom comes out of the home office, saying she needs a break after arguing for an hour on the phone with a plumber they hired for a job. Jackson snuggles up with her on the couch and falls asleep almost instantly.

"What are your plans for the rest of the day?" Mom asks me.

"Just hang out here. Jamie is working a double today, so she can't do anything."

Mom covers Jackson with a blanket, kissing the top of his head. "I have a few errands to run before dinner tonight, would you mind possibly doing a few of them for me?"

"No, not at all," I say eagerly. Getting out of the house and away from Archer is a good idea anyway.

"Great! Archer, why don't you tag along? One of my

errands is to go to the feed store and some of those bags are heavy."

"I can handle it, Mom," I say dryly.

"I'm sure you can, but why not enjoy some company? And I don't think Archer wants to sit in the house with me all day," she adds with a wink. "My list is on my desk."

"I'm going to change first," Archer says, not meeting my eyes. I don't want to hurt his feelings, even though I don't think he considered *my feelings* when he had sex with me three times and then never called.

"Good idea," I say. "It's hot. Out. Outside. It's hot outside, I mean. You should change into something not so hot. Not that what you're wearing is hot like that. I mean in temperature."

Archer nods, smiling slightly at my word vomit and goes upstairs to change. I use the bathroom, shove a few mints in my purse to help my unsettled stomach, and get the list from Mom's desk.

I get into my car, cranking the air to cool it down, and fiddle with the radio until Archer joins me. We leave in silence, with nothing but the radio between us. It doesn't take long to get into town, and since downtown isn't very big, we can park in the middle and walk to most of the stores.

"What's first on the list?" Archer asks once we're out of the car.

"The feed store is right there," I say, pointing across the street. It's been a while since I walked around Eastwood's downtown. It's worlds different than Chicago, and for some reason, the nostalgia is hitting me hard.

Archer nods and follows me to the corner. I can feel his eyes on me and do my best to ignore him. I don't trust myself not to give in to the intense desire to kiss him that's currently crippling me.

We cross the street and go into Henry's Feed and Garden, an old cowbell jingling when I open the door.

"My oh my," Mrs. Miller says, pushing her glasses up on her nose. "Is that you, Quinn Dawson?"

"It is," I say with a smile.

"I haven't seen you in years! Get over here, girl." She opens her arms and wraps me in a big hug. Mrs. Miller and her husband, Henry, have owned this feed store for as long as I've been alive. Back in my youth, I showed goats and horses at the county fair and I spent a decent amount of time in this place. My parents got rid of the goats soon after I graduated high school, and my show horse died five years ago.

I still miss him.

"You look amazing!" Mrs. Miller exclaims, holding me out at arm's length. "I heard about your fancy app and your fancy job. We're all proud of you, hun. This whole town is."

"It was nothing," I say, trying to brush off the compliment. It wasn't nothing, and it took a lot of work to create the app. Selling it was part talent and part luck. The right person saw it at the right time and offered me a deal I couldn't refuse.

"And who is this?" Her eyes go behind me to Archer.

"Hi," Archer says, offering his hand to shake. "I'm Archer. Dean's friend."

He *is* Dean's friend. It's not a lie. But for some reason his words make me feel all stabby. What is up with me today? I must be PMSing hard.

We talk with Mrs. Miller for a bit before getting the things on Mom's list. Archer carries two heavy bags of feed out to the car like it's nothing. I open the door for him and step aside.

"Quinn," he says once the bags of chicken feed are in the car. "I don't want you to be mad at me."

"I'm not mad," I say softly, tempted to go with Mom's favorite and add 'I'm just disappointed' to the end of it. I don't, and instead, I pull the list out of my purse to see what else we need to get. "Mom wants two bouquets of flowers. The florist is just down the block."

I take off, and Archer falls into step next to me. "You seem mad, and I wouldn't blame you."

Coming to a sudden halt, I whirl around. "Really, Archer? You wouldn't blame me? How very generous of you."

I take off again, wondering where the fire inside of me is coming from. I'm not a confrontational person. At all. I know I have feelings for Archer, but I guess they're rooted deeper than I thought for all this snapping.

"Quinn, stop." Archer grabs my wrist, gently pulling me back to him. I let him bring me close, and rest one hand on his firm chest, feeling his heart beat beneath my fingers. I want nothing more than to kiss him, for him to pick me up and press me against the brick wall of Eastwood's only bookstore, not caring who sees.

Tingles make their way through every inch of me, and my pussy aches to feel his touch. I need him.

And I think he needs me too.

I lick my lips and inch in, wanting to feel if his desire matches mine. It's a bit unfair, if you think about it, how women can hide it when they're turned on but guys can't. Especially guys like Archer who have a big dick. Not that I feel sorry for him in that aspect, of course.

"You said you like honesty," Archer says, voice deep, rumbling right through me. "So be honest."

I swallow hard, throat suddenly thick. "Fine. I can be honest." I raise my head, lips inches from his, and open my mouth. Archer tips his head down, and if he doesn't kiss me, I think I might explode.

Archer grips my hips, pulling me to him, and I feel his cock start to harden. I melt into his embrace, remembering how good it felt to have him inside me. Even before that, the way he touched me, the way he looked at me, the way he made me feel like I was a goddess...I miss it and I need it.

I slowly bring my hand down his chest, keeping my eyes locked with his. My fingers dance over his waistband of his athletic shorts, so close to the tip of his cock.

And then the door to the bookstore opens, swinging out and almost hitting us. We jump back, separating just in time.

"Quinn!" Logan exclaims, stopping short. "Didn't expect to see you here."

I blink rapidly, eyes needing to readjust to the bright sunlight around us. Everything faded for a moment there.

"And Archer. I didn't know you were in town." Logan's eyes go from Quinn to me a few times before he pulls Quinn in for a hug. "I'm guessing this is why Mom's having us all come over for dinner tonight."

"Yeah. We're out running errands for her," she says, shuffling back. Sweat breaks out along my back, both from the heat of the day and almost getting caught. My judgment goes out the window when it comes to Quinn, and she got me going from zero to sixty in three seconds flat.

"What'd you buy?" Quinn asks, shifting nervously. She's worried her brother saw us too.

"That thriller that's being made into a movie. I refuse to see the movie until I've read the book."

Out of all her brothers, Quinn and Logan are the most alike. He's the second youngest, even though Owen is a mere handful of seconds older, and I've heard them joke about that bonding them.

"The one about the girl who wakes up from a car accident covered in blood and thinks her husband is a killer?" she asks.

"Yeah, that one." Logan holds up the book. "Well, I'll see you guys later. I need to stop in at the bar and make sure things are set up for tonight. And then find Owen."

Quinn raises an eyebrow. "You lost him?"

"I'm not his keeper."

"He needs you to be," she mumbles. "Do you need me to triangulate his phone again?"

"Nah, I installed a tracking app he hasn't noticed yet. He went home with some girls last night and I'm guessing he's still sleeping it off somewhere."

She shakes her head. "I don't know how you guys can look so alike but be so different."

Logan shrugs. "Beats me. I got all the smarts, and he got all the...you know, there's nothing he has that I don't."

Quinn laughs and moves her gaze from Logan to the buildings surrounding us. I remember Dean saying he was worried about Quinn when she first took her job in Chicago. The rest of her family was here in Eastwood and she moved away, though it's not like anyone could blame her. This is a small town and she has an advanced degree in computer science. There's nothing here for her.

Quinn's hand lands on her stomach and she grimaces. Shit, she's probably feeling sick again.

"You okay, sis?" Logan asks.

"Yeah, I've been so stressed from work it's making me sick," she says, waving her hand in the air. A long list of terminal illnesses rush through my head, and I have to force myself not to diagnose Quinn. There's nothing wrong with her. She's fine.

She has to be fine.

We say bye to Logan and move onto the next stop, and Quinn picks out two bouquets of yellow and white flowers. After that, we go to the vet to pick up medication for Rufus, and lastly, the post office to get a book of stamps.

We leave the post office in silence, and I hate how tense things are. They don't have to be like this. I want to go back to that Friday night when Quinn and I were walking along the river.

"Quinn," I start, mentally yelling at myself to man the fuck up and just tell her how I feel.

"Archer." She unlocks her car and opens her door. I wait until we're both in and buckled to start talking.

"I'm sorry."

She puts the SUV in reverse and flicks her eyes to me. "For what?"

"For not calling you. I should have called or texted or... or...something. Things are complicated, and Dean's been a good friend to me. He's like a brother and I..." I let out my breath, shaking my head. "It's not a good enough excuse, I know. But I am sorry."

Quinn bites her lip, looking out at the road as she leaves the parking space. Her brows come together, and I wish so badly to know what she's thinking.

"Complicated. Right." She turns down the main road out of town. "What does that even mean?"

"I'm not sure," I say honestly.

She tightens her grip on the wheel. "Do you regret sleeping with me?"

"No. Do you regret it?"

Her lips press into a thin line and she shakes her head. Before she can answer, her phone rings. Connected to the Bluetooth in her car, the call comes up over the speakers. It's someone from work, asking Quinn about coding. Her words are technical and lost on me, but I'd be lying if I said hearing her talk like that didn't turn me on. The phone call goes on until we arrive back at the Dawsons' farm, and even though we left our conversation in a very precarious place, going back would be even more awkward.

"Should I take the chicken feed into the barn?" I ask, getting out of the SUV.

"Yeah. Thanks." She gets the other items and heads inside without me. Dean and Kara are here, everyone is in the usual meeting place: the kitchen. Quinn is leaning against the counter snacking on pretzels, Dean looks like he's close to being bored to death, and Kara and Mrs. Dawson are bent over an iPad, intently looking at something.

"Thank the Lord," Dean says when he sees me. "We got important video gaming to do."

Kara looks away from the iPad, giving Dean a glare. He holds up his hands in defeat and sits back down.

"What's going on?" I ask, coming over to the island.

"I'm trying to narrow down poses for these engagement pictures." Kara shakes her head at whatever she's seeing. "What about this one?"

"It's nice," Mrs. Dawson says.

"Just nice?"

"Yes, it's too tame."

Dean raises his eyes. "See what I've been dealing with? This has been going on all day. It's just a photo."

"An engagement photo," Kara counters. "We're only doing this once, babe. Come on."

Dean caves, eyes sparkling as he looks at his fiancée. "I know." He slides the iPad in front of him and scrolls. "I like this one."

"No," Kara and Mrs. Dawson say at the same time. Kara

takes the iPad back, tapping her chin. "I like the ones where you can see the ring, but they look so unnatural with the hand turned out."

"They do," Quinn agrees, breaking a pretzel in half. "A girl from my office got married last year and she had really cute engagement photos with her hand on her fiancée's cheek. It showed the ring and wasn't hokey."

"Oh, I like that idea!"

"I don't," Dean says. "The guy's supposed to cup your cheek. Not the other way around." All the women in the room roll their eyes.

"What about the pose with your hands together," Quinn suggests and tries to demonstrate with her own hands.

"Show me with Archer," Kara says, and no one else blinks an eye. I stiffen and Quinn almost chokes on her pretzels. If either of us balks, it'll look like something is going on. And it is, it so is. But right now, we need to suck it up.

Quinn puts the pretzels down and hesitantly steps forward. She holds up her left hand and motions for me to hold up my right. She puts our hands together, barely interlocking our fingers.

"I like the hand holding, it's really sweet, but you're just standing there," Mrs. Dawson says, really getting into this. "Quinn, step in closer. Archer, put your other hand on her waist."

I swallow hard, praying I can control the reaction from my body, and raise my left arm. Quinn inhales, breasts rising and falling under her t-shirt, and inches closer. She slowly lets out her breath and I put my hand on her hip. The moment my hand flattens against her, she shivers.

"Now look into each others' eyes," Kara instructs, getting up to take our picture. "Act like you love each other."

Quinn's eyes widen and color rushes to her cheeks. This might be awkward for her, above her acting ability, but for me, all I have to do is look at her and not hold back.

All I have to do is look at her the way I've wanted to for the last twelve years.

Closing her eyes, Quinn tips her head up. Her lips part ever so slightly, and the world starts to spin. Then she opens her eyes and everything stops.

"Do something with your hand," Kara tells Quinn. She licks her lips, nodding, and brings her arm up, resting her hand on my chest. I tighten my hold on her waist, bending my fingers in, and shuffle closer. My heart is racing, blood rushing through every part of me.

"Perfect," Kara says, snapping a photo. "Thanks, guys."

It takes another second for us to break apart, and taking my hand off Quinn's waist turns out to be harder than I thought. And finally taking my hand off of hers proves to be almost impossible.

Quinn steps away, lips parted, but with an unreadable expression in her eyes. Messing with her hair, she says she's going to go upstairs to get ready for dinner, whatever that means.

Dean's able to get away from the engagement photo planning, and we go into the living room. Mr. Dawson and Jackson are in there, and Jackson wants me to play cars with him again. I sit on the floor, pushing the cars around and making them talk in silly voices.

Sometime later, Weston arrives, and all the guys go outside with a beer in hand to talk and bullshit while Mr. Dawson grills barbecue chicken. I lean against the patio table, thinking this is how family should be.

How mine could have been.

But it will never be, because my brother is a deadbeat

and there's no chance of him cleaning up his act enough to last more than a couple of weeks. I've had dinner with my parents, of course, but it's obvious the reason why Bobby isn't there. It's not like he's working or busy with his own family.

I look around at Mr. Dawson, Dean, Weston, and Jackson, and vow that when the time comes and I have my own family, we will be like this.

No matter what.

———

QUINN PUSHES HER FOOD AROUND ON HER PLATE, TAKING little bites here and there and only when someone is looking. She still doesn't feel well but is trying to hide it. I'll ask her about it later and make sure she's okay.

"How's life at the hospital?" Mr. Dawson asks. "You're at the biggest one in Indy, right?"

"Yes, I am. And it's hectic and busy, but I really enjoy it."

Owen takes a drink of beer and raises his eyebrows. "Do doctors hook up with hot nurses in break rooms like they do on TV?"

I laugh. "Not that I know of."

"But Archer was seeing a hot nurse for a while," Dean interjects, and I internally wince. "Whatever happened to her?"

"Uh, it was never much of a thing," I deadpan, going for my beer.

"Keeping it casual." Owen nods in approval. "A guy after my own heart."

Quinn looks up at her brother, green eyes full of fire. "Aren't you getting too old for casual relationships?"

The venom in her voice is directed at me, not Owen. He

shrugs her off. "I'll keep it casual as long as I want. Relationships are nothing but drama." He turns to Kara, who's sitting on his other side. "But not yours."

"Thanks," she says dryly. "One day you'll meet a girl who'll change your mind."

Owen smirks. "She'll have to be really good at—"

Logan elbows him hard in the gut, shutting him up. I try to catch Quinn's eye, but she's staring hard at her plate.

"What about you, sis?" Logan asks, and I see him slowly shift his gaze from me to her and back again. "Is there a special someone in your life?"

"He's far from special," Quinn says with a sweet smile. "Though he could have been, but what's done is done, right?"

Her answer only makes sense to me, leaving the rest of the table left wondering. I take a quick look around and feel a lump rise in my throat. Quinn is obviously upset. I hurt her, made her think that weekend was nothing more than dirty sex, and probably fucking blew it.

I'm in love with this woman and I'm pretty sure she never wants to talk to me again.

If the Dawsons knew I was the reason for Quinn's pain... if they knew what I did to her, and what she did to me— three times—they'd line up to beat me up. I can hold my own against Dean. And probably Owen. Logan would give me a run for my money and Weston served two tours in Afghanistan and is a cop. He'd beat the shit out of me.

My only hope would be Quinn, yelling and screaming at them to stop. Though by the look she just gave me, she'd be on the sidelines cheering them on.

"Oh, Archer!" Mrs. Dawson exclaims. "I didn't even ask you about the interview. How do you feel it went?"

"Great," I say honestly. "The chief surgeon is a big

Purdue fan. I think it helped I did my pre-med studies there."

"I knew you'd do great." Mrs. Dawson beams. "If you do get the job, you're welcome to stay here."

"That's very generous, but I can't—"

"Nonsense! We have this big old house full of empty rooms." Mrs. Dawson looks pointedly at Dean as she speaks. She doesn't need to actually say the words for everyone to know what she's talking about: she wants more grandchildren. Her eyes narrow ever so slightly and the temperature shifts down a few degrees. Dean and Kara haven't picked a wedding date yet, which puts more grandchildren farther and farther out of the picture. "We'd be happy to have you until you find something permanent. You can save some money on rent that way too," she adds. "I know how overworked and underpaid resident doctors are." She playfully elbows Mr. Dawson. "I learned that from those romance doctor shows you say are good for nothing."

"They are good for nothing," Mr. Dawson teases, trying his best to convince everyone he really thinks so.

"He watches them too," Mrs. Dawson whisper-talks. "But really, honey, our door is always open."

I can't help but smile at her offer, the generosity of the whole goddamn Dawson clan never failing to surprise me. My phone rings and I reach into my pocket to pull it out and silence it. It's my weekend off, dammit, and I'm not in town to fill in tonight.

But it's not the hospital calling. It's my mom.

19

Archer's face falls when he looks at his phone. Then his eyes narrow ever so slightly with fear.

"Sorry," he says, and stands. "It's my mother. I have to take this."

"Go ahead, honey," Mom says, not catching the worry in Archer's face like I do. My anger goes out the window, and I'm concerned for him now. He mentioned having a sick family member. What if they couldn't fight their illness anymore?

I set my fork down, reaching for my water, and peer into the kitchen, trying to get a read on Archer's face. His back is to me, but his hand lands on his neck. Shit. Something is wrong.

"Quinn?" Dad says in a tone that lets me know it wasn't the first time he said my name. "Earth to Quinn."

"Yeah, sorry. What?"

Everyone laughs. "I asked you how's work going on the Batmobile." He winks and Wes stifles a laugh.

"Dad," I scold. "I told you I can't talk about it in front of others."

Mom shakes her head, and I look past her into the kitchen again. Archer is off the phone now, but still looks stressed. Wanting to put everything behind us and start again, every fiber of my being aches to go to him and ask what's wrong and tell him I'll help however I can.

When he comes back to the table, I look at him, trying to meet his eye, but he keeps his gaze turned down on his plate, eating in silence for a few minutes until Dean brings up stories from their college days.

After dinner, we go outside for drinks and dessert. Weston and Jackson leave first since it's already past Jackson's bedtime. Logan and Owen are the next to leave, and Kara's having a girls' night at her house and invites me to come.

I'm feeling sick again and all I want to do is curl up in bed and watch a movie. And talk to Archer. The nausea gets worse and worse as the night goes on, and when I go upstairs to bed, Dean and Archer move into the living room to play video games. I shower, put on my pajamas, and crash into bed. I doze off and on for a while, eventually getting up to dig a mint out of my purse to try and settle my stomach that won't stop swirling.

I sit back in bed, feeling a little better with the mint in my mouth. Something is off, and I know it. I don't have a fever, and I don't feel like I have the flu. Plus, I'm not nauseous all day. It's just off and on.

Rufus jumps up next to me, resting his head on my stomach. I run my fingers over the sleek fur on his ears, hoping I feel better in the morning so I can hang out with Jamie for a bit before I have to leave. A good night's sleep should do the trick.

Still, something nags at me in the back of my mind. Why am I so nauseous? Maybe from eating too much dessert? I binge on junk food every now and then and it never hits me like that. And eggs? Since when do I like—

"Oh my God." I sit up so fast it freaks out Rufus. In a mad scramble, I grab my phone, pulling up my calendar. I don't track my period, but I remember the last time I had it because I was in a meeting with a bigwig from Microsoft and felt it start. I was wearing a cream-colored pencil skirt that day, so of course it's seared into my mind. I made it out with no bloodstains, but still, it was a close call and I missed half of what was being said because I couldn't stop thinking about the bloodbath happening in my undies.

I flip through my calendar and find the date. Then I count forward. I should have gotten my period by now. I think I might throw up again.

I've been nauseous all week.

My boobs hurt and I've had cramps like my period was going to start.

But it didn't.

I'm exhausted.

And I threw up last night.

Suddenly, I can't breathe. Rufus whines, nudging his nose against my hand. I slide my arms around him, trying to get my heart to stop racing.

Archer and I had sex roughly two weeks after my period started. Two out of the three times, he came inside of me. I didn't think much of it. It wasn't the first time I'd had unprotected sex. The odds are against me. It can take people years to get pregnant when they're trying.

But it can also happen in one shot.

Or twice, in my case. Though I don't know if that's my case. It could be really bad PMS. Yeah, that's what it is. I'm tired from work. Sick from stress. And I'm craving eggs because my body is low on...on...what the hell are in eggs?

In the back of my mind, I know it's more. And there's only one way to find out, and lucky for me, there's a Walmart close by that's open twenty-four hours. I get out of bed, not bothering with clothes. I do put on a bra though, partly because my tank top is white and partly because my boobs hurt.

It's late, and I don't expect Mom or Dad to be up anymore, or at least not in the living room. I can sneak out and back in half an hour. Maybe less. Quietly, I slip down the stairs, purse over my shoulder and keys in my hand.

"Are you going somewhere?" Dean's voice comes from the living room. Dammit. He and Archer are still playing video games, and if I'd come down a minute earlier, he probably wouldn't have looked up from the screen and noticed me.

"Yeah, I just felt like going out."

Dean cocks an eyebrow. "In your pajamas? And I thought you said you felt sick after dinner."

"These PJs are comfy. And I feel better now," I lie. The nausea comes back with a vengeance. I just need to make it outside before I barf again.

"Really?"

"Really." I shift my weight. "I, uh, miss being able to go to Walmart at night. There isn't one close to me downtown."

Archer's watching, not buying what I'm saying, but I know he won't question me.

"We'll go with you," Dean says. "This controller is shit and I need a new one." He holds up the PlayStation controller in his hand and makes a move to stand up.

"Actually," I blurt. "I feel sick again." I really do. I almost trip going down the rest of the stairs in my haste to get into the bathroom. I open the lid just in time and bring up the little food that's left in my stomach into the toilet, throat burning. I slump onto the floor, feeling instant relief after throwing up.

"Quinn?" Archer's voice comes from the doorway.

I look up at him, and my heart skips a beat.

"Are you okay? It sounded like you threw up again."

"I did," I admit. "I'm not sure I'm okay, actually."

"Maybe going out shopping at eleven at night isn't a good idea."

"I know."

Archer reaches for me and I stand up quickly, trying to purposely avoid his touch. I don't think I'm strong enough to resist him at the moment, and after our close encounter in the kitchen earlier, I won't be able to hold out. The movement makes my head spin, and the next thing I know, Archer has his arm around me. He closes the toilet lid and has me sit down.

With furrowed brows, he looks at me. "I think you should let me examine you."

I swallow the lump of vomit rising in my throat. Nerves shoot through me and I try to find the right words to say. Archer, examining me. Removing my clothes and putting his hands all over my body. "I think that was part of the problem in the first place."

"What do you mean?" Archer crouches down and rests his hand on my knee. I'm half-tempted to push it off and half-tempted to slide it up farther. "Quinn, we never got to finish our conversation from earlier, and I know now's not the best time and all, but if I keep waiting for the right time I'm worried I'll never find it."

His fingers gently press into my leg. "When I said I was sorry, I meant it. I never wanted to hurt you. And I don't want to you regret that weekend, because I don't. The only thing I regret is not telling you how much I enjoyed being with you."

His words come out jumbled, but I know he means them. If I weren't internally freaking out over the possibility I'm carrying his baby, they'd have more sentiment.

"So what were you going to the store for?" he asks after a beat passes and I don't say anything.

"Feminine products."

"Oh. Do you want me to go get you some?"

I open my eyes. "You'd go out and get me tampons?"

"Sure. Just tell me what to get. Dean wants to go out anyway. I don't mind grabbing them."

"That's really sweet of you, Archer," I start, mind going a mile a minute. "But that's actually not what I need."

Archer looks at me in question. "Are you trying to sneak out and meet someone?"

"No, not at all." I sigh, debating if I should just tell him. This concerns him as well. Biting my lip, I get up and close the door.

"What's going on Quinn? You're kind of freaking me out, and I don't get freaked out easily."

I nod, nervously twisting my hair in my fingers. Maybe I shouldn't say anything until I know for sure. If the test comes back negative, I'll feel silly for getting him worked up over nothing. Though, it'd be nice to not be alone in this right now.

And mostly, I don't want to lie to Archer.

"I'm not really sure," I start, swallowing hard. "You know I've been sick."

"Yeah, twice now."

I nod. "I've also been exhausted, craving foods I don't normally eat, and have had cramps like my period is going to start, but it hasn't. And it should have over a week ago."

Archer blinks. "Okay."

"Okay? That's all you have to say? You're a doctor! Don't these symptoms add up to you?"

Archer, who's still crouched down on the floor where he was before, stands. His hand goes to his chin as he thinks. He looks at me, lowers his eyes to my abdomen, and looks into my eyes again. "You were going to get a pregnancy test."

"Yes." As soon as the word slips from my lips, panic sets in. Archer takes my hand.

"Quinn." Hearing him say my name calms me. "Look at me."

I turn my head up and look into his deep, dark eyes. It feels so good to have his hand around mine. I want him to pull me close and hug me, to lay me down and kiss me. I'm so scared right now. I don't want to think. Just feel.

"We'll get through whatever happens. Together."

Tears well in my eyes and I nod. "Thanks." I exhale heavily. "I don't know though. Not yet. It could all be from stress, right?"

"When was the date of your last period?" Archer asks, going into doctor mode.

"Sixteen days before we, uh..."

"Hooked up."

"Sure." I frown. It sounds so casual that way, which is all it was to him.

He nods the way TV doctors do when they're thinking. "That puts you at a typical time for ovulating."

"Right."

"It's going to be—" He cuts off when Dean calls his name. "It's gonna be okay," he says quickly. "I'll get the test. Lay down. If you're not pregnant, you have a bug or something and should rest."

He looks at me, and this time his eyes are filled with

longing, reminding me of the way he looked at me when we were walking along the river. I want him to look at me like that again, but because he wants me, not because I might be having his baby.

I turn on the faucet again and rinse my face with cold water, then go into the kitchen to grab a ginger ale before heading upstairs. There's no way I'm going to fall asleep before Archer gets back. And how the heck is he going to get away with buying a pregnancy test without Dean seeing?

Though I guess he could lie and say he's getting it for someone else. Archer's smart. He'll think of something.

Getting into bed, I turn on the TV and make it through half an episode of *Charmed* before passing out.

I WAKE UP, KNOWING EXACTLY WHAT'S GOING ON, BUT STILL bogged down by my dream that everything is perfect. My bedroom door is cracked open just enough to let the dogs in and out, and Rufus moved from my side to the foot of the bed where he could lay under the fan.

Thirsty, I get up to get a drink, and see a small paper bag with my name on it, scrawled out in messy black letters. It's folded down and stapled shut.

Curious, I grab it and rip it open. There are two pregnancy tests inside, along with a note from Archer.

QUINN- *I WASN'T SURE WHAT KIND TO GET, SO I GOT TWO. I CAN be with you when you take it if you want. Whatever happens, it'll be okay.*

-Archer

I LOOK AT THE TESTS AND TRY TO DECIDE WHAT TO DO. IF I AM pregnant, having Archer there will be reassuring. And if I'm not, we can both celebrate together. I put both boxes back in the bag and slip it in a drawer on the nightstand.

It's only seven o'clock, and everyone is still sleeping, I'm sure. Getting out of bed, I pad into the hall and pause outside of Archer's door. My stomach flip-flops, and this time I know it's from nerves. I slowly open the door, set on slipping in and quietly waking Archer up.

My heart lurches when I see him lying there, reminding me of when he fell asleep on my couch. Back before we fucked things up. Rufus runs past me and jumps onto the bed. Startled, Archer sits up, eyes focusing on me.

"Did you take it?" he asks right away.

I shake my head, wrapping my arms around myself. "Not yet. But I do have to pee."

He pets Rufus, gently pushing him back so he can get out of bed. He's only wearing boxers, and the last thing I need right now is to gaze upon his gorgeous body.

"Want me to come with you?"

"Not into the bathroom while I'm peeing, but yeah when we look at the tests."

He's at my side and we quietly walk back to my room, which shares a jack-and-jill bathroom with what is now Jackson's room.

"Where's Dean?"

"Passed out on the couch downstairs," Archer tells me and stands in silence as I rip open the pregnancy tests. I take them both into the bathroom and close the door. I carefully position them under myself and cap them as soon as I'm done. I flip them both over, not wanting to look. It can take a minute or two before the result pops up anyway.

I extend my hand to Archer, who takes the tests. "It says to wait—"

"You're pregnant," he blurts, looking down at the test.

"What?

He holds up the digital test. There's no mistaking the word *pregnant* in bold black letters. "It already said it when I looked. And this one—" he holds up the other "—is faint but it's there. You're pregnant, Quinn," he repeats as if he has to say it again to himself. He stares at the test for a minute. "Fuck." He turns around, gripping the tests in one hand and grabbing the back of his neck with the other.

"I thought you said everything was going to be okay."

"It is, it is," he says too quickly, and closes his eyes for a second. "Let's sit and talk about this."

I wash my hands and join him on the bed. He puts the pregnancy tests on the nightstand, staring at them like they might spontaneously turn into a baby.

"Based on the time of conception, you're around five weeks pregnant," he says, tone level. He's going into doctor-mode again, and it's helping me stay calm. "That's early. I'm, uh, sorry you're having morning sickness already. Is that the right thing to say?" He snaps back to just Archer. "That I'm sorry?" His hand lands on mine. "I don't know what to say. About any of this."

I blink back tears, hand landing on my stomach. "There's a little baby in there," I say slowly. "And it's part of me and it's part of you."

Archer turns his head in, fingers slipping between mine. His lips part and lust sweeps through me. Not stopping to think, I lean forward. Archer lets go of my hand and cups my face, tipping my chin up as he kisses me.

Wasting no time, I grab Archer's sides and pull him onto me. We fall back onto the mattress, with him between my legs. My clit begs to be touched. Now. The need is real, and if Archer doesn't strip me down and fuck me, there's going to be trouble.

I curl one leg around him, arching my back and thrusting my hips against his. His cock hardens and he moves his lips from mine to my neck. I stick my hands down the back of his boxers, squeezing his ass.

"Quinn," he pants. "Are you sure you want this? I mean, I do, but I want to make sure you don't regret it later."

Damn him and his chivalry. Letting out a breath, I bring my hands back up his ass, down his sides, and to his chest. My libido is saying yes, but my mind says no.

And my heart...that poor thing doesn't know what to think.

"It's not what I want, Archer," I pant. "I need you."

That's all he needs to hear from me. Archer dives back down, kissing me hard as he pulls my shorts down. He moves to the side and slips his hand between my legs. I let out a moan only to clamp my hand over my mouth. Archer circles his finger around my entrance, teasing me.

And then the stairs creak.

My door is open, and you can see right into the room when you stand on the landing. Archer moves off me so fast he falls off the bed. I sit up, not bothering with my shorts and pull the blanket over me and look into the hall, expecting to see Dean or my dad.

It's Rufus.

"Seriously?" I shake my head. "He does weigh as much as an adult."

Archer gets back into the bed, but he doesn't move on top of me. Doesn't kiss me. Doesn't touch me.

"You're pregnant," he says, face paling.

"Yeah. I am." I fold my hands in my lap and feel like I

might pass out. "I'm pregnant and you're the father." Slowly, I turn to look at Archer.

His face is pale, and his brown eyes are wide. He swallows hard, and reaches forward, putting his hand on my stomach. "It might be possible to hear a heartbeat already."

The tears I'm holding back start to fall. "So you want this baby?"

"Quinn," Archer says, taking my face in both hands this time. "Yes."

My bottom lip starts to quiver and I burst into tears. Archer pulls me to him, and I bury my face against his shoulder, trying to muffle my sobs. So much rushes through my head right now.

Archer might want this baby, but we're not together. I'm in Chicago and he's four hours away in Indy. I have a full-time job that I love. I live in a busy city away from my parents, and—oh my God. My parents are going to kill me.

I'm a grown adult, but still. Are they going to be disappointed?

"Hey," Archer soothes. "If you don't want it...it's your body."

"I do. I mean I think I do." I put my hand over my stomach, remembering images friends have shown me of early ultrasounds. The baby looks like a blob and nothing more. So why do I already feel attached to it? It has to be these stupid hormones, which explains my mood swinging rage at Archer.

"Take some time," Archer says. "We just found out."

I sit back, wiping my eyes. "You didn't even question me."

"What do you mean?"

"You didn't ask if you were the father."

He tips his head. "Is that a good thing?"

"Yes," I say and start crying again. "I don't know why I'm crying!"

"It's okay. This is a shock. We didn't mean for it to happen. But it did, and we'll figure it out." He kisses me again, and something passes through me, making me relax. "Maybe not today, maybe not tomorrow, but we'll get there."

I let out a breath. "You sound so sure."

"I'm not."

"That's not reassuring."

He smiles. "I thought you liked it when I'm honest."

"Lie to me. Just this time."

He caresses my hair and pulls me back to his chest. "I'm positive things will be fine."

"Thank you." I close my eyes, listening to his heart beat. There's so much to do and even more to say. I'm pregnant, but that's the easy part—and none of this is easy.

What's going to happen when the kid arrives? We don't live together. I work full-time. Archer works more than full-time. I don't want to quit my job, but I don't want to be away from my kid all day.

I get queasy again, and as relaxing as it is to have Archer rubbing my back, I push him away.

"I think I'm going to throw up again."

Archer follows me into the bathroom, and gathers my hair into his hand, holding it back as I lean over the toilet. I close my eyes, not sure if I should will myself not to puke or if I should just let it happen so I feel better.

"You said it's early to have morning sickness," I grumble, throat feeling thick. "Is that bad?"

"No, not necessarily."

I turn my head up only to move it back, getting sick. Archer hands me a wad of toilet paper to wipe my mouth with and then helps me up. I rinse my mouth out with water and crawl back into bed. The sick feeling in my stomach is gone. For now.

"But it could be bad?"

"It's not my area of interest," he says almost guiltily. "But I wouldn't say it's *not* normal. Nausea during pregnancy tends to peak later on, so I hate to think this could get worse for you."

"It can get worse?"

"It might not. And there are great anti-nausea medications you can take."

I put my head in my hands, feeling dizzy. I inhale and get no air. Archer's hands land on my arms, gently pulling me to him. He doesn't kiss me, but he keeps me in his arms and lays back on the bed.

"Do you want to talk about it?"

"About feeling sick?"

"I guess, but I meant you being pregnant and, uh, all it entails."

I bite the inside of my cheek. "That's the adult thing to do, right?"

He runs his fingers up and down my arm. "Right."

I close my eyes, tears rolling down my face. "I'm not ready to be an adult just yet."

"Neither am I."

"Quinn," Archer whispers. I'm not quite asleep, but I'm close to it. Archer rubbed my back for what felt like hours, though it was probably more like twenty minutes. Going into self-preservation mode, I blocked out all thoughts about babies and focused on how good it felt to have Archer touching me.

Which is a different issue altogether.

"Quinn," he repeats. "Someone is awake downstairs."

I open my eyes, wishing I could go back to that Friday night. Would I tell Archer to put on a condom or would I shut him down before the sex even started?

"Don't tell anyone," I rush out.

"I won't. Not until you're ready."

"Thank you, Archer. I mean, I don't even know when this..." I swallow the lump in my throat. "...This baby is due."

"Around March twentieth."

"Oh. Really?"

"Yeah. Give or take a week. Due weeks are the new due days, I've been told."

"March twentieth. That's a good date."

"It's close to my birthday," he says and it hits me that I don't even know when his birthday is. I've known Archer for years, but I don't really know him.

"When is your birthday?"

"March seventeenth," he answers.

"Mine is—"

"December first," he finishes. "I remember."

I tip my head up to look at him, surprised by that. My eyes fill with tears again, but hey, at least I can blame this on the hormones. Though truth be told, I cry when I'm scared and right now I'm fucking terrified.

"I don't know what to do, Archer," I whisper.

He sits up, eyes nervously shifting to the open door. Right. He's worried about Dean seeing him. Oh my God. Dean is going to beat the shit out of Archer when he finds out he knocked me up. And then Logan, Owen, and Weston will all get in line to take a turn throwing punches.

Not only do I have to tell my parents I'm pregnant, I have to tell my brothers.

"We'll figure it out, Quinn. Together."

I pull the blankets up to my chin and close my eyes. Just last night, I was hell-bent on hating Archer Jones for the rest of my life. Now his baby is growing inside of me, and I'm slipping.

"Archer," I start, shifting my eyes to his. "I don't want you to be with me because we're having a baby." I say each word slowly and carefully. Inhaling, I sit up and try to gather my composure. "I'm an adult. I made the adult decision to sleep with you that night. Twice. And then again the next day." Rufus jumps onto the bed again and army crawls his way between Archer and me. I bury my fingers in his thick fur, thankful for the distraction. "And then you went back to Indy, and yeah, I wished you would call, but you didn't and I got over it, and it's okay." I'm rambling again, and there's no end in sight. "Like I said, you don't owe me anything. We're adults and did an adult thing and this happened."

"What are you trying to say?"

"Don't be with me just because I'm pregnant with your baby." Dammit. That sounded way more dramatic than I wanted it to.

"I don't want you to go through this alone."

"I won't. I have no doubt you will be an amazing father, but Archer, I'd rather us not be together and raise this kid the best we can as single parents than try to force something that's not really there." Each word hurts as I say it, but I have to think about this child first.

This. Child.

My child. Archer's child. *Our* child.

And now I'm crying again.

Archer takes me in his arms, soothing me by rubbing my back. "It's going to be okay."

My mother's voice floats up the stairs. She's talking to Dean, chastising him for passing out on the couch and not going upstairs into one of the guest rooms. Archer moves away and wipes a tear from my cheek.

"It's going to be okay," he repeats. I want to believe him, but I can tell he doesn't even believe himself.

20

ARCHER

The bathroom door closes, and I'm still standing there, looking at the white paint until my vision goes blurry. After I reassured her everything will be okay, she smiled and said she was going to take a shower. But I can't move. Hell, I can hardly breathe.

Quinn is pregnant with my baby.

I'm trying to let it sink in, but my defenses are up and I can't think past the fact she's been feeling sick and it's partly my fault. Or all my fault? I know it took both of us to create the baby, and it's not like Quinn wasn't willing. But...fuck. How could I let this happen?

I'm a doctor. I know how the body works. And yet I had sex three times with Quinn within twenty-four hours and only used a condom once. Though it's not like I brought any with me Friday night. I didn't expect to hook up with anyone, and when it finally happened with Quinn, I wasn't thinking straight.

Rufus tips his head, listening to Mr. And Mrs. Dawson move around the kitchen. Knowing it's time for breakfast, he lazily pads out of Quinn's room. Suddenly, sweat breaks out along my forehead and my heart starts to race.

Quinn is pregnant.

I'm going to be a father.

And then it hits me all at once, so hard I have to sink down on Quinn's bed behind me. We're not married. We're not even a couple. Quinn made it pretty clear she doesn't want to be with me just because we're having a baby.

But it's not like I can just stop by after work and help her with the baby. And I don't want to not be with my own child. I want to be involved. I want to be there for everything. I want to feel the baby kicking. I want to set up the nursery. Cut the cord. Read to the kid as soon as he or she is born. Hold her. Cuddle her. Help Quinn with everything after birth and not have her worry because I'm there for her and for our baby.

I want us to be a family.

But Quinn is right, and we can't jump into a relationship just because she's pregnant. I've seen that happen with friends and it doesn't always pan out, and the last thing I want is resentment to grow between us.

I need to be practical and stop thinking about myself. Quinn is pregnant and suffering from symptoms already. Is it going to interfere with her work? And when the baby is born?

My head spins. I shift my eyes to the bathroom door. We have nine months to figure it out. Is that enough time to make Quinn fall in love with me? To be with me because it feels as good for her as it does for me?

It's not just us at stake now, and the bottom line is doing what's best for our child. No matter what.

"You're a quiet bunch," Mr. Dawson comments. Quinn, Dean, and I are sitting at the island counter eating breakfast. Quinn is picking at eggs and bacon, and I hope she's able to keep it down. "Suffering from too much fun last night?"

Quinn flicks her eyes to me and picks up a piece of bacon. "Something like that."

"What's the plan today, kids?" Mr. Dawson pours another cup of coffee and sits at the table. "I take it you're joining us for church?"

"Probably not today," Dean mumbles.

"If you want Father Daniels to marry you, you and Kara should start going to church," Mr. Dawson tells Dean, who nods in agreement.

"We'll start going next week."

"You said that over a month ago too."

"Fine. I'll text Kara. But she had friends over last night and is probably hung over." He picks up his phone and sends Kara a text. A few seconds later, he swears.

"I take it Kara's up and ready for church?" I ask with a laugh.

"Yes," he sighs. "I guess I better get ready."

"What about you, sweetheart?" Mr. Dawson asks Quinn.

"Would you be upset if I stayed home? I don't feel all that well and want to go back to bed before hitting the road."

"You don't feel well?"

Quinn presses a smile. "I think stress from work is catching up with me."

Mr. Dawson nods and tells Quinn to rest. He invites me to church as well, but won't pressure me to join. My family's not religious, and the Dawsons have never pressed. Like Quinn, I make up an excuse, and half an hour later, the house is empty.

Quinn went back to her room and closed the door. I pause outside of it and listen, not wanting to wake her up if she really did go back to sleep. Right as I'm about to knock, the door flies open. Quinn jumps back, startled.

"I was just going to find you."

"You found me," I say with a small smile. "We should talk."

"Yeah. We have a lot to talk about."

She's still in her pajamas and her eyes are red as if she's been crying. We move onto her bed.

"You're not going to be alone in this," I tell her, taking her hand in mine. "I want to be there for you. For our baby."

Quinn nods, biting her lip as she tries not to cry. A moment passes before she's able to talk. "I know, and I believe you, Archer. But...how?"

"What do you mean?"

"We're hours apart. You work a lot, and I'm not saying that's a bad thing, but it makes it harder to see each other because of the whole *we live hours apart* thing."

"I know," I say, tightening my hold on her hand. "Trust me, I've thought about it. I'm in the last year of my residency and will be getting a new job soon. There are lots of hospitals around Chicago."

"You'd move to Chicago for me?"

"Yes," I say with no hesitation. "Quinn, I mean it when I say I want to be involved. I've always wanted to get married and have kids. It's happening out of order and sooner than I thought, but this kid is mine too, and I want to be there."

Tears roll down Quinn's cheeks. "Sorry," she says, wiping them away. "I don't usually cry like this."

"It's understandable. Plus, hormones make you emotional."

"That's only one thing they make me." She raises her

eyebrows and smiles. "At least I know why I've had the sex drive of a teenage boy lately. Is that too much information to tell you? Are we past that now?"

"I think so. And if you need help with your overactive sex drive, I'm more than willing to pitch in."

Quinn gives me a half smile. "Thanks. I'm already pregnant so..." Her eyes fall shut and she rests her hand on her stomach. "I'm going to have to tell my family. Eventually."

Tension builds between my shoulders. "I know. We'll tell them together."

"I want to get an ultrasound and stuff first. Just to be extra sure."

She's putting it off, but I'm okay with that. "Good idea."

"I'll call my OB tomorrow. I'm due for an annual anyway."

"I can come with you to your appointments," I say, and Quinn just nods. We both know that's not possible. I can't take an hour off work to meet her at the doctor's office. I'm too far away.

"What do we do now?" she asks, pulling her hand out of mine. She starts to braid her hair.

"I don't know," I admit. "What do you want to do?"

"I don't know either." She leans back on the pillows, dropping her braid over her shoulder. "I'm hungry again. And kind of nauseated at the same time. This is weird."

"Want me to bring you something?"

"I don't know what I want. I'll go look. You can...do whatever you want."

I want to help her. I want to be with her. And I don't know what else to do to make her believe me.

"WELL," QUINN SAYS, SHIFTING HER WEIGHT. SHE HOLDS HER hand up to her face to block the sun and steals a look at the house behind her. It's a little after noon and I need to leave to make it home on time. I'm on call again tonight and need to try and get some sleep just in case I'm called in. "I'll let you know when I get an appointment."

"Okay." I swallow hard, fighting the urge to grab her and kiss her. I want so fucking badly to tell her I love her, that I've loved her for years, and even though having a baby right now wasn't planned, it'll be okay because in the end, we were meant to be together.

But if I say all that now, she'll think I'm only saying it to make her feel better. She'll think I'm making it up or overexaggerating how I feel in an attempt to show her I really do want this baby.

So I'll wait.

We have nine months.

"And if you need anything, call me. I'm here, Quinn. Even when I'm not."

Her eyes well with tears and she shakes her head, annoyed with herself for getting emotional.

"I know," she says softly and puts her hand over her stomach. "It's still weird to think about."

"Yeah, it is." I step closer and put my hand on top of hers. "We're going to be okay. All three of us."

Her lips curve into a small smile. "Better hope it's not four."

I laugh. "Or—nope. Not even going to say it." She flips her hand over and I lace my fingers through hers. We're in the driveway, right outside the garage, and out of direct line of sight from the house. She puts one hand on my shoulder, fingers pressing into my skin. Her jaw is tight, and she looks right into my eyes. I bend my head down to kiss her, and she looks away.

"Archer," she says softly. "You don't have to pretend to want me."

Her words spur something inside of me, and no amount of self-control can hold me back. I pull my hand from hers, move in, and grab her by the waist. Dipping her back, I kiss her as hard as I did the first time.

"I'm not pretending," I growl, saying each word slowly and deliberately. "I don't pretend, Quinn."

She clings to me, eyes wide and lips parted. "Kiss me again."

I hold her tight and push my tongue into her mouth, knowing this is a dangerous line to cross. Once I get started, it's going to be hard to stop.

"Archer," she moans, running her hand over my chest. I gather my strength and stop kissing her. "This is not helping my issue."

"What issue?"

"You know, the one I told you about."

"Oh, right. Sex drive."

"Yeah." She licks her lips and puts her other hand on my hip, slowly looping her fingers around my belt. "I am so horny," she grumbles, looking at me like she wants to devour me. If only she knew how I felt.

"Do you want me to have sex with you?"

"Seriously? Where is the romance?" She shakes her head but hasn't let go of me yet.

"Well, do you?"

"No," she says, pushing away. "I don't." She crosses her arms and looks me up and down. "Wait, yes, I do. No. No, I don't."

I give her a cheeky grin and I'm pretty sure she wants to slap it off my face. And then maybe slap my ass.

"Is that your final answer?"

She bites her lip then lets out a breath. "Maybe."

"Do you need me to remind you how good we are at sex?"

"I remember. That's part of what's making this so hard for me."

"It's hard for me too," I tease, and Quinn's gaze goes right to my cock. I move away from my Jeep and grab Quinn around the middle, picking her up and pinning her between the driver's side door and my body. Her arms fasten around my neck and lust surges through me.

She tips her head up and kisses me first, arching her back and pushing her hips into mine. I take my mouth off hers and kiss her neck, trailing my way down over her collarbone. I slip my hand under her t-shirt.

"I wish you didn't have to leave," she moans.

"I can spare thirty minutes."

"Okay." She takes my hand to lead me back in. "Wait. This is my parents' house."

"Shit. Right. Do you think we can sneak in unnoticed?"

"Have you met the dogs?"

I run my hands down her arms and interlock my fingers with hers. "Are you above having sex in the barn?" Her blank stare tells me she is.

She lets out a ragged breath. "What are we doing, Archer?"

"Acting like horny teenagers. That's how you described your sex drive, isn't it?"

Pursing her lips, she rolls her eyes. "Yes, those were my words. Thank you for reminding me how ridiculous I'm being."

"It's not ridiculous, Quinn," I say softly. "You can't deny we're good in bed together."

"Being good in bed together is the whole problem," she replies, making things tense again. "And we...we have bigger things to worry about." She rests her head against my chest, and being able to hold her and comfort her is almost better than making love to her. Almost.

My heart lurches in my chest, and I hold Quinn tight against me. Of all the things we talked about earlier, all the life-altering changes coming our way, none of it made me as nervous as I feel now. I inhale, ready to just spit it all out and tell her I think we should really give us a shot.

And then the garage door opens, and Quinn and I jump apart. Quinn crosses her arms, angling her body away from mine.

Mrs. Dawson has all four dogs on leashes and struggles to hold them back when they try to go to Quinn. She hurries over, taking Rufus from her mom, saying something to her that I can't hear over the panting of the dogs.

My heart is in my throat. I don't want to leave without giving Quinn a kiss goodbye, but I don't see what other choice I have. Mr. Dawson comes out of the house and takes Rufus from Quinn.

"Drive safe, Archer," he says and heads down the driveway. Mrs. Dawson and the other three dogs follow, leaving Quinn and I alone. I wait until they're down by the street to turn back to Quinn, cocky grin on my face.

"So, you want to have sex now?"

Quinn's nostrils flare and she crosses her arms, eyes drilling into mine. Then she slowly looks me up and down.

"Meet me upstairs."

She doesn't have to tell me twice.

The door shuts behind me and I turn around, prepared to tell Archer this is silly. But the second I see the look in his eyes, all the air is sucked out of my lungs.

"Quinn," he pants, voice heavy with desire. A shiver runs down my spine and his hands land on either side of my waist. "Are you sure you want this?"

Parting my lips, I hook my arms around his neck. "Yes," I breathe, telling the honest truth. I do want Archer, and I'm not just talking about sex.

I want him to be with me during this pregnancy.

I want him there when I give birth.

I want him to raise this child with me.

I want us. Together.

He wastes no time in kissing me, and I slide my hands down his chest, going right to his belt. His hands go around my back and unhooks my bra.

And then the door opens.

"Motherfucker," I blurt as Archer and I untangle. The

dogs run in ahead of my parents, with Rufus at the rear, limping.

"You should really consider going in and having a specialist look at it," Archer says, eyes narrowing. He holds my wrist in his hands, thumb gently circling over my pulse-point. It's too intimate. Too gentle. But for the life of me, I can't pull away from Archer. "You'll need a referral."

"What's going on?" Mom asks. She's not accusatory, not at all. But knowing how close we were to getting caught makes me clam up.

"Quinn's wrist is still hurting," Archer says, looking into my eyes. "But it won't forever. It'll be okay."

"Right," I say, knowing he's not talking about my wrist right now. "It will."

"And call me if it hurts. At any time."

I bite the inside of my cheek. "Okay."

"Even if the pain isn't that bad. You can always call."

His hand slowly trails down my wrist. "Thank you, Archer."

He nods, struggling to hold back his emotion. "You're not alone in this," he says softly, giving my fingers a squeeze. "I'll see you later."

He says goodbye to my parents, and with one lingering look back at me, he leaves.

"Archer is really concerned about your wrist," Mom says, going into the pantry to get a jar of peanut butter. "You are going to take his advice and get it looked at, right?"

Still staring at the door, I move my head up and down. "Right."

I CLOSE MY EYES, HAND ON MY STOMACH, AND LEAN BACK. IT'S

only eleven o'clock on Tuesday and I'm not sure I can make it through the rest of the day. Yesterday was a challenge. The nausea's getting worse every day, the exhaustion is real, and I feel like I'm lying every time I'm around Marissa for not telling her what's going on.

Archer called me Sunday night to make sure I got home okay and to see how I was dealing. I'm not dealing, and I know the danger of it. But right now, I can't.

I just can't.

Having a baby comes with a slew of ramifications, ones I'm not ready to deal with yet. Thinking about them makes me feel even sicker than I do already, and not being with the man who fathered my child is icing on the cake. We're not at odds with each other. It's not like we were a couple and split up. We're just two people who caved into lust. How does custody work in situations like this? And what about insurance? Is Archer going to want this kid to take his last name?

It's too much to think about. So I just won't. Not yet. I don't have to, not right now, anyway. Deep down, I know I do. I have nine months to figure this stuff out. It seems like a long time, but really, it's not.

Archer and I have texted constantly since then, and while he started the conversation yesterday asking me how I'm feeling, we've gone on to talk about other things. I just sent him a note about some office drama, and he sent me a funny meme about cats.

He's easy to talk to, and I don't feel like I have to try to be anything but myself around him. But we're not in a relationship. We hooked up and then he moved on with no interest in staying in touch with me. I'm pregnant with his baby, and he wants to do the right thing because that's the kind of person Archer is.

I can't keep the thoughts out of my mind every time he texts me, and as much as I'd like to blame this on pregnancy hormones, I know I can't. Archer wouldn't be talking to me if I weren't pregnant, and I don't want him to feel trapped into trying to feel something he doesn't. I'd rather raise this baby on my own than have him or her grow up in a family and watch their parents fight and resent each other.

Besides, he's four hours away.

Opening my eyes, I tear open a bag of Sour Patch Kids, which I started craving Sunday night. I grabbed several bags from a corner store late Sunday night, and have been eating them constantly ever since.

The nausea is pretty constant, yet I'm still craving sour candy. Pregnancy is so weird. And this is just the beginning.

Taking advice I read online, I've been trying to nibble on something throughout the day so my stomach doesn't get empty. I seem to feel the sickest when I have an empty stomach. Other than the candy, the only other thing I can handle right now are saltine crackers, and I have a stash in my desk drawer.

I was able to get into the OB last night for a blood test, and they called this morning to confirm I am indeed pregnant. I have an ultrasound scheduled for Friday afternoon, which I'm pretending not to be nervous about, but I know it'll change everything.

I saw not one, but two positive pregnancy tests. The nurse called just hours ago and told me I'm pregnant. I know I'm pregnant. I know my life is fucked in a way I never thought it would be.

But actually seeing the little blob of a baby on the ultrasound will change everything. I can't refuse to deal and do my best to go about work like everything is normal after that.

I have a few days. No need to panic now.

I trade the Sour Patch Kids for water, wondering if this sore throat is from throwing up or is indicative of getting sick. Stressing out for several days usually leads me to getting a cold, and I've definitely been stressed.

"Hey, lady," Marissa says as she steps into my office. "Do you want to go to lunch early today? I'm starving."

Knowing I should eat something more than crackers and Sour Patch Kids at some point today, I close the baby website I was looking at before Marissa has a chance to see. "Sure. Where do you want to go?"

"Wherever has the shortest wait," she says with a smile. "We can try that new Mexican place that opened a few weeks ago. It's supposed to be really good."

"Yeah, sounds good. We can head out now."

"Perfect!"

I push my rolling chair back and stand, getting hit with dizziness. I grab my desk to steady myself, hoping Marissa doesn't notice. She's looking at something on her phone, thankfully. I grab my candy and follow her into the lobby. Rene comes out from behind her desk and almost runs into me.

"Oh, sorry," she says, eyes narrowing ever so slightly. She's mad at me still because she thinks I stole Archer from her and doesn't think I'm good enough to be a 'doctor's wife.' I know this because she writes and sends emails to her sister on the company server.

"It's okay." I smile politely, wondering what kind of things I'll read when word gets out Archer's baby is growing inside of me.

It's hot and humid today, typical for summer by the lake. Marissa and I walk to the restaurant and get seated pretty quickly.

"Want to order a pitcher of margaritas?" Marissa asks, looking over the menu.

Shit.

"Nah, go ahead and get one though."

Marissa puts down the menu. "They have strawberry. I know how much you love those. Oh, and it's half price!"

"I shouldn't drink at work."

Marissa isn't one to pressure me, but she knows it's weird. I don't drink at work when we have functions, but I usually get a drink with lunch. Especially half-priced strawberry margaritas.

She's going to find out soon enough. I might as well tell her now.

"I can't drink."

Marissa gives me a blank stare. "Are you sick?"

"Not exactly."

"Quinn," she begs when I don't say anything more. "What is going on?"

I close my eyes, not wanting to see her face when I say it. "I'm pregnant."

She bursts out laughing. "No fucking way," she says when she sees I'm serious. "Are you sure?"

"I took two tests at home and got a blood test at the OB office yesterday. I'm sure."

"Who is the fath—oh my God. It's Archer, isn't it? He's the only person you've had sex with recently unless you had another dirty weekend with someone else and didn't tell me."

"It is him."

"Oh my God. He's your brother's friend! Are they even on speaking terms?"

"They're great. Nothing's changed. Because we haven't

told him yet. We haven't told anyone yet. You're the first person to know."

"That makes me feel all sorts of special, but what the hell are you going to do?"

I shake my head. "I know I'm having it, I already decided that."

"What about Archer? How's he handling all this?"

"Better than me," I say with a sigh. "He wants to talk about the future and all that responsible stuff."

"And you don't?"

I shake my head. "I know I have to. It's just..." I trail off, becoming emotional. "That tends to happen when I think about it. Sorry."

Marissa reaches out and takes my hand. "Don't be sorry, Quinn. I'd be a blubbering mess if I were in your shoes. Not that what you're going through is bad, because it's, uh, not."

"It's bad."

Marissa squeezes my hand. "Do you think you'll get together with Archer?"

I sigh and lean back, grabbing a chip. "I don't know. I don't want him to be with me just because I'm pregnant."

"Yeah, that doesn't always work out."

I break the chip in half and let out a breath. "It wouldn't feel right. I want whoever I'm with to love me, you know?"

"Oh, totally." Marissa gives me a sympathetic smile. "Whatever you need, Quinn, I'm here. You're my best friend."

"Thanks. Don't tell anyone yet."

"My lips are sealed."

"It feels good saying this out loud. I've known since Sunday morning and haven't told anyone. Well, besides Archer. He was with me when I took the tests. We want to put off telling my family for as long as possible."

"That's going to be one interesting conversation."

"You're not mad I didn't tell you sooner?"

"Not at all. Archer is your brother's best friend," she repeats, not having to explain for me to know what she's thinking. This is going to cause so many problems, not just between Archer and Dean.

Archer's not the only one who crossed a line. I knew exactly what I was doing, and facing my family and telling them the truth is going to be one of the hardest things I'll ever do.

I WAKE UP WEDNESDAY MORNING WITH A HEADACHE. THERE'S no question about it now: I'm sick. All the cold medications in my cabinet say they're not safe if you're pregnant. I take an extra-long shower, trying to clear my head so I can breathe, and feel a little better.

Until I throw up.

Slumping to the bathroom floor, I can't help the tears. I'm alone, scared, and feel like total crap. I want to call my mom and have her comfort me. Neville comes over instead, rubbing his head against me.

"Hey, buddy," I say quietly, stroking his sleek fur. He jumps into my lap, purring, and I close my eyes and lean against the wall. My phone rings and Neville jumps away when I start to get up.

Thinking it might be Mom and she somehow felt through the universe I need her, I apprehensively look at the name on the screen. It was bad enough lying to Marissa for a day. There's no way I can lie to my own mother. But it's not her. I slowly get to my feet and answer the phone.

"Hello," I say to Archer.

"Hey. How are you feeling?"

"I just threw up again."

"I'm so sorry, Quinn," he says, and I can tell he feels it. "There's medication you can take to help with that. I can write a prescription for you."

I pinch the bridge of my nose and close my eyes. "I read some mixed things online about it not being good for the baby."

"It seems at this point you need it. Being dehydrated isn't good for the baby either."

"I don't think I'm dehydrated."

"You said your blood pressure was low. Are you still dizzy?"

"It is low, and yes, I am. The nurse said it was all normal."

Archer isn't convinced. "Can you send me your lab results? Did they check you for dehydration?"

"Archer," I say, not sure if his concern is endearing or annoying. "The nurse said everything came back normal for pregnancy when I talked to her on the phone. Being dizzy and having morning sickness just comes with it."

"But that was a few days ago. Things can change fast. Maybe you should go in again and have more labs drawn."

Yep. His concern is annoying.

"And even if you're not dehydrated, I don't want you to feel sick all the time. It makes it hard to enjoy anything if you're on the verge of throwing up. You're going through enough and I...I want you to be happy, even though I know it's hard right now."

Well, maybe a little endearing.

"I know," I sigh.

"I miss you," he says, and I can't help but wonder if he actually does or if he's saying that to try and make me feel better. He didn't seem to miss me at all until he found out I'm carrying his baby. "I have the weekend off. I can come see you if you want."

"I did enjoy the last time we spent the weekend together. And we never did have that thirty minutes like you promised me."

"If I come up I'll give you more than thirty minutes."

I smile, body reacting to the mere thought of Archer's touch. "Well, if you're promising that, then, by all means, yes, come up here for a booty call."

"I didn't mean it like that," he says sharply, not finding the humor like I thought he would.

"I was just joking. A booty call is probably a bad idea anyway, though it's not like I can get pregnant again." I move into my bedroom, coughing. "Have you talked to Dean lately?"

"We text occasionally. Have you thought more about when you want to tell your family?"

"No. What about your family?" I ask, realizing I haven't brought it up yet. "Do you want to tell your mom?"

"I will after we tell your parents. Mine have enough going on, waiting isn't a bad thing."

I never got the chance to ask Archer what was wrong the other night at dinner either. Finding out I'm pregnant distracted me from pretty much everything, and now I'm feeling selfish for making things all about me.

"Is everything okay?" I ask.

"It tends to end up that way," he replies softly, and the change in the tone of his voice throws me. "It's nothing to worry about."

"Okay," I say, feeling right back at square one with him. I'm never going to crack Archer Jones, and I don't think he wants me to.

22

ARCHER

I missed a call from Quinn today, and I noticed it right before I went into surgery. I've never had a hard time clearing my head before, but today, as I wash my hands and have my surgical scrubs put on, it's all I can think about. She hasn't called me—ever. What if something is wrong? She didn't leave a message, and she didn't text either.

I'm sure everything is fine with her and the baby. It has to be. As awful as I feel to admit it, there's a small part of me that's glad Quinn is pregnant. The timing couldn't be worse. Dean is going to hate us both. He'll forgive Quinn eventually, but the light he holds her in will forever be dimmed.

But now that she's pregnant, we're talking, and we have a chance. And if anyone was to be the mother of my child, no one is better than Quinn.

Sam puts the patient under and we get started. As soon as I make the first cut, I'm back in the game, and the surgical team and I make small talk as we go about treating the patient.

An hour later, I go into the PACU to check on my patient and get stuck talking to his overly-involved mother, who doesn't think I know what I'm talking about in terms of recovery. I've dealt with my fair share of difficult patients before. I know how to handle them and what to say, but today it's testing my patience.

I need to call Quinn back.

Finally, I get into the break room. I lean against the wall by the window and call Quinn. She answers right away and sounds worse than she did yesterday.

"Hey," she says, voice hoarse.

"How are you feeling?" I ask, though I already know the answer. I've called her every day since Sunday when I saw her last, and Monday, Tuesday, and Wednesday have all been the same in terms of morning sickness, and it seems to be getting worse and worse as the days go on. And now she has a nasty cold that went from bad to worse overnight.

"I'm pretty congested. I actually went home from work. I just got in. But I'm fine," she adds quickly, like she always does. She doesn't want sympathy and is one of the toughest people I know. She's going through this all alone, and I hate it.

I should be there with her. When she's throwing up, I should be holding her hair, rubbing her back, and bringing her water and a cloth to wipe her face. It kills me to be hours away, unable to go to her, showing up within a moment's notice to bring her whatever she's craving.

"Rest should help. That cough doesn't sound too good though."

"I'll be fine. I get colds like this every now and then. How are you?"

"I'm good. Just got out of surgery. I miss you, Quinn," I tell her, heart aching. I miss her so much it hurts, but I don't know how to make her believe me. I fucked up, and I know it. I should have called her after I left all those weeks ago. I should have manned up and told her how I really felt.

It might not have changed this situation, but at least she'd know I saw her—that I still see her—as more than a booty call. She wasn't a convenient piece of ass for me just because I was in Chicago. Sleeping with Quinn meant more to me than she'll ever know.

But I can't tell her now. She won't believe me. She already thinks I'm only talking to her because she's pregnant.

"If I'm sick, will they still do the ultrasound?" she asks.

"Yeah, though coughing might make things a little painful."

"Really? Don't they just put that thing on my belly?"

I push off the wall and go to the coffee pot to pour myself another cup. "They will, but they also do an internal one this early."

"Internal?" She pauses for a second. "Oh, right. Some girls at the office talked about it before. They called it a *dildo cam*. Now I get it."

I laugh. "That's pretty much what it is. I was able to get tomorrow off."

"Really? So you can be there with me?" I can tell she's smiling when she's talking. She starts to say something else but cuts off, coughing. "Ugh, I feel like shit. Can I call you back later?"

"Of course. You need rest. Have you taken anything for the cold?"

"Everything I have in my medicine cabinet says it's not safe to take during pregnancy. I'll go out later."

My stomach starts to knot. She's sick. Pregnant. I want to

be the one to bring her medication. "Do you have a humidifier? That'll help with the congestion."

"No. I'll get one too." She starts coughing again, and it's the kind of cough I hear when patients have bronchitis or pneumonia. "I'm going to take a nap first. I feel like I was hit by a truck. Sorry for complaining."

"You're not complaining, Quinn."

"I am, and it annoys me when people complain, so I'm sorry."

I set my jaw, looking at the clock. Technically, I'm done with my scheduled surgeries for the day. It'll be asking for a miracle, but for Quinn, I'll make it happen.

I STAND OUTSIDE QUINN'S DOOR, BAG IN MY HAND, AND PULL out my phone. I'm lucky I didn't get pulled over for speeding on the way here, and it had to be divine intervention for the lack of traffic.

Quinn's phone rings once. Twice. Three times. I don't think she's going to answer. That's okay. I'll wait. I waited to get into the building, sneaking in behind someone like a creep. But I wanted to surprise Quinn.

"Hello?" she answers, sounding like she just woke up.

"Hey, are you home?"

"Yeah," she says, and she sounds sicker than before. "I'm trying to muster up the energy to go out and get medicine. I feel worse now."

"You don't have to go out. Just open your door."

"What are you talking about?"

I knock on the door and wait. A few seconds later, Quinn opens the door, phone still pressed to her ear. She looks at me in shock. And then she starts crying.

"Quinn," I say, putting the bag and my phone down. I step in, taking her in my arms. "Sorry. I thought surprising you was a good idea."

"It is. It's a really good idea," she sniffles, then turns her head to cough. "I don't know why I'm crying."

Chuckling, I wrap Quinn in a tighter hug and kiss the top of her head. The moment I felt her against me, everything clicked into place. This is where I'm supposed to be.

With Quinn.

Pregnant or not, she's the only one for me. I've known it for years. Fought it as hard as I could. There was never any point because everything always went back to her.

We move inside, and I get out the medicine I brought for Quinn. "This is all safe for pregnancy," I tell her. "I don't know how much it'll help, but it's better than nothing."

Quinn sits on the couch, pulling a blanket around her shoulders. She looks sick, with bags under her eyes and pale skin.

"I can't believe you came. How did you get off work?"

"I was able to switch on-call days with another surgical resident. I'm working Sunday instead."

"You gave up your weekend for me?"

"I'd give up a lot more than that for you, Quinn." I go to her, wrap her in my arms again, and lay down on the couch. Quinn coughs, turning her head away from me, and then lays down. I rub her back and cover her back up with the blanket.

"This is nice," she mumbles, eyes closed.

"It is." This is how it should be. Every day. "Are you tired?"

"Yeah. I tried to take a nap but didn't sleep very long. It's hard to sleep when I'm all stuffy like this."

"Take a hot shower to break up some of the congestion. I'll set up the humidifier in your room and will rub your back until you fall asleep."

Quinn looks at me, eyes full of emotion. She's glad I'm here, but she's also confused. I know it's my fault. I promise myself right then and there that I'm going to fix it. I sit up with her in my arms, and stand, helping her to her feet. Quinn grabs a tissue and blows her nose.

"Sorry. It's gross, I know."

"I spent an hour in surgery this morning draining abscesses and it was oddly satisfying," I tell her. "So blowing your nose doesn't gross me out in the least."

"Good." She gives me a small smile. "Thank you, Archer." She grabs another tissue and goes into the bathroom.

The cats follow me around when I go into the kitchen. There are a few dirty dishes in the sink, so I rinse them and put them in the dishwasher. I fill a glass with water and take it along with the medicine into Quinn's room, setting it on the nightstand. I bring a chair in from the dining table and put the humidifier on it next to Quinn's bed.

I sit on the edge of the bed, petting Neville until Quinn comes out of the shower. Her hair is twisted in a messy bun on the top of her head, and she's wearing a loose-fitting t-shirt that barely covers her ass. She's not wearing pants, and her pink and black panties show when she walks.

I swallow hard, looking her over. She's so fucking gorgeous, even when she's sick. She comes to the bed, sitting heavily, and lays back.

"Is this okay?" she asks, reaching for the blanket.

"What do you mean?" I pull the blankets over both of us.

"Wearing this. I mean...you've seen me naked before. I've seen you naked. But we're not...we're not dating," she says, almost wincing at the words. "And I wasn't sure if I should put on pants or not. I either just wear underwear or shorts to bed."

"Oh, right. I, uh, don't know. I'm fine with it as long as you're comfortable."

She rolls over, facing the humidifier. "I'm comfortable. Around you, I mean."

I lay down next to her, spooning my body next to hers, and put my hand over her abdomen. Quinn's hand lands on top of mine, and she lets out a deep breath.

"Archer?" she says softly.

"Yeah?"

"I'm glad you're here."

I kiss the back of her neck. "Me too."

———

WAKING UP WITH QUINN IN MY ARMS IS THE BEST FEELING IN the world. The sun is setting, and we've both been asleep for hours. Quinn is still asleep, snoring slightly through her stuffy nose. I brush loose strands of her hair back from her face and kiss her softly.

Slowly, I get up and use the bathroom, then climb back into bed with Quinn. In her sleep, she rolls over and wraps her arm around me. I hold her close, never wanting to let go.

Then she starts coughing, waking herself up. Groaning, she sits up and reaches for the glass of water, but hesitates. I smile, remembering her saying she won't drink out of a glass that's been sitting unattended.

"I'll get you a fresh glass," I offer and get out of bed. I go into the kitchen, Neville winding around my feet the whole way, and get a clean glass from the cabinet.

"Thanks," Quinn says when I get back, taking the water from me.

"How are you feeling?"

"I think a little better. I don't have a headache anymore."

"That's good. Are you hungry?"

"Kind of. I don't really have an appetite. Though I do want Sour Patch Kids." She sets the glass down and lays back in my arms. I kiss her neck and pull her onto my chest.

"I like this," she says softly, blushing as if I'm going to think it's stupid.

"I do too, Quinn." Taking a breath, I look into her eyes. "I like being with you, and I'm not saying that because you're pregnant," I add. "I should have called you. You have no idea how much I regret not calling you."

Her brows pinch together, and she nods and splays her fingers over my chest. "I wished you called. I got mad at you when you didn't."

"I noticed," I say with a smile, thinking back to seeing her walk into her parents' house over the past weekend.

"And I feel like I should still be mad at you, but there's so much else going on I don't have the energy to."

"I guess that's good for me? If you want to be mad, I can't blame you. But if you want to give this a shot—give us a shot—it'd make me really happy."

She sits up, looking into my eyes. "You mean like be a couple?"

"Yes."

Quinn bites her lip, considering my words. "Are you sure you want to date me?"

"Hmmm...let me think about it. Okay, thought about it. Yes."

Quinn smiles. "I feel like you're only getting half of me

though and it won't be a fair representation of who I really am."

"What are you talking about?" I run my hand up the back of her thigh.

"I can be really annoying when I'm drunk. And I can't drink."

My fingers edge along the hem of her panties. "I don't think that will be a determining factor. At all. You don't drink very often, right?"

"No."

"See? Not a problem at all."

She smiles. "I don't want you to feel like you have to be with me because I'm pregnant."

"I don't at all. I know I left and didn't call and that doesn't help my case, but I promise you, Quinn, I wouldn't have slept with you the first time if I didn't like you." I swallow hard, heart beating fast. "I kind of panicked after."

"Really?" Quinn lifts her head up, looking at me incredulously.

"Really. Dean's been my best friend for over a decade. Your family is like my family, and I knew the mess it would make if they found out about us."

Quinn lets out a strangled snort of laughter. "Oh, it's going to be very messy. Dean's not going to be happy to hear that we're dating, let alone that you knocked me up."

"I know." I slide my hand over her ass and close my eyes. "But it's worth it, Quinn. You're worth it. I mean, we have a lot at stake now."

"Yeah, we do."

"I want to raise this child together." *Because I love you.*

"Me too." She rests her head back on my chest. "You said you work next weekend, right?"

"Yeah, why?"

"We need to tell my family."

The thought makes my stomach knot up. "Yeah. We do."

"Maybe we can take it in stages. Tell them we're dating first, then drop the baby-bomb."

"Good idea." I squeeze Quinn's ass again. She's finally my girlfriend, and though it didn't happen the way I thought, I have a good feeling about us. "I work Saturday and Sunday, but I'm off Thursday evening and all of Friday."

"I can leave early Thursday and take Friday off."

"So, dinner at your parents' Thursday night?"

Quinn lifts her head, looking into my eyes. "Yeah. We'll tell everyone in a week."

23

QUINN

I wake up in Archer's arms, and for the first time since I found out I'm pregnant, everything feels like it's going to be okay. He made me dinner last night, and went out and got me more Sour Patch Kids before we went to sleep.

I carefully roll over, moving closer to him. It feels so good to have him next to me. Physically, his presence is comforting on its own. But having him here for everything else is almost enough to do me in.

We jumped into a relationship and need to take things slow. He said he likes me but held off moving forward out of respect to Dean, but things are bigger than their friendship now. We have less than a week before we drop the bomb on my family, and I'm fairly sure all four of my brothers are going to have a few choice words for Archer.

Early morning sun filters through the large windows. I forgot to close the blinds last night, and the light is shining right in on Archer. I reach over and take my phone from the nightstand. My blinds are powered, and I can open and close them with an app on my phone.

The room darkens, and I lay back down next to Archer. Two of the cats are in bed with us, and it might be silly to take it as a sign, but I do: the cats like Archer. I'm completely aware of how much I'm becoming a crazy cat lady, but hey, at least I'm not currently single. That has to count for something, right?

"Quinn?" Archer asks softly some time later. I hadn't quite fallen back asleep on account of an overactive mind. All those things I didn't want to think about kept popping into my brain. "Are you awake?"

I tighten my arm around him and tip my head up. "Yeah."

He smiles and kisses my forehead. "I like waking up next to you."

"I like it too. But you, not me. Because saying I like it too means I like waking up next to myself, right?"

He laughs softly. "Sure. Are you hungry? I'll make breakfast. Just tell me what you want."

I wrinkle my nose. "Breakfast and I don't really get along too well at the moment."

"Oh, right."

"But a smoothie sounds good, and easy to digest."

"I can go get you one." He smooths my hair back. Neither of us makes a move to get up. Lounging around in bed with Archer—who's now my boyfriend—feels so damn good.

"There's stuff in the freezer for it. I used to make smoothies every morning in an attempt to eat healthy. We have donuts and coffee cake at work all the time, and bringing a smoothie with me helped me resist the temptation."

"I think I went into the wrong line of work," Archer jokes. "You have parties and donuts at your office."

"The first Monday of every month we have massages too."

"Yep. Definitely the wrong line."

I GRIP ARCHER'S HAND AND EXHALE SLOWLY, EYES ON THE large TV screen mounted on the wall in front of us. The room is cold, and I'm blaming that on why I'm trembling. But really, I'm nervous as fuck.

"Try and relax," the ultrasound tech tells me. Archer gives my hand a reassuring squeeze. I tear my eyes away from the screen to look at his face, needing to see into his deep, brown eyes for a second.

Because this is it.

The moment I know will change everything.

"All right, Mom and Dad," the tech says with a smile on her face. "There's your baby."

Archer and I both look at the screen, watching a little white blob come in and out of focus. Something flickers inside of it, and I don't have to be told to know what it is.

It's the heart.

Tears well in the corners of my eyes, and I tighten my hold on Archer's hand. The tech takes a few pictures and then switches something over so we can hear. I turn my head, looking at Archer as the sound of our baby's heartbeat fills the room. He's smiling, looking at the screen with emotion in his eyes.

And now I'm a goner.

The tears roll down my cheeks, but I don't try to stop them. Everything hits me all at once, and my mind races from *I'm going to have a baby* to *that's my baby's heart beating* and I'm scared and panicked while at the same time maternal instincts are kicking in and I'm feeling incredibly protective of that little flickering heartbeat.

After the ultrasound, we meet with my OB. I think I'm in a state of shock, not really absorbing any of the information the doctor gives me. Thank goodness Archer is there and in doctor-mode himself. Everything looks good with the baby, and we're given the official due date of March eighteenth, one day after Archer's birthday. I get a prescription for anti-nausea medication and leave with a spinning head.

"Quinn?" Archer says carefully when we get into the elevator to go back down to the main floor of the building. "Are you okay?"

I swallow hard, hearing the baby's heartbeat echo over and over again in my head. Archer recorded a clip on his phone and sent it to me, so I have it to reference later, though I don't think I'll need to.

"My mom keeps talking about how excited she is to someday plan my wedding." My jaw starts to tremble and I lose my resolve. Archer takes me in his arms, cradling me against his chest. I press my face into his shirt, not wanting anyone to see me cry. We're alone in the elevator for now, but that'll change soon, I'm sure.

I don't expect Archer to understand my train of thought. Hell, I hardly understand it. But he does.

"I know things didn't happen the way you thought it would, and I'm sure your parents will be upset. But it's only because they love you, and because they love you, they'll come around. Dean too. All your brothers will be there for you, and eventually your mom is going to be pretty damn excited to get another grandchild. Hell, I bet even Jackson will be happy to have a cousin."

I pull a tissue from my purse and mop up my face before

blowing my nose again. Stifling a cough, I turn my face up to Archer's. "Yeah, I guess you're right."

"And as for your wedding..." He trails off, hand going to the back of his neck. If he were to suggest to me right now that we get married, I'm telling him no. Though for the last ten years I've been convinced there is no one more perfect in this world than Archer, I can't do that to him. I want him to marry someone he's head over heels in love with, not the girl who got knocked up during an attempted one-night stand. Yeah, he likes me. But liking someone isn't enough to get married.

"You'll still plan it. And it will be perfect. Maybe having your kid there will make it more special. They can, uh, bring the ring down the aisle or something."

"Or be a flower girl," I say quietly. I close my eyes, trying to imagine it, and I can't. I can always see things panning out, and that vision drives me.

I saw myself getting into MIT. And I did.

I envisioned working at one of the best new software companies in the country. And I do.

Living alone in the city? Yeah, I could see myself doing that before I even took the job.

But having a baby? I can't picture it. At all. I can hardly even see myself with a big belly. I'd give anything for a cheat code to get around this mental blockage in my head. I have to play the game to get to the end, but if I could at least see how it works out, I'll be fine.

Not knowing is killing me.

"Breathe, Quinn," Archer says, hands landing on my shoulders. I let out a breath, just now becoming aware that I'm hyperventilating. "It'll be okay."

"You keep saying that, but how? How is it going to be okay?"

"I don't know. But I do know I want it to be okay, so I'll find a way." He moves his hands to my face and looks me in the eye. "We'll figure it out, Quinn. I promise."

The elevator dings and the doors open. Archer keeps a steady hold on my hand as we get out, walking through the lobby and stepping out into the summer sun. We grab lunch to bring back to my apartment and sit on the couch once we're done.

I'm coughing again and feeling run down, and cuddling up with Archer is exactly what I need. We put on a movie and even though there are a million and one thoughts running through my brain, I doze off and fall asleep before the movie ends.

———

TWO AND A HALF HOURS LATER, I WAKE UP, NEEDING TO PEE. Archer is asleep, and I slip off the couch without waking him up. The ultrasound photos are on the coffee table, and I pick them up when I get back into the living room, staring at them as I go into the kitchen to get more candy.

"You're going to be a big sister," I tell Lily, the biggest of all my cats. And by biggest, I mean fattest. She's been on a diet for over a year and hasn't lost a single pound. "He or she won't be here for a while, but I thought I'd let ya know." Lily lets me pet her for a minute before walking away.

I take my candy back to the living room, sitting on the edge of the couch by Archer's feet. After a few minutes of me searching through Netflix for something to watch, Archer wakes up, smiling as soon as he sees me.

He runs a hand through his hair, and that messy-sexy look is doing bad things to me. We never did get our thirty minutes like he promised.

"How are you feeling?" he asks right away.

"Better. Taking a nap helped."

"Yeah. You needed it."

"You did too."

He chuckles. "I haven't been this well-rested in a while. I forgot what it feels like to not be dead tired." He sits up, stretches, and swings his legs over the edge of the couch. "If you're not feeling up to it, then please tell me. But if you are, I'd like to take you out on a date."

I smile. "I am feeling up to it. Can I have like an hour to get ready? I want to pull out all the stops tonight and look good for you."

"You don't have to do anything to look good. But sure, you can have as much time as you want."

He pulls me in for a kiss before I get up and go into my bathroom. I gather my hair up into a bun and get in the shower to shave myself smooth. Archer *is* my boyfriend now. We're going on a date. Even though I wanted to take things slow, I'm okay with sleeping together tonight. Because I am so fucking horny.

"Thanks, baby," I mumble, looking down at my stomach. I move quickly, curling my hair once I'm out of the shower. I put on my usual makeup, but go for my best pushup bra that makes my already large boobs look ridiculous.

I pull a black dress on top of that, finger comb out my curls to relax them more into loose waves, and finish off with a few pumps of perfume. The smell instantly makes me gag, dammit. I scrub as much of it as I can off my skin, grab my heels, and meet Archer in the living room.

He also changed and looks incredible in dark jeans and a blue button-up shirt. Turning around when he hears me come into the room, Archer's eyes widen when he sees me.

"You look beautiful."

My lips curve into a smile. "You don't look so bad yourself."

He takes me by the waist, pulls me in, and kisses me. I melt at his touch, heat growing between my legs as his tongue slips into my mouth. It's tempting to suggest staying in instead of going out. Something tells me Archer won't object.

"Where did you want to go?" I ask, stopping for air.

Archer seems to have as hard of a time moving away from me as I do from him. "What about Navy Pier? I've never been."

"You'll love it."

"Good." He takes my hand and heads toward the door. "I want to make sure our second date is as memorable as our first."

I keep the smile on my face, not letting Archer know my confidence is wavering. Not specifically in him, but in this whole situation. If our second date isn't anywhere near as good as the first, we can forget about a third.

Normally, it wouldn't be a big deal. But I don't normally go on a second date with a guy who already knocked me up.

24

ARCHER

Panting, I roll to the side, flopping down onto the mattress. My heart is still racing, and sweat covers my brow. Quinn is breathing just as hard, and her bare breasts rise and fall as she gulps in air.

I didn't think it was possible to have better sex that we did the first time, but I feel confident to say we just topped it. Reaching for the water bottle on the nightstand, I take a drink and grab the sheet, pulling it up over us. We're both hot and sweaty now, but with the ceiling fan going on high, we'll cool off fast and I don't want Quinn to get a chill. She's still fighting a cold and has to be worn out after the marathon sex we just had.

I know I am.

"That was more than thirty minutes," she says once she catches her breath and moves onto her side. I wrap her in my arms.

"I'm not sorry about that."

"You've set a high standard for yourself," she says with a coy smile.

"I always aim to please, babe."

Quinn laughs and runs her fingers through my hair. "You did. Multiple times."

"Once is never enough. You're so fucking sexy when you come."

She smiles, and a little dimple forms on her cheek. I didn't know it was possible for someone to be as hot and sexy as she is while at the same time being fucking adorable. They're opposite qualities and yet Quinn exhibits them both at the same time.

"And you're sexy when you make me come."

I kiss the side of her neck and feel my heart start to slow. We got dinner from a food truck, and Quinn introduced me to a Chicago-style hot dog. We sat along the lake as we ate, talking and laughing, and finished the date with a ride on the Ferris wheel at Navy Pier.

Everything was perfect.

"I don't want you to go," Quinn says softly.

"I don't want to go either."

"I've never been in a long-distance relationship before," she tells me, tracing a line of muscle on my chest with her fingertips.

"I haven't either. And I feel like I should tell you I've only had one long-term relationship before."

"Really?" She doesn't try to hide her shock. "Why? I mean, don't get me wrong, I'm glad it's my bed you're in right now, but you're a total catch, Dr. Jones."

"I never found that right person, I guess," I say, holding back the words that want to come up. She wants to take things slow. Telling her I've never been able to date anyone because I've been in love with her is the opposite of slow, right?

I'm not good with this stuff.

"And I guess I could say the same."

I push myself up on my elbow, tucking her hair behind her ear. This is my in, the perfect timing to tell her the fate of the universe was holding out on us all this time because together is where we're meant to be.

But then her phone rings and Quinn's face pales when she sees the name on the caller ID.

"Dean," we both say together, feeling like we got caught red-handed.

"He never calls me," she mumbles, sitting up. The blankets fall off her breasts, and even though I was up close and personal with every inch of her mere minutes ago, the sight of her naked causes my dick to jump and my heart to race. "I'm not going to answer."

"See what he wants," I rush out, conflicted myself about not answering and being curious about what he has to say. "He's not going to yell at you, Quinn. Not yet at least."

She makes a face and answers the phone. "Hello?" She pauses. "Oh, hey, Kara. Really? That's exciting. Yeah, my work email is fine. It's the one I check most often anyway. Next weekend?" She looks at me, nodding along to whatever Kara is saying. "I was thinking of coming into town anyway. Would Thursday night work instead? I'll be in Thursday night and Friday morning instead this time." Another long pause. "Great, see you then."

Quinn hangs up and tosses the phone on the bed. She falls back onto the pillows and reaches for me.

"What was that about?"

"Kara said she wants to look at bridesmaid dresses and was wondering if I'm coming into town next weekend. At least we have a cover."

I pull her into an embrace, resting my hand on top of her slender abdomen. She told me she thinks she's started to look bloated, but I can't tell the difference yet. I close my eyes, hearing our baby's strong heartbeat echo in my head.

"It's going to be okay," I promise. "We'll get through it together."

"DUDE. WHAT THE HELL IS WRONG WITH YOU?" SAM TURNS away from the TV, eyeing me as he waits for an answer. It's Thursday afternoon, and I'm packed and ready to drive north to Eastwood. I promised Quinn everything would be okay, and I really believe it will, but damn I'm starting to get nervous.

"What are you talking about?"

"Don't bullshit me. You know what I'm talking about. You disappeared for a few days last week and you're going away again. Not that I care, and I only hope you're getting laid, but this isn't you, man."

I look at Sam, let out a breath, and lean against the wall. Sam and I got paired together during surgery enough back when we were new residents to become friends. We roomed together more out of convenience since neither of us planned to stay here long-term and we both wanted to pay off our student loans as fast as possible, but we've become good friends over the years and knowing we have to part ways soon sucks.

"You know how you told me to fuck Quinn out of my system?"

"Are you finally taking my advice?"

I shake my head. "I already did."

"No shit! When?"

"Remember that conference I went to? It was in Chicago. Quinn lives in Chicago."

"Right, you mentioned that. But that was weeks ago. Don't tell me my method didn't work. It's foolproof."

"I'm not even going to get into that right now."

"I was right, wasn't I?" he goes on. "You found out she was a dirty whore or something. I told you, you had her on a pedestal."

Sam is, well, Sam, and he's always crude. He plays the hot-shot doctor more often than he doesn't, and thinking of Quinn hiding a giggle when she meets him and flashing me a telling look helps to calm me down.

"Don't talk about her like that," I snap.

"Then what the hell is wrong?"

"She's pregnant."

Sam stares at me for a good ten seconds. "And you're the..."

"Yep."

Sam blinks, leaning back on the couch. "Fuck. Did she just tell you?"

I shake my head. "I've known for a while."

"So those trips you took 'for interviews' were bullshit."

"The last one was. I've been seeing her. We're together now and are telling her family tonight."

"Isn't her brother your friend?"

"Yeah."

Sam laughs. "Good luck."

"Fuck you."

He grabs his beer from the coffee table. "When you've been beat to shit and go in for surgery, ask for me."

"You think you're so fucking funny."

"I know I am." He takes a long swig of beer. "Fuck. Just— fuck. She's keeping it?"

"Yeah. We both want it. Her brothers, and her dad, and

probably her mom, are going to hate me, but yeah, I definitely want it. And I want her."

Sam looks away from the TV, turning around to face me. "You really love this chick, don't you?"

"I have for years," I admit out loud for the first time.

"Then go get her. Start your family."

———

THERE ARE ONLY TWO PLACES TO STAY WHEN VISITING Eastwood if you don't have a friend or family member to crash with. One is the Whippoorwill Bed and Breakfast, and the nicer of the two options. It's where I stayed weeks ago, the first time I came back to Eastwood in years. And it might be where I'm staying tonight, based on how the situation goes when Quinn and I break the news to her parents.

Currently, I'm parked on the street downtown, waiting for Quinn. No one knows I'm coming into town with her, and she thought it was best to arrive together. She's getting panicked about this, and as much as I'm trying to tell her—and myself—that it's really not that big of a deal, her anxiety is getting to me.

Not because I'm worried what will happen to my friendship with Dean. I already know he's not going to react well. It'll hurt to lose him. Hell, it'll hurt to lose Owen and Logan, but it's not me I'm worried about.

I can handle it.

But Quinn...it'll kill her to have her family upset at her. And she really needs them right now. Quinn is a family-oriented person, and even though she hasn't said anything to me, I know how upset she is to not be going through this pregnancy with her mother.

I look up, feeling Quinn's presence before I see her. She

parks across the street, smiling when she sees me. I grab my bag and get out of the car.

"Hey," I say as I slide into the passenger seat, leaning in to kiss her. A quick peck turns into something more, and I can't pull away. Blood rushes to my cock, and the pain of being separated from Quinn for days rushes back. Long-distance relationships suck ass.

"You know," she says, unbuckling so she can turn in and kiss me back. "There's a cornfield on the way to my parents' house that's a notorious make-out spot."

"I want to fuck you, Quinn," I growl and kiss her hard. Quinn lets out a moan and reaches over the center console, slipping her hand between my thighs.

"On second thought, I think we should both stay at the bed and breakfast tonight."

"I said I want to fuck you, and I plan on it no matter where we are."

Quinn cups my balls through my pants and bites her lip. "I enjoyed phone sex this week, but it's not as good as the real thing."

"Not at all. Though those pictures you sent...you are so hot, Quinn."

"I like when you say my name, Archer Jones." She grabs the hem of my shirt and pulls it up.

"As much as I hate saying this, we need to stop." I take Quinn's hand. "Or Weston will get a call that his sister is being arrested for indecent exposure."

Quinn blushes. "Sorry. I got carried away."

"Don't apologize."

She pulls her seatbelt back across her body and gets her phone from her purse. "Owen and Logan just got to my parents'. Ready?"

I reach over and take Quinn's hand. "Let's go."

Quinn puts her Porsche in drive and fiddles with the radio the entire way to her parents' house. We park behind Weston's squad car, and I take Quinn's hand and we walk inside together.

The dogs come running, and the smell of chicken enchiladas fills the air. Laughter echoes through the house, and that instant feel-good aura the Dawson farm holds sets in. This place is safe and warm. It's welcoming and full of comfort. It was my reprieve in college when Bobby was at the height of his addiction.

"Quinn!" Kara says, looking up from the wine she's trying to open. "And Archer?"

"Hey, Kara," I say. Quinn pets each dog and goes over to give Kara a hug. She pulls a bottle of wine from her large purse.

"Oh!" Kara squeals. "That's the good stuff!"

"Yeah, from that little winery in Chicago you all love."

"Let's crack it open."

I crouch down and pet Rufus, noticing more and more gray fur around his eyes. He leans into me, turning his head up so I can scratch under his chin. Kara grabs two wine glasses, and Quinn fills them both up. Kara takes one, and Quinn takes the other. I look at the wine and then at Quinn.

"You can't drink," I whisper.

She rolls her eyes at me. "Should have told me that sooner, doctor. I've been boozing it up every night." She waits a beat for Kara to step farther ahead. "It's for my mom. I figure liquoring her up won't hurt."

Now that I'm here, I'm no longer nervous. The timing isn't right, and we might have started things a little backward, but it'll work out in the end.

I know it will.

"There you are!" Mrs. Dawson says, smiling when she

sees Quinn. And then her eyes go to me, brows furrowing for just a split second. She's surprised to see me, but not in a bad way. "Archer!" She gets up, giving Quinn a quick hug and coming over to me. "What are you doing here? Does this mean you took the job at our county hospital?"

"Not quite," I say, though I did get invited back for a second interview.

"Here, Mom." Quinn shoves the glass of wine into her mom's hand. "It's from that place in Chicago you like."

Mrs. Dawson takes a sip. "I do like this. Thanks, Quinn. Go ahead and sit, kids. I'll grab another place setting for Archer."

"Finally," Owen grumbles to Quinn. "Mom's been making us wait for you."

Quinn raises her eyebrows. "You've only been here for like ten minutes, and your beer is still full. You guys just sat down."

"You're too damn smart," Owen says with a smile.

"Language," Mr. Dawson reminds him, looking at Jackson. "Little ears are at the table tonight."

Quinn goes around to Jackson, picking him up and giving him a big hug. I don't mean to smile as I watch her, thinking how she'll get to do the same with our kid.

"Hey, man," Dean says. "Didn't know you were coming. Are you taking that job?"

Quinn looks over the table at me. She knows about the second interview, but the last time we talked, we both agreed it wasn't for me. Though seeing her with Jackson, surrounded by her family is making me reconsider.

"It hasn't been offered yet, but I don't know."

"It's a small hospital," Quinn says, setting Jackson down. "And you want to get into a trauma fellowship."

"More school?" Logan asks, eyebrows raised. "You like torture, don't you?"

"I guess I do."

Quinn comes back around the table, taking a seat next to me. Weston eyes Quinn and then me several times, and I pretend like I don't notice. Mrs. Dawson sets a placemat, a plate, a full glass of ice water, and silverware down in front of me. Quinn scoots her chair a little closer to mine, and I slip my hand into hers and give it a squeeze. Meals at the Dawsons' are always served family-style, and we all fill our plates. Quinn pushes her food around, not eating. She's still dealing with constant nausea, and the nerves aren't helping.

"Well, since you're all here," Kara starts, a big smile breaking out over her face. She turns to Dean, smile growing even more. "We picked a date for the wedding!"

Mrs. Dawson cheers and Quinn looks relieved she has some time. "When?"

"March sixteenth. I know it's a little soon, but it falls on my spring break and the arboretum just happened to have a cancelation. I got on the wait list the day after Dean proposed and when they called to see if I wanted the date, I knew it was fate!"

Quinn turns her head down, eyes wide. March sixteenth is two days before our baby's due date.

25

QUINN

I need a drink. A big one. With lots and lots of alcohol. I close my eyes in a long blink, praying I misheard Kara.

"That's less than a year away!" Mom exclaims. "Do you think you can get everything ready in time?"

March isn't that far away, she's right. And there is a lot to do before then, and I'm not thinking about the wedding.

"I think we can swing it," Kara says. "I'll have to get right to work, I know, and my mom's already on it." She looks back at Dean, smiling. "We don't want anything fancy, anyway."

I bring my hand to my head, subconsciously rubbing the space between my jaw and my ear. It's been hurting off and on since last weekend, and I knew I should have listened to Archer about a sinus infection lingering for longer than normal now that I'm pregnant.

"Are you okay, hun?" Mom asks, and I flick my eyes up to her.

"Oh, yeah. I think I have an ear infection, that's all," I blurt. I should have made something up, but I've never been a good liar and not telling the truth is as bad as lying in Mom's book.

"I thought you said you were feeling better," Archer says, turning to me.

"I was," I say guiltily. "But I got busy with work and started feeling crappy again. You were right about the cold turning into something more."

"Wait a minute," Weston says, eyes narrowing. It clicks in my mind right before he says it. "Why does Archer know you were sick?"

Dean stares at me before shifting his gaze to Archer. "Is he your doctor or something now?"

Shit. Shit. Shit. This isn't how it was supposed to go. Damn you, Archer. Stop being so genuinely concerned for me, why don't ya?

I inhale, look at Archer, and give him a tiny nod. "No, he's not my doctor now. He's my boyfriend."

Dean lets out a snort. "Funny."

Archer puts his arm around me, and I lean in, needing his support. "Quinn and I are dating," he says, voice steady. "That's why I came to dinner tonight. We wanted to tell you."

Silence falls over the table. No one talks. No one breathes. And then Dean's fist comes down on the table.

"You're dating my sister?"

"Dean," Mom scolds, sticking to her *don't raise your voice at the dinner table* rules.

"My sister?" Dean repeats, looking at Logan, Owen, and Weston. He expects them to be outraged like he is. Weston gives me a guilty look, feeling bad for outing us. Logan's expression is unreadable, and Owen, that asshole, is amused.

"What the hell, man?" Dean waves his hand out in front

of him. "Did you even think to stop and ask my permission before you made a move on her?"

"Permission?" I echo. "Seriously, Dean? Like I need your approval before I date someone. Like I need any of your approval."

Wrong choice of words. Everyone starts talking at once. Jackson gets up from the table, running into the kitchen while no one is looking.

"You don't own me," I retort, narrowing my eyes at my brother. "Or Archer. We can see whoever we want and we want to see each other."

"But he's my best friend," Dean says, turning from the table.

"So now you're mad at me?" My voice gets higher pitched than I'd like. "Oh, I'm sorry I didn't ask for your permission to date Archer. I forgot he belongs to you and you alone."

"Dean," Archer starts, and Jackson runs back into the dining room, holding a bag of Sour Patch Kids he took from my purse.

"Can I have these, Aunt Winnie?"

"Sure, if your daddy says it's okay."

Jackson jumps up and down and toddles over to Weston, asking him if he can have the candy.

"Enough," Dad says, voice booming over everyone. "You both have valid points."

"Really, Dad?" I throw up my hands. "Oh, I'm sorry. I forgot we went back fifty years and I needed approval from the men of the house before I can date someone. Why don't you arrange my marriage and line up a dowry too?"

"Quinn, you're overreacting," Mom says softly. I have a tendency to do that, and it never went unmentioned growing up. "Calm down, everyone. This is a sensitive subject, but yelling and pointing blame isn't going to solve anything."

I lean back, heart racing. Archer's arm is still around me, and I rest my head on his shoulder. I'm starting to feel sick again.

"Dean," Mom starts. "Quinn is right, and she and Archer are free to date whoever they want, including each other. Quinn, you have to understand the shock it gives to all of us to find out you two are a couple. I certainly didn't expect it, though I can't say I'm surprised."

"What is that supposed to mean?" Dean rounds on Mom. "And how are you okay with this?"

Mom gives Dean a stern look, silently telling him to calm the fuck down and stop being such a possessive asshole. Archer is his own person and doesn't need Dean's permission to do anything.

"Who wouldn't want to date Quinn?" Mom asks seriously, and if things weren't so tense, I'd tell her to stop. "And Archer...I hope this means we'll be seeing you more often."

"Seriously, Mom?" Dean spits out. "She's dating my best friend."

"I'm sorry, Kara," Owen says seriously. "I think the truth is coming out. Clearly, Dean doesn't want anyone else getting in with the good doctor because he wants him all for himself."

"Shut up," Dean deadpans, annoyed with Owen already.

Owen makes a face like he doesn't understand Dean's disdain. "Why else would you be so possessive of Archer? What really went on behind closed doors in that dorm?"

"You'd be pissed if she was dating your best friend."

"I would be too," Logan interjects, a smirk on his face. "We'd have bigger problems than this if Quinn wanted to date Owen's best friend." He turns to me and winks. "But I think I'm safe there, right sis?"

"You are all ridiculous." I shake my head. "Archer and I are a couple, Dean, deal with it."

"Look," Archer starts, looking across the table at Dean. "I should have told you, and I'm sorry for that. But I really care about Quinn, and we're happy together."

"That's what matters," Mom presses. "You both deserve to be happy. Yes, it's a surprise, but we love you both and want you to be happy."

"How long has this been going on?" Dean asks through gritted teeth.

I open my mouth just to snap it shut again. We slept together before we became a couple, and once Dean knows I got knocked up from what was basically a one-night stand, he'll be even more pissed.

"A while," Archer answers for me. He turns in, looking into my eyes. "Your mom is right. Who wouldn't want to date Quinn? She's the most amazing woman I've ever met, and I've wanted to ask her out for years but didn't because I didn't want to piss you off," he admits, selling it so well I almost believe it.

"What changed?" Weston interjects.

I got her pregnant, I imagine Archer saying. Instead, he tightens his arm around me. He doesn't feel tense though, not like I do. "I caved and kissed her. I haven't been able to look back since."

He's telling the truth, to an extent. Is he telling the truth about liking me for years too?

"Grammy, Grammy," Jackson says, tugging on my mom's sleeve. He's holding something else now and is asking her what it is.

"I don't like this," Dean huffs. "You don't have my blessing."

I shake my head. "Sorry to tell you I'm not losing sleep over it. I haven't before, and I won't now." I take a small drink of water, hoping to settle my stomach. Dean will come around eventually, like Archer said. It's going to be a rough road, but we'll get down it.

Well, until they find out about the baby. Last night, Archer told me not to worry about my family's approval, and it hit me how much I seek it. My whole life they've supported me, told me how proud they are of me, and protected me. My parents worked their asses off for me, and all four of my brothers would take a bullet for me in a heartbeat.

I'm a grown woman with a good job, a healthy bank account, and my own place. It's not like I'm sixteen and pregnant. And as far as baby daddies go, I hit the jackpot with a sexy surgeon.

Still, I'm terrified to see the disapproval in their eyes. Maybe we should wait until tomorrow, deviating from my plan to further liquor my parents up, remind my mom how much she desperately wants another grandchild, and then spring the news on her.

My stomach protests and my throat feels sick. I'm definitely not ready to tell them now. I just need to make it through dinner and then go lay down, preferably with Archer's arms around me.

Jackson gives my mom something, and I realize what it is a moment too late. He was digging through my purse to get the candy, but that's not the only thing he took from there.

And now Mom is holding the ultrasound pictures.

The air leaves my lungs, and if it weren't for Archer's arm around me, I might have fallen over. Mom's eyebrows pinch together, and she tips her head looking at the images.

"Where did you get—" Mom tips her head, eyeing the photos. The blood drains from my face, and I can't open my mouth to form the words to warn Archer.

"This has your name on it, Quinn," she says quietly. And then it hits her. Her mouth opens, and she lets out a gasp. The ultrasound pictures fall to the table, and Dad picks them up.

It doesn't take him long to come to the same conclusion. He stands up so fast his chair scoots out from behind him and falls over.

"You knocked up my daughter?"

A hush falls over the room, and I swear even the dogs stopped sniffing around the table to look.

"Quinn," Mom starts, still looking confused. She picks up the chair and reaches up for Dad's wrist, pulling him back down. "What...when...are you sure?"

"Wait a minute," Owen says, reaching across the table for the ultrasound pictures. "You're pregnant?"

I cover my face with my hands, unable to deal right now. Archer's arm tightens around me. Now he's tense. Stunned silence holds the room in an awkward pause, and the calm before the storm is even worse than one-hundred-mile-per-hour winds.

"Yes," Archer says, and I don't know how he's able to sound so calm and certain. It must come with the territory of being a doctor. He has to deliver bad news and can't come undone when he talks to patients. "She is."

"You. Knocked. Up. My. Sister," Dean says slowly, letting it sink in. And then he jumps up, fists curled. Weston's faster and stronger and easily shoves Dean back into his chair.

I peel my hands away from my face, heart in my throat. Mom is looking at the ultrasound photos again, but her expression is unreadable. Dad grinds his jaw, eyes narrowed as his gaze shifts back and forth between Archer and me.

"How far along are you?" Kara asks quietly.

"Almost seven weeks," I reply, having a hard time finding my voice.

"First you date my sister, then you get her pregnant," Dean says through clenched teeth. "Fuck you, man."

No one scolds him for his language. Jackson went into the living room anyway, and I can hear him playing with some sort of Mickey Mouse toy.

"Grow up, Dean," I snap. "It's not like we did this on purpose."

Dad shakes his head. "How did this happen?"

"You don't know how babies are made?" Owen says, trying to lighten the mood. "You have five of them, I thought you'd have figured it out."

Dad sits back down, finally giving into Mom's persistent

tugging. "Can you explain how the two smartest people I know could do something so stupid."

"Harold," Mom scolds. "That's enough. We didn't plan our first one either."

"Seriously?" Weston exclaims, then shakes his head. "That's not important right now."

Dad waves his hand at Owen. "Your brother's slept with half of Eastwood and he's never knocked anyone up."

"Not that we know of," Logan mutters under his breath.

"Quinn," Dad says, exasperated, and I see it. The worry behind the anger. The questioning of my future, the *disappointment*. "You're smart. And Archer," he practically growls Archer's name. "You're a doctor. Don't you know how the human body works?"

"I do," Archer replies, still calm. "And I'm aware that Quinn and I didn't make the best choices, but we can't go back and now all we can do is focus on moving forward."

I straighten up, hand going to my mouth. Archer takes his arm from around me and scoots my chair out, knowing I'm about to get sick. He comes with me as I run into the bathroom, gathering my hair into my hand as I crouch down and throw up.

Archer closes the bathroom door and grabs a tissue from the back of the toilet. I wipe my mouth and let out a sigh.

"Besides feeling sick, how are you holding up?" he asks, helping me to my feet. I rinse out my mouth and think I might throw up again.

"This didn't go as I planned."

Archer's lips pull into a small smile and he looks at my stomach. "None of this did." He closes the distance between us and takes me in his arms. "It'll be okay."

"Dean is about ready to rip your head off."

"Let him try. He won't succeed, I promise you that."

I rest my head against his chest. "They all look so disappointed in me."

"They're surprised. You can't blame them for that. And they're concerned because they care about you."

He has a point, and I totally get it. Archer and I are both successful, independent adults, but we don't live together. Even if we'd been dating for a few months, the news of me having his baby would still come as a shock.

We have a lot to do before this baby is born.

"You're going to have to talk to them eventually. Let's go back out."

I take another breath and nod, letting my arms fall away from Archer's firm body. He smooths back my hair and kisses me on the forehead.

"We're in this together," he reminds me, and the knot in my chest loosens a bit. Holding my hand in his, he opens the bathroom door and we step out. A tumult of voices come from the dining room, and everyone stops talking when Archer and I come back into the room.

Mom's holding the ultrasound photos and is starting to look a little emotional. Phase one might not have happened like we planned, but I might still be able to get her into phase two soon, and she'll start getting excited about another grandbaby.

"Are you okay?" she asks me, blinking back tears.

"Yeah." I step closer to Archer. "I've been really nauseous this whole time."

Mom takes in a shaky breath. "I was only sick with you. I bet you're carrying a girl."

I haven't really let myself think too far ahead, but hearing Mom say it makes me emotional. I grip Archer's hand tighter, imagining him holding our baby wrapped in a little pink blanket.

"Sit down, honey." Mom rubs her lower eyelid with her knuckle. Yep. She's getting emotional. Archer pulls out my chair for me, and Dean glowers at us both with his arms crossed. Kara looks annoyed with him, Weston's holding Jackson, trying to distract him with videos on his phone. Owen and Logan look both concerned and pissed. And Dad won't even look at me.

"You had the ultrasound almost a week ago." Mom taps the date on the image. "And you're just now telling me?"

"We wanted to tell you in person. Together," Archer says, moving his chair closer to mine.

Mom nods and picks up the images again. "I can understand that."

"Have you two thought this through?" Dad addresses the question to us both but looks right at Archer. "How are you going to raise this baby?"

"Together," I tell him.

"How?" Dad fires another question. "You don't live together. You don't even live near each other. I take it Archer is going to do the right thing and move to Chicago before the baby is born. Right, Archer?"

"We haven't talked about it yet," I say.

"You need to start talking about it."

"I know."

"It's more than just wanting to raise it together." Dad's voice gets louder as he keeps talking. "You have to figure out insurance and what are you going to do about work?"

"Dad," Logan interjects. "Go easy on her."

"I think I was too easy on her and that's why this happened."

"She's not a kid anymore," Logan presses and I'm so grateful for my brother right now. "Stop treating her like one."

"*Thanks*," I mouth to Logan when he looks over.

"I'm twenty-six," I remind my father in case he forgot. "A lot of my friends are married and have kids."

"Exactly. They're married. You're not."

"Thanks for reminding me. I forgot I never walked down the aisle."

"Enough," Mom says, voice tight. "You said it yourself, Harold, Quinn and Archer are smart. I'm sure they've discussed everything. It's overwhelming for us all, and getting worked up isn't going to help anything, especially with Quinn having morning sickness."

Jackson looks up from the phone. "You sick, Aunt Winnie?"

"No, I'm okay," I tell him with a smile. If my kid turns out to be half as sweet as him, we'll be just fine.

"Why is Papa mad?" he asks, turning around to look at Weston, who doesn't know how to answer.

"He's not mad," Weston finally says. "Why don't you go play in the living room?"

"Okay," Jackson says and slides off Weston's lap. He runs around to Archer. "Play trucks with me?"

"Uh," Archer starts, knowing he's in hot water with my family right now. But it's not like he's a bad person. We're equally at fault here.

"Go play," Mom says with a smile. "Consider it practice."

Archer gets up, letting Jackson tug him along. I sit back in the chair, arms wrapped around myself. Logan moves into Archer's spot and puts his hand on my shoulder. He's always the one I go to first if I need advice or just someone to vent to.

"That's going to be one smart kid," he says with a grin. "With a computer genius and a doctor for parents."

"If it's a boy, I hope he gets our good looks," Owen joins in.

I smile and look up. "As long as that's all he gets from your set of genes."

Logan leans back, giving me an encouraging nod.

"I have a video from the ultrasound," I say, flicking my gaze to Mom's. "You can see the heart beating and everything. I can show you if you want."

Mom's eyes light up. "Of course I want to see it." She turns to Dad. "We want to see it," she corrects.

Dad sighs and gets up to start clearing the table. Tears fill my eyes and I turn my head down.

"Hey," Logan says, seeing a fat tear splash onto the table. "Don't cry. He'll come around."

"See what that asshole did," Dean mumbles to Kara. "He hurt her. Fucking no good piece of shit."

"Archer didn't hurt me," I sniffle.

"You're crying," Dean goes on, extending his hand at me.

"Even I'm not that dense," Owen quips. "Dad's being an ass about this. And so are you."

"Are you happy with what he did to her?"

"Stop," I say, but my voice gets lost in a sob.

"Of course not," Owen shoots back.

"It takes two," Kara offers. "I think you are all being unfair to Archer."

"Thank you," I say, using my napkin to mop up my tears. "We both had an equal part in this, okay? So just stop. I'm already pregnant and hating me isn't going to change anything."

"Nobody hates you, hun," Mom says.

"Dad does." This time I know I'm overreacting.

"He doesn't," Mom presses.

Owen leans forward. "Dad knows we're all fuck-ups, but

he still thinks you're little Miss Innocent Quinn. You basically crushed his hopes and dreams for the family, but he doesn't hate you."

I look up, giving Owen a glare. He cracks a smile and picks up his fork, digging into what's left on his plate.

"Honey." Mom gets up and comes around to me, shooing Logan from the chair. She takes my hands in hers and looks into my eyes. "We all love you. It's a shock, and having a baby with someone you haven't been with for a long time can be difficult. But I know you and I know Archer. You're both responsible, mature adults and will be great parents. I mean, look at him." She motions to Archer in the living room. He's on the floor with Jackson, and whatever he's saying to the kid is making him crack up.

"He's a natural."

My hand lands on my stomach without me even thinking about it. Archer is good with Jackson. He's been excited about this baby since the beginning.

I can only hope we're natural together too.

"All things considered, that went as well as I thought it would." I put my arm around Quinn and push off the ground, sending the glider back. It's getting late, and everyone but Weston and Jackson have left already. Wes is working the night shift tonight, so Jackson is staying here with Quinn's parents.

Quinn rests her head on my shoulder and closes her eyes. She looks exhausted. Physically, I know she will be for the rest of the first trimester at least. Emotionally, she's spent.

And I still think she's one of the fucking strongest people I know.

"Yeah. Only my dad and Dean want to take you out back and cut off your testicles. But don't worry, I won't let that happen. I happen to like them. Well, more so what they're attached to."

I laugh and press my lips against the top of Quinn's head. "Thanks for looking out for my balls." The sound of katydids and crickets echo through the yard, reverberating off the tall corn that surrounds us. The sounds of a country summer night surround us, and it takes me back to the time I spent with the Dawsons in the summer.

The first time I saw Quinn was when we were moving into our dorm. She was wearing a tight black dress that hugged her curves and showed off her tits. She was in the middle of an argument with her father about the dress being inappropriate when I walked into the dorm with a box full of stuff. I could tell right away she wasn't in college, but I pegged her to be sixteen, maybe even seventeen.

She was beautiful, and with her ample breasts and supple ass to match, she looked more mature than she was. I became nonverbal at the sight of her, trying to surreptitiously watch her move about the tiny room and hoped the dress would ride up on her ass a little bit more than it already was.

And then Dean came in, carrying a box of his own supplies, and introduced me to his dad and his baby sister.

Who was fourteen.

I felt dirty for weeks, but hey, I didn't know. I was a horny eighteen-year-old then, and Quinn didn't look her age at the time.

That summer, Bobby went to his first rehab center, and I stayed with the Dawsons for most of June. Quinn was fifteen then, but still too young. And I was still too attracted to her.

I shift my weight, allowing Quinn to lean back on me more. She tucks her feet up under herself and turns in.

"Are you cold?" I ask, feeling goosebumps break out along her arms.

"Yeah. A little."

"Do you want to go in?"

"No, it's nice out here. I can tough it out. Which really means I'm too lazy to go inside and get a blanket."

Chuckling, I take my arms from around her and get up. "I'll get you one."

"Don't get murdered in there."

"I'll do my best."

The back door we came out of leads into the kitchen, and the lights are off. The dogs are outside with us, and only Carlos follows me in, probably cold too, and slips inside when I open the sliding glass door. I pause when I step in, listening to see if anyone is up. Quinn and I came outside right as Weston was putting Jackson down to sleep, so the house should be pretty quiet regardless.

I go into the living room and take a blanket off the back of the couch. A light turns on upstairs, and Weston's voice echoes over the stairs.

"I'd put it off if I were them too," Weston says to someone. "Can you blame them? Look at how everyone reacted tonight."

"It wasn't our finest moment," Mrs. Dawson replies with a heavy sigh. "We're worried. Being a single parent isn't easy, as you know."

"I do. And I know getting married first and then having kids might sound like the right way to do things, but look how that turned out for me."

"I know, it just came as such a shock."

"Archer seems to really care about her."

"He does. He's always been good to her, he's been good to all of us. I've always liked him and thought of him like a fifth son." The floorboards in the hall upstairs creak.

"Then get Dad to stop being a jerk. Telling the family life-altering news isn't easy. I put off telling you guys about Daisy for over a week."

"He's worried right now. And shocked. Very shocked. And Dean...I'll call him. He owes both Quinn and Archer an apology." The light above the stairs turns on. "I did say I wanted more grandchildren. I didn't think it would happen this way, but when does life go according to plan?"

At least Weston's on our side. With his military training and no-nonsense attitude, I haven't seen this version of Wes very often. With an eight-year age gap between him and Quinn, he's always had a strong sense of responsibility over her and was the most overprotective of his little sister, with Dean coming in at a close second.

I take the blanket and go back into the kitchen, hurrying back out to Quinn. I wrap the blanket around her shoulders, running my fingers through her hair.

"What if Dean kicks you out of the wedding?" she asks softly.

"Then he kicks me out of the wedding. Nothing is more important to me than this baby, Quinn. If being with you pisses Dean off that much, then fuck him."

She sits up. "You'd choose me over him?"

"I'd choose you over anything." It kills me not to tell her I love her. She's not ready to hear it, and definitely not ready to say it back.

The sliding glass door opens, and Mrs. Dawson steps out onto the deck. "I just put on a pot of coffee and got out a plate of cookies. Do you two want any?"

"She's giving you an olive branch," I whisper to Quinn. We get up and go inside, joining Mrs. Dawson in the kitchen.

"Are you still drinking coffee?" she asks Quinn.

"Yeah. Just half a cup in the morning though." Quinn sits at the counter, blanket still wrapped around her shoulders. "I've been exhausted since day one."

"And you've had morning sickness?"

Quinn nods. "That was the telltale symptom that made me realize something wasn't right."

I stand behind Quinn, rubbing her shoulders. She folds her arms on the counter and rests her head on top.

"I was the same way with you." Mrs. Dawson puts a kettle on the stove to boil and pulls out a bag of loose-leaf peppermint tea. "I didn't have a single symptom with any of the boys. But I swear I started throwing up the day I conceived you." She looks at Quinn with a smile on her face. "I knew right away I was having a girl. As much as I love my boys, I was so excited to have a little princess. Little did I know you'd be just as rough—and probably twice as tough—as all four of those boys combined."

Quinn looks up, blinking from the bright lights, and pulls the stool out next to her for me to sit down.

"I kind of want a girl," she says, and my heart does a weird skip-a-beat thing. We haven't talked about the baby like this before.

Like we're a couple about to start our family.

"What about you?"

"I don't think I care," I tell her. "If it is a girl, I hope she's just like you."

"And if it's a boy, I really hope he takes after you and not my brothers." She smiles, and I lace my fingers through hers. "You don't have any weird family names that have to be passed down, do you?"

"Nope. We're good to pick anything."

Mrs. Dawson puts a plate of cookies in front of us and comes around the counter to hug Quinn.

"You never did show me that video."

"ARCHER, CAN I HAVE A WORD?" MR. DAWSON STEPS OUT OF his office. It's Friday afternoon and I'm getting ready to head out. Quinn is staying for dinner, and then is leaving too. It kills me thinking about her driving back up to Chicago alone and I hate that we're headed in separate directions.

"Yes, sir," I say and stand from the couch where Quinn and I were sitting.

"Close the door," Mr. Dawson says when I get into his office. "Quinn is my only daughter. My youngest. My *baby*. She'll always be those things to me, do you understand?"

"I do."

"Now, I know this wasn't planned, but I expect you to be there for her. No matter what."

"I plan to. I care about her more than anything, and now that she's carrying my baby, she's my priority."

Mr. Dawson rubs his chin and nods. "Do you love her?"

"Yes."

"Does she love you?"

"Not yet."

Mr. Dawson's frown slowly turns. He steps around his desk and gives me a pat on the back. "Being a father is one of the most difficult things you'll ever do, but it's also the most rewarding. You don't know love until you've held your own child in your arms."

I nod. "I've heard that before, and I'm looking forward to the day when I can hold our child."

"Now...speaking of that day. What are your plans for the future? Have you and Quinn discussed it at all?"

"Not in full detail."

"March seems far away, but there's a lot to get squared away before then, and once Quinn hits the seventh month, she might not be up for any of those big discussions. And there's a chance the baby could come early."

"I've thought about it," I tell him. "There are a lot of great hospitals in the Chicago area I'd be honored to work for."

Mr. Dawson's thin smile grows, and he lets out a sigh of relief. "That's good to hear. I don't doubt you," he says, words sounding forced. Thinking back to Weston and his mother's conversation last night, I'm pretty sure what's to come next was scripted by Mrs. Dawson.

He lets out his breath, giving up on what he was supposed to say. "Don't hurt Quinn."

"I won't. All I want is to make her happy."

Mr. Dawson sets his jaw and nods. "I'll hold you to it. We all will."

"I expect you to, sir."

His smile turns genuine this time, and he waves his hand at the door. "Drive safe, Archer. I assume we'll see you again soon."

I go back to Quinn, who's anxiously waiting for me back on the couch.

"What was that about?" she asks. "Did he yell at you?"

"No. He's being a good dad, that's all. Wants to make sure I'm here for you."

She smiles and loops her arms around my shoulders. "You are."

And I always will be.

"Dean still hasn't talked to you?" Quinn asks, moving around her kitchen. It's Monday evening and I just got out of a long surgery. I'm sitting in the break room with my dinner, resting my feet while I can.

We're FaceTiming, and I miss her like crazy. "No. I texted

him this morning, but he doesn't always reply right away anyway."

"He's being a drama queen over this, way more than me, and I'm the pregnant one."

I laugh. "He's always been dramatic."

Quinn shakes her head. "Try growing up with him." She sets the phone down for a moment to feed the cats. "The smell of cat food is killing me today." Covering her nose, she goes into the living room and sits on the couch. I'd do anything to be there next to her.

"You work this weekend, right?" she asks.

"I have scheduled procedures for Saturday and I'm on call Sunday."

"So there's a chance you could be home Sunday?"

"A small one, but yes."

She bites her lip and smiles. "I can come visit you."

"That's a long drive."

She cocks an eyebrow. "Do you not want to put your hands on these?" She lifts her shirt, revealing her perfect round tits.

"You're fucking killing me, Quinn. Yes, I want to see you, but I don't want to make you drive."

"You're not making me. I'm offering. And I have access to a private jet that can fly me there in like an hour."

"Really?"

"Perks of building the Batmobile." She flashes a smile. "You look hot in your doctor clothes, by the way."

"They're called scrubs," I say with a chuckle. "Would you leave Friday night?"

"Yeah, probably around six or seven my time."

"That seems so far away now."

"It does." She sits up, grimacing, and reaches for something in front of her. I get another good view of her tits, though this time she didn't do it on purpose. Sipping a ginger ale, she leans back on the couch.

And then I'm paged for surgery.

"I have to go."

"Already?"

"Yeah. Someone needs an emergency gallbladder removal. It's the second one I've done today."

"Go save lives, Dr. Jones. I'm probably going to go to bed."

"I'll call you tomorrow then. Take care, Quinn."

We hang up and I take a few quick bites of my sandwich, use the bathroom, and head to the OR. My patient is in bad shape, having refused to listen to his general practitioner's advice for several weeks now, and going under is going to take a toll on his body.

The surgery takes longer than normal, but he pulls through. Though as soon as I get into the recovery room to talk to him, I can tell I'll be seeing him again soon. There's nothing that irritates me more than someone who refuses to listen to post-op instructions and ends up back in a few days to get re-stitched.

I have a missed call, and I assume it's from Quinn, calling to say goodnight or something like that. It's from my mother, and for some reason, I already know it's bad news.

I move by a window in the hall to get better reception, and put the phone to my ear. I meant to call her today and talk to her, maybe even invite them down from Michigan to meet Quinn and I in Chicago for dinner.

My parents will be surprised to find out I not only have a girlfriend, but a pregnant one at that, but I don't expect their reaction to be anything like the Dawsons'. My parents have been desensitized to shocking information, and being told

Quinn is having my baby is nothing compared to getting a call that Bobby has been arrested for the fifth time.

"Archie," Mom's voice comes through my voicemail. "Call me when you can. Bobby relapsed, and I don't know where he is."

"Can you tell?" I smooth my shirt over my stomach and turn to the side.

"No." Marissa shakes her head. "I know you and you've always been a skinny bitch, so I guess I'm able to pick up on that slight bump you claim is the baby, but to anyone else, you look like you ate a big meal."

"It's weird," I say, wrinkling my nose, and grab my shoes. I take off my heels and put on my running shoes, not caring how silly it looks with my dress pants and blouse. It's Friday, and we're leaving work for the week. "I'm almost looking forward to showing."

"Just don't turn into Bethany."

I widen my eyes and shake my head, showing my horror. "If I do, slap me." Bethany works with us and had her first baby last year. She made sure everyone knew everything about the pregnancy and complained nonstop about her symptoms. Though I can emphasize now, and after throwing up three times yesterday, I broke down and took an anti-nausea pill this morning.

I still feel sick, but I haven't puked. It's a small victory, but I'll take it.

"Your brother still won't talk to Archer?" Marissa asks.

I shake my head. "Nope. And now Kara won't reply to my texts since she realized my due date and her wedding date don't exactly mesh."

"Ouch."

I close my office door, locking it behind me. Marissa and I head to the elevators. "I get it, though. It's terrible timing. What happens if I go into labor on her wedding day? I told my mom she's to stay at the wedding if it happens, but it'll be a big distraction for everyone."

"And she's not going to move her date?"

I shake my head. "Nope. The place she wants to get married at is booked solid until the next year."

"Can you call and bribe someone?"

"I didn't think of that. I think I will."

"I was joking." Marissa pressed the elevator button. "But if it works…"

"Right? Anything to quell the drama."

We step into the elevator. "Are you all packed and ready for your weekend with the sexy doctor?"

"I am. I just have to stop by home and check on my cats before I head out."

"You're so lame."

"Hey," I say, trying hard to sound offended. "I love my kitties."

"Your other kitty is going to be happier."

I laugh. "Oh yeah, it will be."

ARCHER GOT CALLED INTO EMERGENCY SURGERY AND IS sending his friend Sam to come pick me up from the airport. He apologized over and over, and while I'm anxious to see him, I don't mind. It comes with the territory of dating a doctor.

Sam is nice, a bit talkative, and if he's Archer's friend, then I want to get to know him too. We pick up Chinese takeout on the way home, and I order extra for Archer.

"Make yourself at home," Sam tells me when we step into the apartment. I take a quick second to look around. Everything is nice and neat with minimal decorations. Archer told me he always viewed this place as temporary, knowing he'd leave after he finished at the hospital here and finds a permanent position.

Sam sits on the couch, setting his food on the coffee table. I follow suit and take a seat on the opposite side.

"Do you like Game of Thrones?" he asks, picking up the remote.

"Do I like Game of Thrones?" I echo. "Do I like breathing? Yes!"

"I've been watching the behind-the-scenes footage."

"Oh, I love that stuff! It always amazes me to see all the work they put into it."

An hour later, we're coming up with names for our houses, and Archer walks in. His face lights up when he sees me, and he rushes over. I stand and throw my arms around him. He brushes my hair back and kisses me, sending a jolt right through me.

"I brought you food," I tell him, sliding my hands over his arms. "But do you want to have sex first?"

"I'm officially jealous," Sam laughs. "She's a good one, Jones."

Archer picks me up in a swift swoop, answering my

question with another kiss. He carries me into his bedroom, and we fall onto his bed together.

"I missed you," Archer says, pulling his shirt over his head.

"I missed you too." I shimmy out of my leggings. "I think the hormones are kicking in harder or something. All I can think about is sex right now."

Archer gives me a cocky grin. "It's because I'm so good at it."

I nod. "You are. But don't go and get complacent on me. I told you, I have very high standards."

"I aim to please." He grabs my ankles and pulls me to the edge of the bed. He drops onto the floor, kneeling between my thighs.

"If you fucking tease me tonight, Archer Jones, I might murder you."

He smirks and slowly kisses his way up my thigh. His fingers dance over my panties, pressing oh-so gently against my clit. I lay back, body humming with anticipation. Archer takes his sweet time, kissing my thighs, making me squirm as he trails his nails up and down my legs.

"Archer," I moan, reaching down and taking a tangle of his hair in my fingers. I guide his head back between my legs and arch my back. He grabs the sides of my panties and pulls them down, dropping them onto the floor.

"Take your shirt off," he tells me. "I want to watch you undress."

I give him a coy smile and sit up, moving back onto the bed. Slowly, I pull my shirt over my head and toss it at Archer. I run my hands over my breasts, pushing my bra straps off my shoulders one at a time.

And then Archer advances, taking me in his arms. He kisses me and unhooks my bra with one hand. We lay back, and I scramble to remove his boxers and pants. His cock is hard, and the tip is wet with precum. I wrap my fingers around his big dick, spreading the wetness down his shaft. Archer relishes my touch, eyes falling shut as I stroke him.

He moves away, pushing me back onto the mattress and kisses his way to my pussy, tongue lashing out as soon as he gets there. I fall back, letting out a moan as he gets to work. It doesn't take long before I come, writhing against him as wetness spills from me. Archer doesn't let up and moves his mouth faster. I'm so sensitive, so overtaken by pleasure that I push him away.

He grabs my wrists, pinning them down against the mattress as he continues to eat me out until I come again, even harder than before.

"I don't do complacent," he pants, slowly moving over top of me. My heart is still racing, pussy spasming, and I'm seeing stars. There was nothing complacent about that. Not at all.

"And by the way." He tips my chin to the side and kisses my neck. "I'm not done with you yet."

He moves on top of me, nuzzling my neck and playing with my breasts. I'm still floating in bliss, body on overdrive. Feebly, I wrap my arms around Archer, feeling every pound of muscle beneath my fingers. I feel closer to Archer than ever before, and it's not just because of the two intense orgasms he gave me. He gets me, and I'm starting to think I get him too.

It's complicated, trying to sort out my feelings for the man who's fathering my child. The man I've had an innocent crush on since the day I saw him. I want us to work out. I'm falling for Archer, and though I'm doing my best to resist, I can't fight gravity.

Archer lines his cock up with my core, and I widen my

legs as he enters me. He moans, pushing that big dick all the way inside, then circles his hips, hitting me in the right spot.

I don't know how he does it every single time.

"Ohhh," I groan. "That feels so good, Archer."

He likes when I say his name during sex. I've never been much of a dirty-talker, and usually would turn into a giggling mess if I tried, but nothing is awkward with Archer.

"Fuck me harder," I pant, and Archer responds with an animalistic growl and thrusts in harder and faster, not stopping until I'm coming again. He holds his cock inside me, waiting until I'm finished, and then pulls out and picks me up, turning me over and pushing me down on all fours.

It's the most forceful he's ever been with me, and fuck, I love it. He enters me from behind, pushing his cock in and out with fury. He reaches around, fingers sweeping over my clit. His touch is soft and gentle, knowing I'm already at the point of no return. Moving his fingers in swift circles, he slows his movements until another orgasm takes over.

He grabs me by the waist and fucks me hard, falling against me as he climaxes. We both collapse onto the mattress after that.

"I counted four orgasms," he pants, taking my hand.

"Are you keeping score?" I ask, breasts rapidly rising and falling as I gulp in air.

"Maybe." He smiles and rolls over so we're facing each other and places his hand on my ass. "It's fun when I win like this."

"If that was me losing, I'm a lucky girl."

He smiles, kisses my forehead, and gets up to get a towel for me to clean up with. He gets back into bed and covers us with a blanket.

"Are you tired?" I ask, curling up in his arms.

"Yeah. It was a long day. I know you are." He flattens his

hand over my stomach. "You're growing a person. *Our* person."

"Sex and sleep pretty much make up our relationship," I muse, nestling in deeper into Archer's embrace. It's Sunday morning, and I'm feeling too queasy for sex right now, but could easily fall back asleep.

"You say that like it's a bad thing."

"It's not. Give me a few more weeks and we can probably throw in eating."

"Sex, food, and sleep. Sounds pretty perfect to me." He pushes my messy hair back out of my face. "But next weekend when I'm in Chicago, let's do something else. I still plan on having plenty of sex though."

"Oh, me too. What do you want to do?"

"I've always wanted to go to the Science Museum there, unless you think that's lame."

"I love the museum. You can really come next weekend?"

"Yeah. And if you want to hook me up with your private jet connection, I wouldn't object."

I laugh. "I'll see what I can do."

"I was joking. I don't mind driving, actually."

"It'll get old."

"We won't be making that drive forever," he says and then stops short, realizing what he's insinuating. He tried to bring it up a few times, and my parents keep pestering me about it. I'm only eight weeks, and a lot of women wait until they're out of the first trimester to start any sort of planning.

"I know." I swallow the lump in my throat, debating if I should take another pill or not. There are so many things on the 'do not eat or use' list for pregnancy, I'm scared just to breathe. "What about your parents? You haven't told them yet, have you?"

He tenses. "No. But I will."

"Are you worried they'll be mad?"

"They won't be. My mom will be pretty excited, I'm sure. And they'll love you."

I nod, not understanding why he hasn't told them yet. "Are they still in Michigan?"

"They live there," he says hesitantly. "But they're...they're out of town. I'll tell them when they get back. I thought we could all go out for lunch together or something."

"I'd like that." There's more we need to talk about on the subject, but before I can delve into it, I groan, not sure if I'm going to win or lose this morning sickness battle.

"Feeling sick?"

I push up, nodding.

"What can I do?" Archer's hand lands on my back.

"Can you get me some water?"

"Of course, babe." He gets out of bed and heads out of the room.

"And Sour Patch Kids, if there are any left."

"I think you ate them all, but I'll go get you some."

I feel like I'm about to throw up stomach bile, but I smile, heart skipping a beat. My hand lands on my stomach. "You have a good daddy," I whisper. "I think things are going to work out after all."

Leaning back against the pillows, I close my eyes and think about anything else other than the sick feeling in my stomach. Archer comes back with a glass of cold water, remembering me telling him ice cold water seems to help for some strange reason.

"Do you want to take one?" Archer asks, holding up a pill bottle.

I make a face. "I need your honest opinion, not your doctor one. Do you think it's okay to take?"

"This is commonly prescribed—sorry. That's a doctor opinion. *My* honest opinion is if you can get by without it, then don't take it. But if you need to, then take it."

"That doesn't help me much."

"I know. Sorry. You need to be able to eat and keep food down for obvious reasons, and feeling like you're on the verge of puking all day is pretty fucking awful. I want you to be happy."

"I am happy," I say honestly. "Even with all the drama going on, I am happy."

Archer moves back into his spot next to me. "Good. Because I'm happy too. I know things happened out of order, but I'm glad we're together."

I take another sip of water, set the glass down, and rest my head against Archer's shoulder. "This could go on for another month." I reach for the water again, not sure how I can make it through four more weeks of throwing up.

"It's kind of crazy that's all there's left in the first trimester," Archer says. "It'll probably go by fast." He's trying to comfort me, not cause me to panic. The first trimester will be over before we know it, and we'll be that much closer to the due date and needing to figure things out.

On a rational level, I know I need to process everything. I'm a logical person. A problem solver. I know I can't ignore something and make it go away.

But I'm so fucking scared.

"If you feel better later, do you want to go out and see the city? I still feel bad for yesterday. I hope you weren't too bored sitting around here waiting for me to get off work."

"I told you I wasn't. Going through all your personal possessions kept me busy."

"Too bad I keep all my incriminating stuff in a storage locker."

"So that's what the weird little key is for. You're busted now, Dr. Jones." Speaking of Dr. Jones, my eyes go to the Indiana Jones hat I got for Archer as a joke. He has it on his dresser, and his room is too neat and tidy for it to have just been discarded there.

"Though really, I wasn't bored yesterday. I hung out with Sam in the morning, and then I worked on building a laptop."

"I thought you said you didn't want to even think about work."

"I don't, and I didn't. I've been working on this gaming PC for a while and haven't had much time to devote to it lately. I used to build them all the time in my youth. It's like my comfort food now since real food makes me vomit."

"Building a computer is comfort food?"

"I told you I'm a nerd."

"You really are," he says with a smile and grabs his phone, turning it off silent. His on-call hours start soon. "I'm making breakfast. What do you want?"

"An omelet."

"You're still craving eggs?"

"Yeah. It's so weird."

Archer's lips curve into a smile. "I think it's pretty damn cool. You're growing a person in there, and it's making you crave things you normally don't like. It was a little ball of cells and now it has a heartbeat and an influence over what you eat. You say you're a nerd, but you haven't heard me get excited about biology yet. I have a degree in biology if you didn't know. I'm sure that turns you on."

"It does. And since you love biology so much, you should give me a lesson."

"I plan to at least one more time before you have to leave." He kisses me and tells me to lay back down while he makes breakfast. I snuggle up under the covers, loving how the blankets smell like Archer's cologne. I doze off, waking up only when Archer comes back into the bedroom. He's carrying two plates of food, and it smells delicious.

I push myself up, fluffing the pillow behind my back. "I wonder if I'll still like eggs when I'm not pregnant anymore."

Archer hands me my plate. "I don't know. I'd guess no, but it'll be interesting to see."

After breakfast, we shower, get dressed, and go downtown to see the monument circle. It's ungodly hot and humid today, ending our walk along the canal early. We're eating lunch when Archer gets a call from the hospital. We wrap things up quickly and go back to his apartment.

Sam has the day off again today but isn't home at the moment. Archer gives me a kiss goodbye and hurries to work, promising to call as soon as he can. I put our leftovers from the restaurant in the fridge, and go back into Archer's room, changing out of my dress and back into my booty shorts and a t-shirt from Archer's closet.

Ready for a nap, I turn on the TV and snuggle in bed. My phone rings and I grumble when I remember I left it on the dresser and I have to get out of bed to answer it.

"Hey, Mom," I say, flopping back onto the mattress.

"Hey, honey. How are you feeling?"

"Tired and nauseous, but overall good."

"Are you able to take a nap?"

"Yeah, I'm in bed, actually."

"Oh, good." Mom's been checking on me almost daily since we told her about the baby, and things are good between us. "Try and get as much rest as you can now. You'll need it."

"Good point. How's Rufus?"

"The new meds seem to be helping. Poor old guy. What about Archer? Have you seen him recently?"

"Yeah, a few minutes ago. I'm at his house."

"How has he been treating you?"

I don't take it as an insult. I know she's concerned and wants to make sure Archer is committed. "Like a princess. He's been great, really, and is excited for the baby."

"Is he there? I wanted to talk to you guys about the baby shower."

"It's way too early to talk about that, Mom."

"Not plan it, just talk about it. You're my baby and you're having a baby. I'm not going to apologize for being excited."

"I like that you're excited now, and no, Archer isn't here. He just got called in for surgery. He thinks he'll be back in a few hours at least."

We chat for a few more minutes before we hang up, and I don't even bother finding something to watch. I roll over and fall asleep in minutes.

———

A LOUD POUNDING SOUND WAKES ME UP WITH A START. I sit up, confused for a split second, and then remember I'm at Archer's. I look at my phone; I've only been asleep for forty-five minutes.

Someone knocks on the front door again, hard, heavy, and desperate. I unlock my phone and call Archer, not expecting him to answer. He doesn't, and I swing my legs over the bed, peering out into the hall. The door is locked. Archer made sure of it before he left.

A few seconds go by, and I think whoever was outside must have left. I let out a breath and prepare to go back to sleep. And then the person outside knocks again.

"Archer!" the man outside the door yells. "Are you in there?"

They know Archer?

"I know you're in there, man!"

And they're angry. What the hell?

The pounding on the door starts again, so loud I'm scared they're going to bust through the door. Swallowing my pounding heart, I unlock my phone, thinking I might need to call the cops about this crazy guy.

"Look, Arch," the guy says, voice muffled. "I'm sorry for all that shit I did before. Can we talk about it?"

I leave the bedroom, going through the small living room toward the front door. Should I open it? This guy seems to know Archer...Nope. No way I'm opening the door.

"Come on, Archer. Stop being such a fucking asshole."

He kicks the door.

"And I'm calling the cops," I whisper, hands starting to shake. I get my phone unlocked.

"Who the hell are you?" Sam's voice is so welcome right now. "And what are you doing here?" I hurry to the door and unlock it to let Sam in before that guy does something to him. But as soon as I throw back the deadbolt, the door is shoved open, and the doorknob hits me right in the stomach. I fall back, tripping over the entryway rug. I catch myself with my bad wrist, and pain shoots up my arm.

"Shit, Quinn," Sam says, dropping his gym bag and going in after the guy who was pounding on the door.

"Archer," he calls. "Are you here?"

Sam helps me to my feet and rounds on the guy, shoving him against the wall. "What the fuck are you doing?"

"Where's Archer?"

"I'm not telling you shit."

The guy turns, eyes red and bugged out. He's on something, and it scares me even more. My hands go to my stomach on their own accord, protecting this little life inside of me. I know it takes a lot to hurt a baby at this time, but getting whacked by the door hurt.

Bad.

"Sorry. I didn't mean to hurt you," the guy says, twitching slightly. "Duke University," he mumbles, reading the words on my shirt. "Archer went there."

So this guy really does know Archer, or at least knows Archer went to med school at Duke for some reason. Then his eyes go to my hands clutching my stomach, and he tips his head.

"Who the fuck are you?" Sam demands, arms held out at his sides. "I'm calling the cops."

"No need, I'm leaving. Sorry. I thought Archer lived here."

"Why?" I rush out. "Why are you looking for him?"

The guy turns at me, giving me a blank stare for a few seconds. "Haven't seen him in a while." He sidesteps away from Sam, who's pulling out his phone. "Tell Archer I was here." He looks right into my eyes, and there's something familiar about his brown eyes.

"I don't know your name."

"Robert," he says with a twitch. "But everyone calls me Bobby."

Stay tuned for the conclusion of Quinn and Archer's story.

Only time will tell if everything Quinn and Archer fought to have will be lost. As Archer finds himself going to lengths he never imagined possible to protects what his, going to lengths he never thought he'd go ... Will this be the end game?

END GAME, available now!

ABOUT THE AUTHOR

Emily Goodwin is the New York Times and USA Today Bestselling author of over a dozen of romantic titles. Emily writes the kind of books she likes to read, and is a sucker for a swoon-worthy bad boy and happily ever afters.

She lives in the midwest with her husband and two daughters. When she's not writing, you can find her riding her horses, hiking, reading, or drinking wine with friends.

Emily is represented by Julie Gwinn of the Seymour Agency.

Stalk me:
www.emilygoodwinbooks.com
emily@emilygoodwinbooks.com

ALSO BY EMILY GOODWIN

First Comes Love

Then Come Marriage

Outside the Lines

Never Say Never

One Call Away

Free Fall

Stay

All I Need

Hot Mess (Luke & Lexi Book 1)

Twice Burned (Luke & Lexi Book 2)

Bad Things (Cole & Ana Book 1)

Battle Scars (Cole & Ana Book 2)

Cheat Codes (The Dawson Family Series Book 1)

Made in the USA
Monee, IL
11 May 2023

33473427R00157